THE INVENTION OF MOREL

and Other Stories (from *La Trama Celeste*)

THE TEXAS PAN AMERICAN SERIES

THE INVENTION OF MOREL

by *Adolfo Bioy Casares*
translated by Ruth L. C. Simms

illustrated by Norah Borges de Torre
with a prologue by Jorge Luis Borges

UNIVERSITY OF TEXAS PRESS ⚘ AUSTIN

AND OTHER STORIES (from *La Trama Celeste*)

International Standard Book Number 0-292-73840-4
Library of Congress Catalog Card Number 64–10312
Copyright © 1964 by Adolfo Bioy Casares
All rights reserved
Printed in the United States of America

First Paperback Printing, 1985

La invención de Morel was first published in 1940
by Editorial Losada, Buenos Aires, Argentina.

La trama celeste was first published in 1948 by Sur,
Buenos Aires, Argentina.

*Requests for permission to reproduce material from this
work should be sent to Permissions, University of Texas
Press, Box 7819, Austin, Texas 78713.*

The Texas Pan American Series is published with the assistance of a revolving publication fund established by the Pan American Sulphur Company and other friends of Latin America in Texas. Publication of this book was also assisted by a grant from the Rockefeller Foundation through the Latin American translation program of the Association of American University Presses.

CONTENTS

The Invention of Morel 1
Stories from *La Trama Celeste* 91
    "In Memory of Pauline" 93
    "The Future Kings" 108
    "The Idol" 120
    "The Celestial Plot" 144
    "The Other Labyrinth" 174
    "The Perjury of the Snow" 209

THE INVENTION OF MOREL

To Jorge Luis Borges

PROLOGUE

Around 1880 Stevenson observed that the adventure story was regarded as an object of scorn by the British reading public, who believed that the ability to write a novel without a plot, or with an infinitesimal, atrophied plot, was a mark of skill. In *La deshumanización del arte* (1925) José Ortega y Gasset, seeking the reason for that scorn, said, "I doubt very much whether an adventure that will interest our superior sensibility can be invented today" (p. 96), and added that such an invention was "practically impossible" (p. 97). On other pages, on almost all the other pages, he upheld the cause of the "psychological" novel and asserted that the pleasure to be derived from adventure stories was nonexistent or puerile. That was undoubtedly the prevailing opinion of 1880, 1925, and even 1940. Some writers (among whom I am happy to include Adolfo Bioy Casares) believe they have a right to disagree. The following, briefly, are the reasons why.

The first of these (I shall neither emphasize nor attenuate the fact that it is a paradox) has to do with the intrinsic form of the adventure story. The typical psychological novel is formless. The Russians and their disciples have demonstrated, tediously, that no one is impossible. A person may kill himself because he is so happy, for example, or commit murder as an act of benevolence. Lovers may separate forever as a consequence of their love. And one man can inform on another out of fervor or humility. In the end such complete freedom is tantamount to chaos. But the psychological novel would also be a "realistic" novel, and have us forget that it is a verbal artifice, for it uses each vain precision (or each languid obscurity) as a new proof of verisimilitude. There are pages, there are chapters in Marcel Proust that are unacceptable as inventions, and we unwittingly resign ourselves to them as we resign ourselves to the insipidity and the emptiness of each day. The adventure story, on the other hand, does not propose to be a transcription of reality: it is an artificial object, no part of which lacks justification. It must have a rigid plot if it is not to succumb to the mere sequential variety of *The Golden Ass,* the *Seven Voyages of Sinbad,* or the *Quixote.*

I have given one reason of an intellectual sort; there are others of an empirical nature. We hear sad murmurs that our century lacks the ability to devise interesting plots. But no one attempts to prove that if this century has any ascendancy over the preceding ones it lies in the quality of its plots. Stevenson is more passionate, more diverse, more lucid, perhaps more deserving of our unqualified friendship than is Chesterton; but his plots are inferior. De Quincey plunged deep into labyrinths on his nights of meticulously detailed horror, but he did not coin his impression of "unutterable and self-repeating infinities" in fables comparable to Kafka's. Ortega y Gasset was right when he said that Balzac's "psychology" did not satisfy us; the same thing could be said of his plots. Shakespeare and Cervantes were both delighted by the antinomian idea of a girl who, without losing her beauty, could be taken for a man; but we find that idea unconvincing now. I believe I am free from every susperstition of modernity, of any illusion that yesterday differs intimately from today or will differ from tomorrow; but I maintain that during no other era have there been novels with such admirable plots as *The Turn of the Screw, Der Prozess, Le Voyageur sur la terre,* and the one you are about to read, which was written in Buenos Aires by Adolfo Bioy Casares.

Another popular genre in this so-called plotless century is the detective story, which tells of mysterious events that are later explained and justified by a reasonable occurrence. In this book Adolfo Bioy Casares easily solves a problem that is perhaps more difficult. The odyssey of marvels he unfolds seems to have no possible explanation other than hallucination or symbolism, and he uses a single fantastic but not supernatural postulate to decipher it. My fear of making premature or partial revelations restrains me from examining the plot and the wealth of delicate wisdom in its execution. Let me say only that Bioy renews in literature a concept that was refuted by St. Augustine and

Origen, studied by Louis Auguste Blanqui, and expressed in memorable cadences by Dante Gabriel Rossetti:

> I have been here before,
> But when or how I cannot tell:
> I know the grass beyond the door,
> The sweet keen smell,
> The sighing sound, the lights around the shore.

In Spanish, works of reasoned imagination are infrequent and even very rare. The classicists employed allegory, the exaggerations of satire, and, sometimes, simple verbal incoherence. The only recent works of this type I remember are a story of *Las fuerzas extrañas* and one by Santiago Dabove: now unjustly forgotten. *The Invention of Morel* (the title alludes filially to another island inventor, Moreau) brings a new genre to our land and our language.

I have discussed with the author the details of his plot. I have reread it. To classify it as perfect is neither an imprecision nor a hyperbole.

JORGE LUIS BORGES

The Invention of Morel

Today, on this island, a miracle happened. The weather suddenly grew very warm, as if summer had come ahead of time. I moved my bed out by the swimming pool, but then, because it was impossible to sleep, I stayed in the water for a long time. The heat was so intense that after I had been out of the pool for only two or three minutes I was already bathed in perspiration again. As day was breaking, I awoke to the sound of a phonograph record. Afraid to go back to the museum to get my things, I ran away down through the ravine. Now I am in the lowlands at the southern part of the island, where the aquatic plants grow, where mosquitoes torment me, where I find myself waist-deep in dirty streams of sea water. And, what is worse, I realize that there was no need to run away at all. Those people did not come here on my account; I believe they did not even see me. But here I am, without provisions, trapped in the smallest, least habitable part of the island—the marshes that the sea floods once each week.

I am writing this to leave a record of the adverse miracle. If I am not drowned or killed trying to escape in the next few days, I hope to write two books. I shall entitle them *Apology for Survivors* and *Tribute to Malthus*. My books will expose the men who violate the sanctity of forests and deserts; I intend to show that the world is an implacable hell for fugitives, that its efficient police forces, its documents, newspapers, radio broadcasts, and border patrols have made every error of justice irreparable. So far I have written only this one page; yesterday I had no inkling of what was going to happen. There are so many things to do on this lonely island! The trees that grow here have such hard wood! And when I see a bird in flight I realize the vastness of the open spaces all around me!

An Italian rugseller in Calcutta told me about this place. He said (in his own language): "There is only one possible place for a fugitive like you—it is an uninhabited island, but a human being cannot live there. Around 1924 a group of white men built a museum, a chapel, and a swimming pool on the island. The work was completed, and then abandoned."

I interrupted him; I wanted to know how to reach it; the rug merchant went on talking: "Chinese pirates do not go there, and the white ship of the Rockefeller Institute never calls at the island, because it is known to be the focal point of a mysterious disease, a fatal disease that attacks the outside of the body and then works inward. The nails drop off the fingers and toes; the hair falls out. The skin and the corneas of the eyes die, and the body lives on for one week, or two at the most. The crew of a ship that had stopped there were skinless, hairless, without nails on their fingers or toes—all dead, of course—when they were found by the Japanese cruiser *Namura*. The horrified Japanese sank their ship."

But my life was so unbearable that I decided to go there anyway. The Italian tried to dissuade me; but in the end I managed to obtain his help.

Last night, for the hundredth time, I slept in this deserted place. As I looked at the buildings, I thought of what a laborious task it must have been to bring so many stones here. It would have been easy enough—and far more practical—to build an outdoor oven. When I was finally able to sleep, it was very late. The music and the shouting woke me up a few hours later. I have not slept soundly since my escape; I am sure that if a ship, a plane, or any other form of transportation had arrived, I would have heard it. And yet suddenly, unaccountably, on this oppressive summerlike night, the grassy hillside has become crowded with people who dance, stroll up and down, and swim in the pool, as if this were a summer resort like Los Teques or Marienbad.

From the marshlands with their churning waters I can see the top of the hill, and the people who have taken up residence in the museum. I suppose someone might attribute their mysterious appearance to the effect of last night's heat on my brain. But there are no hallucinations or imaginings here: I know these people are real—at least as real as I am.

The fact that their clothes are from another era indicates that they are a group of eccentrics; but I have known many people who use such devices to capture the magic of the past.

I watch them unwaveringly, constantly, with the eyes of a man who has been condemned to death. They are dancing on the grassy hillside as I write, unmindful of the snakes at their feet. They are my unconscious enemies who, as they corner me against the sea in the disease-infested marshes, deprive me of everything I need, everything I must have if I am to go on living. The sound of their very loud phonograph—"Tea for Two" and "Valencia" are their favorite records—seems now to be permanently superimposed on the wind and the sea.

Perhaps watching them is a dangerous pastime: like every group of civilized men they no doubt have a network of consular establishments and a file of fingerprints that can send me, after the necessary ceremonies or conferences have been held, to jail.

But I am exaggerating. I actually find a certain fascination in watching these odious intruders—it has been so long since I have seen anyone. But there are times when I must stop.

First of all, I have so much work to do. This place could kill even a seasoned islander. And I have not been here long; I have no tools to work with.

Secondly, there is always the danger that they may see me watching them, or that they may find me if they come down to this part of the island; so I must build some sort of shelter to hide in.

And, finally, it is very difficult for me to see them. They are at the top of the hill, while I am far below. From here they look like a race of giants—I can see them better when they approach the ravine.

Living on these sandbanks is dreadful at a time like this. A few days ago the tide was higher than any I have seen since I came to the island.

When it grows dark I make a bed of branches covered with leaves. I am never surprised to wake up and find that I am in the water. The tide comes in around seven o'clock in the morning, sometimes earlier. But once a week there are tides that can put an end to everything. I count the days by making gashes in a tree trunk; a mistake would fill my lungs with water.

I have the uncomfortable sensation that this paper is changing into a will. If I must resign myself to that, I shall try to make statements that can be verified so that no one, knowing that I was accused of duplicity, will doubt that they condemned me unjustly. I shall adopt the motto of Leonardo—*Ostinato rigore*—as my own, and endeavor to live up to it.

I believe that this island is called Villings, and belongs to the archipelago of the Ellice Islands.[1] More details can be obtained from the rug merchant, Dalmacio Ombrellieri (21 Hyderabad Street, Ramkrishnapur, Calcutta). He fed me for several days while I hid in one of his Persian rugs, and then he put me in the hold of a ship bound for Rabaul. (But I do not wish to compromise him in any way, for I am naturally very grateful to him.) My book *Apology for Survivors* will enshrine Ombrellieri in the memory of men—the probable location of heaven—as a kind person who helped a poor devil escape from an unjust sentence.

A card from the rug merchant put me in contact with a Sicilian at Rabaul who gave me instructions and a stolen boat as we stood in the metallic gleam of the moonlight (I could smell the stench of the fish

---

[1] Doubtful. He mentions a hill and several kinds of trees. The Ellice, or Lagoon, Islands are flat. The coconut is the only tree that grows in their coral sands. (Editor's Note.)

canneries). I rowed frantically, and arrived, incredibly, at my destination (for I did not understand the compass; I had lost my bearings; I had no hat and I was ill, haunted by hallucinations). The boat ran aground on the sands at the eastern side of the island (the coral reefs must have been submerged). I stayed in the boat for more than a day, reliving that horrible experience, forgetting that I had arrived at my journey's end.

The island vegetation is abundant. Spring, summer, autumn, and winter plants, grasses, and flowers overtake each other with urgency, with more urgency to be born than to die, each one invading the time and the place of the others in a tangled mass. But the trees seem to be diseased; although their trunks have vigorous new shoots, their upper branches are dry. I find two explanations for this: either the grass is sapping the strength from the soil or else the roots of the trees have reached stone (the fact that the young trees are in good condition seems to confirm the second theory). The trees on the hill have grown so hard that it is impossible to cut them; nor can anything be done with those on the bank: the slightest pressure destroys them, and all that is left is a sticky sawdust, some bland splinters.

The island has four grassy ravines; there are large boulders in the ravine on the western side. The museum, the chapel, and the swimming pool are up on the hill. The buildings are modern, angular, unadorned, built of unpolished stone, which is somewhat incongruous with the architectural style.
The chapel is flat, rectangular—it looks like a long box. The swimming pool appears to be well built, but as it is at ground level it is always filled with snakes, frogs, and aquatic insects. The museum is a large building, three stories high, without a visible roof; it has a covered porch in front and another smaller one in the rear, and a cylindrical tower.
The museum was open when I arrived; I moved in at once. I do not know why the Italian referred to it as a museum. It could be a fine hotel for about fifty people, or a sanatorium.
In one room there is a large but incomplete collection of books, consisting of novels, poetry, drama. The only exception was a small

volume (Bélidor, *Travaux: Le Moulin Perse,* Paris, 1737), which I found on a green-marble shelf and promptly tucked away into a pocket of these now threadbare trousers. I wanted to read it because I was intrigued by the name *Bélidor,* and I wondered whether the *Moulin Perse* would help me understand the mill I saw in the lowlands of this island. I examined the shelves in vain, hoping to find some books that would be useful for a research project I began before the trial. (I believe we lose immortality because we have not conquered our opposition to death; we keep insisting on the primary, rudimentary idea: that the whole body should be kept alive. We should seek to preserve only the part that has to do with consciousness.)

The large room, a kind of assembly hall, has walls of rose-colored marble, with greenish streaks that resemble sunken columns. The windows, with their panes of blue glass, would reach the top floor of the house where I was born. Four alabaster urns (six men could hide in each one) irradiate electric light. The books improve the room somewhat. One door opens onto the hall; another opens onto the round room; another, the smallest one, is concealed by a screen and opens onto a spiral staircase. The principal staircase is at the end of the hall; it is elegantly carpeted. There are some wicker chairs in the room, and the walls are lined with books.

The dining room measures approximately forty feet by fifty. There are three mahogany columns at each side, and each group of columns supports a stand with a figure of a seated divinity that appears to be Indian or Egyptian, of ocher terracotta. Each god is three times larger than a man, and is garlanded by dark plaster leaves. Below them there are large panels with drawings by Foujita, which present a discordant aspect (because of their humility).

The floor of the circular room is an aquarium. Invisible glass boxes in the water incase the electric lights that provide the only illumination for that windowless room. I recall the place with disgust. Hundreds of dead fish were floating on the water when I arrived, and removing them was an obnoxious task. Now, after letting the water run for days and days, I can still smell the odor of dead fish when I am in the room (it reminds me of the beaches in my country, where huge quantities of fish, dead and alive, emerge from the water to contami-

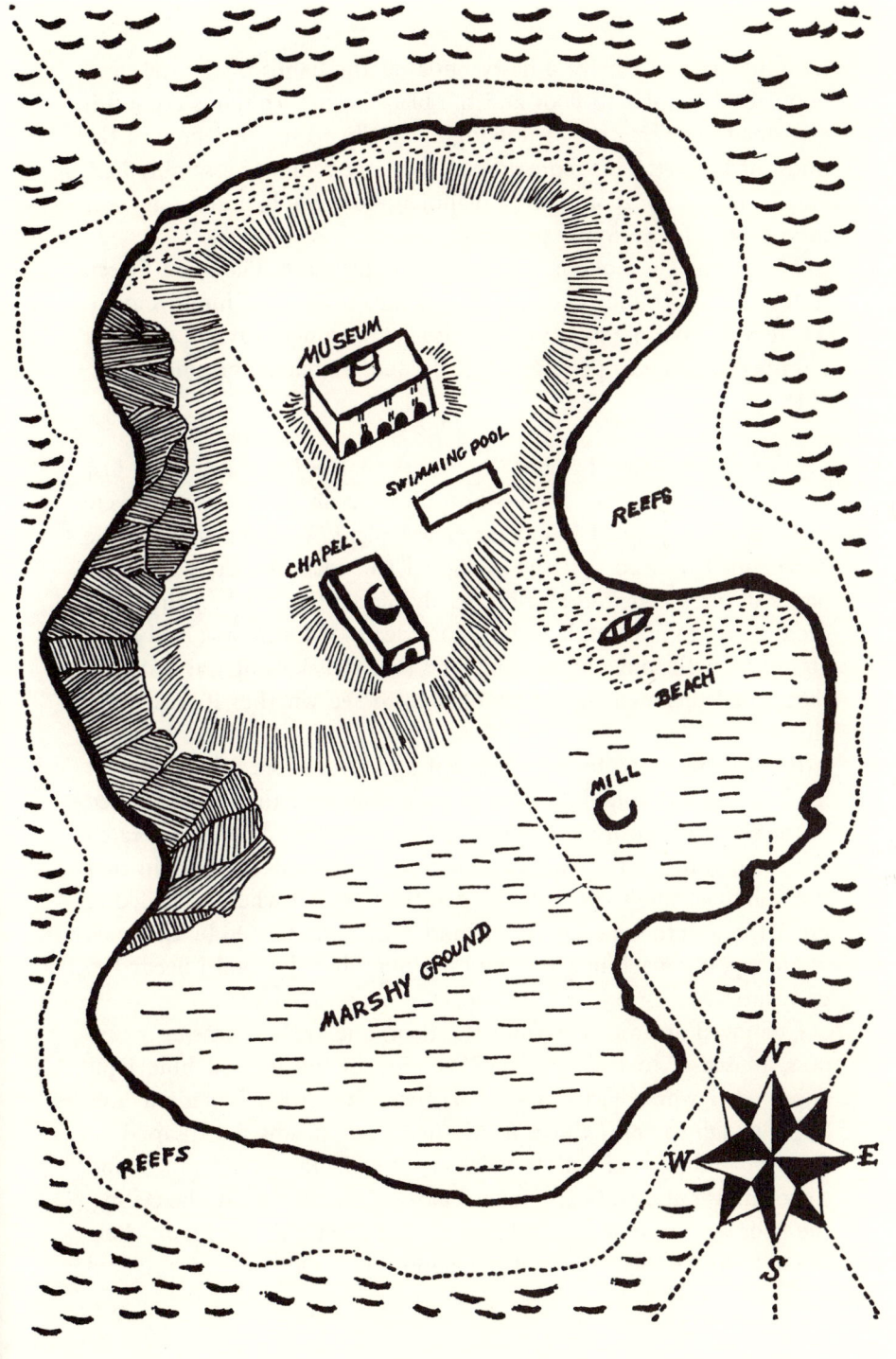

nate the air, and receive a hasty burial at the hands of the outraged populace. The lighted floor and the black-lacquer columns around it give one the impression of walking magically on top of a pool in the midst of a forest. This room adjoins the large room, or assembly hall, and a small green room with a piano, a phonograph, and a screen of mirrors, which has twenty panels or more.

The rooms are modern, pretentious, unpleasant. There are fifteen suites. Clearing mine out completely made only a slight improvement. There were no more paintings by Picasso, or smoked crystal, or books inscribed by famous people, but still I felt wretched and uncomfortable.

On two occasions I made discoveries in the basement. The first time I was looking for food—the provisions in the storeroom were growing scarce—and I found the power plant. Walking through the basement, I noticed that the skylight I had seen outside, with thick panes of glass and iron grating, partly hidden by the branches of a cedar tree, was not visible from the inside. As if I were involved in an argument with someone who insisted that the skylight was not real, that I had dreamed it, I went outside to see whether it was really there.

It was. I returned to the basement and after some difficulty I got my bearings and found, from the inside, the place that corresponded to the skylight's position. I looked for cracks, secret doors. The search was to no avail, for the wall was smooth and very solid. I thought that the wall must surely conceal a hidden treasure; but when I decided to break the wall to see what was behind it I was motivated by the hope of finding, not machine guns and munitions, but the food I needed so desperately.

I removed an iron bolt from the door, and with increasing weariness, I used it to make a small opening in the wall: a blue light appeared. I worked with a kind of frenzy and soon I made a hole large enough to crawl through. My first reaction was not disappointment at finding no food, or relief at recognizing a water pump and a generator, but ecstatic, prolonged amazement: the walls, the ceiling, the floor were of blue tile and even the air itself (in that room where the only contact with the outside world was a high skylight obscured by the branches of a tree) had the deep azure transparency of a waterfall's foam.

I know very little about motors, but even so I was not long in getting them started. Now when the rain water is all gone I can turn on the pump. It surprises me that the machines are relatively uncomplicated and in good condition and, especially, that I knew what to do with them. But I was not completely successful and I have come to feel, more and more, that perhaps I may never be. For I have not yet been able to discover the purpose of the green motors, in the same room, or the reason for the mill wheel I saw in the lowlands at the southern tip of the island (it is connected to the basement by an iron pipeline, and if it were not so far from the coast I should imagine it had something to do with the tides; could it possibly charge the storage batteries of the power plant?). My ineptitude makes me very frugal; I turn on the motors only when it is absolutely necessary to do so.

But once I had every light in the museum burning all night long. That was the second time I made discoveries in the basement.

I was ill. I hoped that I might find a medicine cabinet somewhere in the museum. There was nothing upstairs, so I went down to the basement and—that night I forgot my sickness, I forgot the horrible, nightmarish existence I was leading. I discovered a secret door, a stairway, a second basement. I entered a many-sided room, like those bomb shelters I have seen in movies. The walls were covered with strips of a material that resembled cork, and with slabs of marble, arranged symmetrically. I took a step: through stone arches I saw the same room duplicated eight times in eight directions as if it were reflected in mirrors. Then I heard the sound of many footsteps—they were all around me, upstairs, downstairs, all through the museum. I took another step: the sounds faded away, as if they had been muffled. (It reminded me of the way a snowstorm on the cold highlands of my Venezuela deadens all the noises within earshot.)

I went upstairs, back to the silence, the lonely sound of the sea, the quiet movement of the centipedes. I dreaded an invasion of ghosts or, less likely, an invasion of the police. I stood behind a curtain for hours, perhaps minutes, irked by the hiding place I had chosen (I could be seen from the outside; and if I wanted to escape from someone in the room I would have to open a window). Then, mustering my courage, I searched the house, but I was still uneasy, for there was no mistake about it: I had clearly heard myself surrounded by moving footsteps all through the building, at different levels.

Early the next morning I went down to the basement again. The same footsteps seemed to surround me again, some close, others farther away. But this time I understood them. Annoyed, I continued to explore the second basement, intermittently escorted by the diligent swarm of echoes, many dimensions of the same echo. There are nine identical rooms in the second basement, and five others in a lower basement. They appear to be bomb shelters. Who built this place in 1924 or thereabouts? And why did they abandon it? What sort of bombings were they afraid of? And why should men who could plan such a well-constructed building make a shelter like this, which tries one's mental equilibrium: when I sigh, for example, I can hear the echoes of a sigh, both near and faraway, for two or three minutes afterward. And when there are no echoes, the silence is as horrible as that heavy weight that keeps you from running away in dreams.

From my description the attentive reader can obtain a list of more or less startling objects, situations, facts; the most startling of all, of course, is the sudden arrival of the people who are up on the hill as I write. Are these people connected in some way with the ones who lived here in 1924? Did these visitors build the museum, the chapel, the swimming pool? I find it difficult to believe that one of them ever stopped listening to "Tea for Two" or "Valencia" long enough to design this building, which abounds in echoes, but which is bombproof.

One of these people, a woman, sits on the rocks to watch the sunset every afternoon. She wears a bright scarf over her dark curls; she sits with her hands clasped on one knee; her skin is burnished by prenatal suns; her eyes, her black hair, her bosom make her look like one of the Spanish or gypsy girls in those paintings I detest.

(Although I have been making entries in this diary at regular intervals, I have not had a chance to work on the books that I hope to write as a kind of justification for my shadowy life on this earth. And yet these lines will serve as a precaution, for they will stay the same even if my ideas change. But I must not forget what I now know is true: for my own safety, I must renounce—once and for all—any help from my fellow men.)

I had nothing to hope for. That was not so horrible—and the acceptance of that fact brought me peace of mind. But now the woman has changed all that. And hope is the one thing I must fear.

She watches the sunset every afternoon; from my hiding place I watch her. Yesterday, and again today, I discovered that my nights and days wait for this hour. The woman, with a gypsy's sensuality and a large, bright-colored scarf on her head, is a ridiculous figure. But still I feel (perhaps I only half believe this) that if she looked at me for a moment, spoke to me only once, I would derive from those simple acts the sort of stimulus a man obtains from friends, from relatives, and, most of all, from the woman he loves.

This hope (although it is against my better judgment) must have been whetted by the people who have kept me away from her: the fishermen and the bearded tennis player. Finding her with the latter today annoyed me; of course I am not jealous. But I was not able to see her yesterday either. As I was on my way to the rocks, the people who were fishing there made it impossible for me to come any closer. They did not speak to me, because I ran away before they saw me. I tried to elude them from above—impossible. Their friends were up there, watching them fish. The sun had already set when I returned: the lonely rocks bore witness to the night.

Perhaps I am leading myself into a blunder that will have dire consequences; perhaps this woman, tempered by so many late afternoon suns, will betray me to the police.

I may be misjudging her; but I cannot forget the power of the law. Those who are in a position to sentence others impose penalties that make us value liberty above all things.

Now, harassed by dirt and whiskers I cannot eradicate, feeling inordinately the weight of my years, I long for the benign presence of this woman, who is undoubtedly beautiful.

I am certain that the greatest difficulty of all will be to survive her first impression of me. But surely she will not judge me by my appearance alone.

There were three large floods in the past two weeks. Yesterday I almost drowned. The water catches me off guard. I studied the marks on the tree, and calculated the tide for today. But if I had been asleep early this morning I would be dead now. The water rose swiftly with that unusual intensity it has once a week. I cannot account for these surprises; they may be due to mistakes in my calculations, or to a temporary change in the schedule of the high tides. If the tides are always subject to such variations, life in this area will be even more precarious. But I shall survive it. After all, I have been through so much already!

I was sick, in pain, feverish, for a long time; very busy trying not to die of hunger; unable to write (and hating my fellow men).

When I arrived at the island, I found some provisions in the storeroom of the museum. In a very old, charred oven I made an inedible bread of flour, salt, and water. Before very long I was eating flour out of the sack (with sips of water). I used everything that was there, including some spoiled lamb tongues. I used up the matches, allowing myself just three a day. (I feel the deepest respect for the men who first learned how to kindle fires; how much more advanced they were than we!) I had to work for many days, lacerating myself in the process, in an effort to make a trap. When I finally succeeded, I was able to add fresh, bloody birds to my diet. I have followed the tradition of recluses: I have also eaten roots. I learned to recognize the most poisonous plants by the pain I suffered, the attacks of fever, the dreadful discoloration of my skin, the seizures that obliterated my memory, and the unforgettable fears that filled my dreams.[2]

I am miserable. I have no tools down here. This region is unhealthy, sinister. But a few months ago the mere thought of a life like this would have seemed too good to be true.

The daily tides are neither dangerous nor punctual. Sometimes they lift the leafy branches I sleep upon, and I wake up in a mixture of sea water and the muddy water of the marshes.

I hunt during the afternoons; in the morning the water is up to my waist, and the submerged part of my body feels so large and heavy

---

[2] He must have been living under coconut trees. Why, then, does he not mention them? Is it possible he did not see them? Or is it more probable that, since they were diseased, the trees did not produce fruit? (Editor's Note.)

that I can scarcely move. In compensation for these discomforts, there are fewer snakes and lizards. But the mosquitoes are present the whole day, the whole year long.

The tools are in the museum. I hope to be brave enough to try to go and get them later. But that may not be necessary after all—perhaps these people will disappear; perhaps they are merely hallucinations.

The boat, on the beach at the eastern part of the island, is inaccessible now. But my loss of it is not important; all I have really lost is the satisfaction of knowing that I am not a captive, that I can leave the island if I wish to. But was I ever really able to leave? That boat has been a kind of inferno to me. When I came here all the way from Rabaul, I had no drinking water, no covering for my head. The sea is endless when you are in a rowboat. I was overwhelmed by the sun, by fatigue. I was plagued by a burning sensation and by dreams that never ceased.

Now I spend my days trying to distinguish the edible roots. I have come to manage my life so well that I do all my work and still have time to rest. This makes me feel free, happy.

Yesterday I lagged behind; today I worked continuously; still there is more work left for tomorrow. When there is so much to do, I do not have time to think about the woman who watches the sunsets.

Yesterday morning the sea invaded the sandbanks. I never saw a tide of such proportions. It was still rising when the rain started (the rains here are infrequent, very heavy, and accompanied by strong winds). I had to find shelter.

I climbed the hill in spite of the odds against me: the slippery terrain, the intense downpour, the strong wind, and the dense foliage. I thought that perhaps I could hide in the chapel (it is the most unfrequented place on the island).

I was in one of the anterooms where the priests eat breakfast and change their clothes (I have not seen a member of the clergy among the occupants of the museum), and all at once two people were standing there, as if they had not arrived, as if they had appeared only in my sight or my imagination. I hid—nervously, stupidly—under the altar, among the red silks and laces. They did not see me. I am still amazed at that.

Even after they had gone I kept on crouching there uncomfortably,

21

frozen, peering cautiously between the silk curtains beneath the main altar, concentrating on the sounds of the storm, watching the dark mountains of the anthills, the undulant paths of large, pale ants, the agitation on the tile floor. I listened to the rain pelting against the walls and the roof, the water stirring in the eaves, the rain pouring on the path outside, the thunder. I could hear the confused sounds of the storm, the rustling trees, the pounding surf resounding on the shore, and I strained my ears to isolate the steps or the voices of someone who might be approaching my hiding place, for I did not want to be taken by surprise again—

I began to hear the fragments of a concise, very faint melody. Then it faded away completely, and I thought of the figures that appear, according to Leonardo, when we look fixedly at damp spots on a wall for any length of time. The music came back; and I listened to it, still crouching, my vision blurred, my body agitated, but thrilled by the beauty of its harmony. In a little while I dared to edge my way over to the window. The water was white on the glass, and opaque, and it was almost impossible to see— I was so taken aback that I was not even afraid to look out through the open door.

The people who live here are dreadful snobs—or else they are the inmates of an abandoned insane asylum! Without any audience (or perhaps their performance has been for my benefit from the beginning), they are enduring discomfort, even risking their lives, in an attempt to be original. And I am not saying this because of my own bitterness: it is the truth. They moved the phonograph out of the green room next to the aquarium, and there they are, men and women together, sitting on benches or sprawling on the ground, chatting, listening to music or dancing, in the midst of a torrential downpour that threatens to uproot all the trees!

Now the woman who wears the scarf has become indispensable to me. Perhaps my "no hope" therapy is a little ridiculous; never hope, to avoid disappointment; consider myself dead, to keep from dying. Suddenly I see this feeling as a frightening, disconcerting apathy. I must overcome it. After my escape I managed to live with a kind of indifference to the deadly tedium, and as a result I attained peace of mind. Now I am contemplating a move that may send me back to my past or to the judges; but anything would be preferable to the utter purgatory I am living in.

It all started a week ago. That was when I first observed the miraculous appearance of these people; in the afternoon I stood by the rocks at the western part of the island, trembling. I told myself that all this was vulgar: like any recluse who had been alone too long, I was falling in love with a woman who was nothing but a gypsy. I went back to see her the next afternoon, and the next. She was there, and her presence began to take on the quality of a miracle. After that came the awful days when I did not see her because the fishermen and the bearded man were there; then the flood came, and I tried to protect myself from its devastation. This afternoon—

I am afraid. But more than that I am angry at myself. Now I must wait for those people to come and get me at any moment. If there is a delay it can only mean they are setting a trap for me. I shall hide this diary, invent some explanation, and wait for them near the boat, ready to fight, to escape. But I am not so worried about the dangers I am facing—I am most concerned about the mistake I made—it can deprive me of the woman forever.

After I had bathed, and was clean but more unkempt looking than ever (the humidity has that effect on my beard and hair), I went down to see her. This was my plan: I would wait for her by the rocks, and when she arrived I would be watching the sunset. That would change her surprise, her probable suspicion, to curiosity. Our common devotion to the setting sun would make a favorable impression on her. She would ask my name, we would become friends—

It was very late when I arrived. (My lack of punctuality exasperates me—to think that in the civilized world, in Caracas, I was always late deliberately; that was one of my most personal characteristics!)

I ruined everything. She was watching the sunset, and suddenly I jumped out from behind some boulders. With my hairy face, and standing above her, I must have appeared more hideous than I actually am.

I imagine they will be coming to get me any moment now. I have not prepared an explanation. I am not afraid.

This woman is not just a gypsy. Her aplomb astounded me, for she gave no indication that she had seen me. She did not blink an eye, or make the slightest movement of any kind.

The sun was still above the horizon, hovering as a kind of mirage. I hurried down to the rocks. I saw her: the bright scarf, her hands clasped on one knee, her glance, enlarging my little world. My breathing became uncontrollable. The rocks, the sea, everything seemed tremulous.

As I watched her, I could hear the ocean with its sounds of movement and fatigue close at hand, as if it had moved to my side. My agitation diminished somewhat. And I began to doubt that she could hear my breathing.

Then, while waiting to speak to her, I was reminded of an old psychological law. It was preferable to address her from a high place; that would make her look up to me. The elevation would compensate, at least in part, for my defects.

I climbed higher on the rocks. The effort made me feel weak. Other things that made me weak were:

My haste: I felt obliged to speak to her that very day. If I wanted to keep her from feeling afraid of me—we were in a lonely place and it was growing dark—I could not wait a minute longer.

The sight of her: As if she were posing for an invisible photographer, she surpassed the calm of the sunset. And I did not wish to interrupt that.

Speaking to her would be an alarming experience. I did not even know whether I had any voice left.

I watched her from my hiding place. I was afraid that she would see me, so I came out, perhaps too abruptly. Even so, her composure was not altered; she ignored me, as if I were invisible.

I hesitated no longer. "Please, young lady," I said, "will you please listen to me," but I hoped she would not listen, because I was so excited I had forgotten what I was going to say. The words "young lady" sounded ridiculous on the island. And besides, my sentence was too imperative (combined with my sudden appearance there, the time of day, the solitude).

I persisted: "I realize you may not wish—"

But I find it impossible now to recall exactly what I said. I was almost unconscious. I spoke in a slow, subdued voice with a com-

posure that suggested impropriety. I repeated the words, "young lady." I stopped talking altogether and began to look at the sunset, hoping that the shared vision of that peaceful scene would bring us together. I spoke again. The effort I was making to control myself pitched my voice even lower, and increased the indecency of my tone. After several more minutes of silence, I insisted, I implored, in what was surely a repulsive manner. And finally I became ridiculous. Trembling, almost shouting, I begged her to insult me, to inform against me even, if only she would break the terrible silence.

It was not as if she had not heard me, as if she had not seen me; rather it seemed that her ears were not used for hearing, that her eyes could not see.

She did insult me, in a sense, by showing that she was not afraid of me. Night had fallen when she picked up her basket and walked slowly up the hill.

The men have not come to get me yet. Perhaps they will not come tonight. Perhaps the woman is unusual in this respect, too—she may not have told them about seeing me. It is very dark tonight. I know the island well: I am not afraid of an army, if it tries to find me at night.

It has been, again, as if she did not see me. This time I made the mistake of not speaking to her at all.

When the woman came down to the rocks, I was watching the sunset. She stood there for a moment without moving, looking for a place to spread out her blanket. Then she walked toward me. If I had put out my hand, I would have touched her. This possibility horrified me (as if I had almost touched a ghost). There was something frightening in her complete detachment. But when she sat down at my side it seemed she was defying me, trying to show that she no longer ignored my presence.

She took a book out of her basket and sat there reading. I tried to control my nerves.

Then, as she stopped reading and looked up, I thought, "She is going to ask me a question." But the implacable silence continued. I understood the serious implications of not interrupting it; but still, without any obstinacy, for no reason, I remained silent.

Her companions have not come to get me. Perhaps she has not told them about me. Or they may be worried because I know the island so well (and perhaps they send the woman back each day to make me think she is in love with me, to put me off my guard). I am suspicious. But I am sure I can ferret out any scheme, no matter how cunning it may be.

I have found that I usually imagine that things are going to turn out badly. This tendency started about three or four years ago; it is not accidental; but it is annoying. The fact that the woman comes back each day, that she wants to be near me, all this seems to indicate a change that is too good to be true— Perhaps I can forget my beard, my age, and the police who have pursued me for so long—and who, no doubt, are still searching for me stubbornly, like an effective curse. But I must not let myself be too optimistic. As I write these lines, I have an idea that gives me some hope. I do not believe I have insulted the woman, but still it would not do any harm to apologize to her. What does a man usually do on these occasions? He sends flowers, of course. I have a ridiculous plan; but any gift, no matter how trivial, is touching if it is given in the spirit of humility. There are many flowers on the island. When I arrived I saw some of them growing near the swimming pool and the museum. I should be able to make a small garden for her down by the rocks, enlisting nature's help to gain her confidence. Perhaps the results of my efforts will put an end to her silence and her reserve. It will be a poetic maneuver! I have never worked with colors; I know nothing about art. But I am sure I can make a modest effort, which will be pleasing to her.

I got up very early this morning. My plan was so good that I felt it surely would not fail.

I went to gather the flowers, which are most abundant down in the ravines. I picked the ones that were least ugly. (Even the palest flowers have an almost animal vitality!) When I had picked all I could carry and started to arrange them, I saw that they were dead.

I was going to change my plan, but then I remembered that up on the hill, not far from the museum, there is another place where many flowers grow. As it was early in the morning, I felt certain that the people would still be sleeping, so it would be safe to go there.

I picked several of these very small and scabrous flowers. It seemed that they did not have that monstrous urge to die.

Their disadvantages: they are small, and they grow near the museum.

Almost all morning I exposed myself to the danger of being seen by anyone brave enough to get up before ten o'clock. But while I was gathering the flowers, I kept an eye on the museum and did not see any signs of life; this allows me to suppose, to be certain, that I was not observed either.

The flowers are very small. I shall have to plant literally thousands of them if I want my garden to be noticed.

I spent a long time preparing the soil, breaking the ground (it is hard, and I have a large surface to cover), and sprinkling it with rain water. When the ground is ready, I shall have to find more flowers. I shall try to keep those people from seeing me, or from seeing my garden before it is finished. I had almost forgotten that there are cosmic demands on the life of a plant. And after all my work, the risk I have taken, the flowers may not even live until sunset.

I see that I have no artistic talent whatever, but I am sure my garden will be quite touching, between the clumps of grass and hay. Naturally, it will be a fraud. Although it will look like a cultivated garden this afternoon, it will be wilted by tomorrow, or, if there is a wind, it may have no flowers at all.

It rather embarrasses me to reveal the design of my garden. An immense woman is seated, watching the sunset, with her hands clasped on one knee; a diminutive man, made of leaves, kneels in front of the woman (he will be labeled *I*). And underneath it I shall make this inscription:

> Sublime, close at hand but mysterious
> With the living silence of the rose.

My fatigue almost sickens me. I could sleep under the trees until this evening, but I shall not do it. It must be my nerves that make me feel this urge to write. And the reason I am so nervous is that everything I do now is leading me to one of three possible futures: to the woman, to solitude (or the living death in which I spent the past few years, an impossibility now that I have seen the woman), or to a horrible sentence. Which one will it be? Time alone will tell. But still I know that writing this diary can perhaps provide the answer; it may even help produce the right future.

When I made this garden, I felt like a magician because the finished work had no connection with the precise movements that produced it. My magic depended on this: I had to concentrate on each part, on the difficult task of planting each flower and aligning it with the preceding one. As I worked, the garden appeared to be either a disorderly conglomeration of flowers or a woman.

And yet the finished garden is quite beautiful. But I was not able to create it exactly as I had planned. In imagination it is no more difficult to make a woman standing than to make one seated with her hands clasped on one knee; but in reality it is almost impossible to create the latter out of flowers. The woman is shown from the front view, with her head in profile, looking at the sunset. A scarf made of violet-colored flowers covers her head. Her skin is not right. I could not find any flowers of that somber color that repels and attracts me at the same time. Her dress and the ocean are made of blue and of white flowers. The sun is composed of some strange sunflowers that grow on this island. I am shown in profile view, kneeling. I am small (a third of the size of the woman) and green, made of leaves.

I had to modify the inscription. The first one was too long to make out of flowers. I changed it to this:

> You have awakened me from a living death on this island.

I liked the idea of calling myself a dead man who suffered from insomnia. I liked it so well, I almost forgot to be courteous—she might have interpreted the phrase as a reproach. But I believe I was blinded by my wish to appear as an ex-corpse, and I was delighted with the discovery that death was impossible if I could be with the woman. The variations with all their monotony were almost monstrous:

> You have kept a dead man on this island from sleeping.

or:

I am no longer dead: I am in love.

But I lost my courage. The inscription on the flowers says:

The humble tribute of my love.

The way things turned out was natural enough, but unexpectedly merciful. I am lost. My little garden was a dreadful mistake. When Ajax—or some other Hellenic name I have forgotten now—slaughtered the animals, he made a mistake of equal magnitude; but in this case, I am the slaughtered animals.

This afternoon the woman came earlier than usual. She left her book and basket on a rock, and spread out her blanket close to the shore. She was wearing a tennis dress and a violet-colored head scarf. She sat there for a moment, watching the sea, as if she were only half awake; then she stood up and went to get her book. She moved with that freedom we have when we are alone. As she passed my little garden she pretended not to notice it. I did not mind, for the moment she arrived I realized what an atrocious failure it was, and I was miserable because it was too late to do anything about it. When the woman opened her book, put her fingers between the pages, and continued to watch the sunset, I began to feel less nervous. She did not go away until night had fallen.

Now I derive consolation from thinking about her disapproval. And I wonder whether it is justified. What is there to hope for after this stupid mistake I have made? But since I can still recognize my own limitations, perhaps she will excuse me. Of course, I was at fault for having created the garden in the first place.

I was going to say that my experiment shows the dangers of creation, the difficulty of balancing more than one consciousness simultaneously. But what good would that do? What solace could I derive from that? Everything is lost now: the woman, my past solitude. Since I cannot escape, I continue with this monologue, which now is unjustifiable.

In spite of my nervousness I felt inspired today when I spent the afternoon sharing the undefiled serenity, the magnificence of the woman. I experienced the same sense of well-being again at night, when I dreamed about the bordello of blind women that Ombrellieri and I visited in Calcutta. In the dream I saw the woman of the sunsets and suddenly the bordello changed into an opulent Florentine palace. I was dazzled by it all, and I heard myself exclaim, "How romantic!" as I sobbed with complacent joy.

But I slept fitfully, remembering that I did not measure up to the woman's strict demands. I shall never be able to forget it: she controlled her distaste and pretended, kindly, not to see my horrible little garden. I was miserable, too, hearing "Tea for Two" and "Valencia," which that blatant phonograph repeated until sunrise.

All that I have written about my life—hopefully or with apprehension, in jest or seriously—mortifies me.

I am in a bad state of mind. It seems that for a long time I have known that everything I do is wrong, and yet I have kept on the same way, stupidly, obstinately. I might have acted this way in a dream, or if I were insane— When I slept this afternoon, I had this dream, like a symbolic and premature commentary on my life: as I was playing a game of croquet, I learned that my part in the game was killing a man. Then, suddenly, I knew I was that man.

Now the nightmare continues. I am a failure, and now I even tell my dreams. I want to wake up, but I am confronted with the sort of resistance that keeps us from freeing ourselves from our most atrocious dreams.

Today the woman was trying to show me her indifference, and she succeeded. But why is she so cruel? Even though I am the victim, I can view the situation objectively.

She was with the dreadful tennis player. His appearance should discourage any feelings of jealousy. He is very tall and was wearing a wine-colored tennis jacket, which was much too large for him, white slacks, and huge yellow and white shoes. His beard seemed to be false, his skin effeminate, waxy, mottled on his temples. His eyes are dark; his teeth, ugly. He speaks slowly, opening his small round mouth wide, vocalizing in a childish way, revealing a small round crimson tongue, which is always close to his lower teeth. His hands are long and pallid—I sense that they are slightly moist.

When I saw them approaching I hid at once. The woman must have seen me; at least, I suppose she did for not once did she look in my direction.

I am quite sure that the man did not notice the little garden until later. And, as before, she pretended not to see it.

They were speaking French. They stood, simply watching the sea, as if something had saddened them. The man said a few words I could not hear. Each time a wave broke against the boulders, I took two or three quick steps in their direction. They were French. The woman shook her head. I did not hear what she said, but it was clearly a negative reply. She closed her eyes and smiled sweetly.

"Please believe me, Faustine—" began the bearded man with obvious desperation, and I found out her name, at last! (Of course, it does not matter now.)

"No— Now I know what you really want—"

She smiled again, with no bitterness or ecstasy, with a certain frivolity. I know that I hated her then. She was just playing with us.

"What a pity that we cannot come to an understanding! We have only a short time left—three days, and then it will all be over."

I do not know what he meant. All I know is that he must be my enemy. He seemed to be sad; but I should not be surprised to learn that this was merely a pose. Faustine's behavior is grotesque; it is almost driving me mad!

The man tried to mitigate the gravity of his statement. He said several sentences that had approximately this meaning: "There's nothing to worry about. We are not going to discuss an eternity—"

"Morel," said Faustine stupidly, "do you know that I find you mysterious?"

In spite of Faustine's questions he remained in his light-hearted mood.

The bearded man went to get her scarf and basket. She had left them on a rock a few feet away. He came back shaking the sand out of them, and said, "Don't take my words so seriously. Sometimes I think that if I am able to arouse your curiosity— But please don't be angry."

When he went to get her things, and then again on the way back, he stepped on my garden. Did he do it deliberately, or did he just not happen to notice it? Faustine saw it, I swear that she did, and yet she would not spare me that insult. She smiled and asked questions with a great show of interest; it was almost as if she surrendered her whole being to him, so complete was her curiosity. But I do not like her attitude. The little garden is no doubt in wretched taste. But why should she stand there calmly and let a disgusting man trample on it? Have I not been trampled on enough already?

But then—what can you expect of people like that? They are the sort you find on indecent postcards. How well they go together: a pale bearded man and a buxom gypsy girl with enormous eyes— I even feel I have seen them in the best collections in Caracas.

And still I wonder: what does all this mean? Certainly she is a detestable person. But what is she after? She may be playing with the bearded man and me; but then again he may be a tool that enables her to tease me. She does not care if she makes him suffer. Perhaps Morel only serves to emphasize her complete repudiation of me, to portend the inevitable climax and the disastrous outcome of this repudiation!

But if not— Oh, it has been such a long time now since she has seen me. I think I shall kill her, or go mad, if this continues any longer. I find myself wondering whether the disease-ridden marshes I have been living in have made me invisible. And, if that were the case, it would be an advantage: then I could seduce Faustine without any danger—

Yesterday I did not visit the rocks. I told myself over and over again that I would not go today either. But by the middle of the afternoon I knew that I had to go. Faustine was not there, and now I am wondering when she will come back. I suppose that her trampling of my garden has brought her fun with me to an end. Now I will bore her like a joke that was amusing once but does not bear repeating. And I will see to it that it is not repeated!

But, as I sat on the rocks waiting, I was miserable. "It's all my fault," I said to myself (that Faustine did not come), "because I was so sure *I* was not coming!"

I climbed the hill, hoping for a glimpse of her. I came out from behind a clump of bushes, and found myself facing two men and a woman. I stood still, I did not dare to breathe; there was nothing separating us but twenty feet of empty, crepuscular space. The men had their backs to me, but the woman faced them, and she was looking right at me. I saw her shudder. She turned quickly and looked toward the museum. I crouched down behind some bushy plants. I heard her say, "This is not the proper time for ghost stories. We'd better go in now!"

I still do not know whether they were actually telling such stories, or if she mentioned ghosts only to announce a strange occurrence (my presence).

They went away. I saw a man and woman strolling by, not far away. I was afraid they would see me. As they approached, I heard a familiar voice say, "Today I didn't go to see—" (I began to tremble violently. I was sure that she was talking about me.)

"And are you sorry?"

I did not hear Faustine's answer. I noticed that the bearded man had made some progress, because they were using the intimate form of address.

I have come back to the lowlands. I have decided to stay here until the sea carries me away. If the intruders come to get me, I shall not surrender; I shall not try to escape.

My plan not to let Faustine see me again lasted for four days (and was helped by two tides that gave me a lot of work to do).

The fifth day I went to the rocks early. Then I saw Faustine and that damned tennis player. They spoke French correctly, too correctly—like South Americans.

"So you no longer trust me?"

"No."

"But you used to have faith in me—"

There was a coolness between them now. I was reminded of persons who slip back into their old habits of formal speech soon after beginning to speak with intimacy. Their conversation might have made me think of that. But I thought about the idea of a return to the past in a different sense also.

"Would you believe me if I said I could take you back to a time before that afternoon in Vincennes?"

"No, I could never believe you again. Never."

"The influence of the future on the past," said Morel enthusiastically, almost inaudibly.

They stood together, looking at the sea. The man seemed to be trying to break an oppressive tension between them.

"Please believe me, Faustine—"

I remember thinking what a stubborn person he was. He was repeating the same demands I had heard him make the week before.

"No— Now I know what you really want—"

Conversations are subject to repetition, although one cannot explain this phenomenon. I would not have the reader attribute that statement to any bitterness on my part, nor to the very facile association of the words "fugitive," "recluse," "misanthrope." But I gave the matter some study before my trial—conversations are an exchange of news (example: meteorological), of joy or irritation already known or shared by the participants (example: intellectual). But all conversations spring from the pleasure of speaking, from the desire to express agreement and disagreement.

Watching Morel and Faustine, listening to them, I felt that something strange was happening; I did not know what it was. All I knew was that Morel infuriated me.

"If I told you what I really wanted—"

"Would I take offense?"

"No, I think it would help us to understand each other better. We have only a short time left. Three days. What a pity that we cannot come to an understanding!"

I began to realize that the words and movements of Faustine and the bearded man coincided with those of a week ago. The atrocious eternal return. But today one element was missing. My little garden, mutilated by Morel's footsteps, is a mudhole now, with parts of dead flowers crushed into the ground.

I felt elated. I thought I had made this discovery: that there are unexpected, constant repetitions in our behavior. The right combination of circumstances had enabled me to observe them. One seldom has the chance to be a clandestine witness of several talks between the same people. But scenes are repeated in life, just as they are in the theatre.

After hearing Faustine and Morel speak, I turned back to the page (in my diary) where I reported their previous conversation, and I was able to verify that their words and actions were, essentially, the same (the few minor lapses I noticed were due to my own inaccuracy in reporting).

And then I began to suspect angrily that they were merely putting on a comic performance as a joke at my expense.

But let me explain. I never doubted for a minute the importance of trying to make Faustine realize that she and I were all that mattered (and that the bearded man had no place in our plans). I had begun to feel the desire to castigate him in some way—I played with the idea without acting upon it—to insult him by making him look ridiculous to her.

Now I had the chance. But how could I take advantage of it? I found it hard to think because of my anger.

I stood still, pretending to be lost in thought, waiting for the moment when I would be face to face with him. The bearded man went to get Faustine's scarf and basket. He came back shaking the sand out of them, saying (as he had said before): "Don't take my words so seriously. Sometimes I think—"

He was only a few feet away from Faustine. I was not sure what I was going to do. Spontaneity is the mother of crudity. I pointed at the bearded man, as if I were introducing him to Faustine, and shouted, "La femme à barbe, Madame Faustine!"

It was a very bad joke; in fact, it was not even clear whether I was speaking to her or to him.

The bearded man kept on walking toward Faustine, and if I had not moved in time he would have walked right into me. The woman did not stop asking questions; she did not interrupt her look of contentment. Her serenity still appalls me.

Since that moment I have been miserable and ashamed, and I have felt an urge to kneel at Faustine's feet. This afternoon I could not wait until sunset. I went straight to the hill, ready to give myself up, certain that if all went well I would soon be involved in a sentimental scene with Faustine. But I was wrong. There is no explanation for what has happened. *The hill is deserted now!*

When I saw that there was no one on the hill, I was afraid that this was some sort of a trap, that they were really hiding, lying in wait for me. Overcome with dread, I searched the whole museum, exercising extreme caution. But I had only to look at the furniture and the walls, which seemed to be invested with isolation, to be convinced that no one was there. What is more: to be convinced that no one was ever there. It is difficult, after an absence of almost twenty days, to be able to state positively that all the objects in a house with a great many rooms are exactly where they were when one went away; but it seems clear that these fifteen people (and an equal number of servants) did not move a bench, a lamp, or if they did they put everything back in its place, in the exact position it occupied before. I have inspected the kitchen and the laundry room; the meal I left twenty days ago, the clothes (stolen from a closet in the museum) that I hung up to dry twenty days ago, were there; the former spoiled, the latter dry, both untouched.

I shouted in the empty building, "Faustine! Faustine!"

There was no reply.

(I can think of two facts—a fact and a memory—that may be an explanation for these strange occurrences. Recently I started to experiment with new roots. I believe that in Mexico the Indians make a drink from the juice of certain roots, and—if I remember correctly—it causes a person to become delirious for several days. The conclusion, used to explain the presence of Faustine and her friends on this island, is logically admissible; but I do not seriously believe it applies in this case. Now that I have lost Faustine I should like to submit these problems to a hypothetical observer, a third person.)

And then I remembered, incredulously, that I was a fugitive and that justice still had its infernal power. Perhaps these people were playing an outrageous trick on me. If so, I must not give up now, or weaken my powers of resistance, for a horrible catastrophe could result.

I inspected the chapel, the basements. I decided to look at the whole island before going to bed. I went to the rocks, to the grassy part of the hill, to the beaches, the lowlands (my caution was excessive). I had to accept the fact that the intruders were not on the island.

But when I returned to the museum it was almost dark, and I felt nervous. I wanted the brightness of the electric light. I tried many switches; there was no illumination. This seems to confirm my belief that the tides furnish the energy for the motors (by means of that hydraulic mill or water wheel I saw in the lowlands). Those people must have wasted the light. There has been a long period of calm since the last two tides. It ended this very afternoon, when I went back to the museum. I had to close all the doors and windows; I thought that the wind and the sea were going to destroy the island.

In the first basement, standing alongside motors that looked enormous in the shadows, I felt very depressed. The effort needed to kill myself was superfluous now, because with Faustine gone not even the anachronous satisfaction of death remained.

To justify my descent into the basement, I tried to make the machinery work. There were a few weak explosions and then everything was quiet again, while outside the storm raged and the branches of the cedar tree scraped against the thick glass of the skylight.

When I came upstairs I heard the hum of a motor; with incredible speed the light touched everything and placed me in front of two men: one in white, the other in green (a cook and a manservant). They were speaking Spanish.

"Do you know why he chose this deserted spot?"

"He must have his reasons!"

I listened anxiously. These were not the same people. These new ghosts were Iberian (did they exist only in my brain, tortured by the privations I had suffered, by the poisonous roots and the equatorial sun, or were they really here on this deadly island?); their words made me conclude that Faustine had not returned.

They continued to converse in low tones, as if they had not heard my footsteps, as if I were not there.

"I don't deny that; but how did Morel happen to think of it in the first place?"

At this point they were interrupted by a man who said angrily, "Say, when are you coming anyway? Dinner has been ready for an hour!"

He stared at them (so intently that I suspected he was trying to resist an urge to look at me), and then ran off shouting excitedly. He was followed by the cook; the servant hurried away in the opposite direction.

I tried hard to control my nerves, but I was trembling. I heard a gong. In a situation like this, anyone, no matter how brave, would have been afraid, and I was no exception. Fortunately, though, I soon remembered that gong. I had seen it many times in the dining room.

I wanted to escape, but I restrained myself, because I knew I could not really run away; that was impossible. The storm, the boat, the night: even if the storm had ended, it would have been horrible to be out at sea on that moonless night. Besides, I was certain that the boat would not be long in capsizing. And surely the lowlands were flooded. If I ran away, where could I go? It would be better to listen; to watch the movements of these people; to wait.

I looked for a place to hide and chose a little room that I found under the stairway. (How stupid! If they had tried to find me, they would have looked there first!) I stayed in my hiding place for a while not daring to think, feeling slightly more relaxed but still bewildered.

Two problems occurred to me:

How did they get to this island? With a storm like this no captain would have dared to approach the shore; it was absurd to imagine that they had transferred to small boats while out at sea, and then used them to land on the island.

When did they come? Their dinner had been ready for a long time; yet when I went down to inspect the motors, less than fifteen minutes ago, there was no one on the island.

They mentioned Morel. Surely, it all had something to do with a return of the same people. It is probable, I thought tremblingly, that I shall have a chance to see Faustine again after all!

I peered out, expecting that someone would be waiting to seize me and then my dilemma would be over.

No one was there.

I went up the stairs and walked along the narrow balcony; then I stood behind one of the terracotta idols, and looked down on the dining room.

About a dozen people were seated at the table. I took them for a group of tourists from New Zealand or Australia; they appeared to be settled here, as if they did not plan to leave for some time.

I remember it well: I saw the group; I compared these new people with the others who had been here; I discovered that they did not appear to be transients, and only then did I think of Faustine. I searched for her and found her at once. I had a pleasant surprise: the bearded man was not at her side; a precarious joy, which I could scarcely believe: the bearded man was not there (but soon afterward I saw him across the table).

The conversation was not very animated. Morel brought up the subject of immortality. They spoke about travel, parties, diets. Faustine and a blond girl talked about different kinds of medicine. Alec, a young man, whose hair was carefully combed, an Oriental type with green eyes, tried to interest them in the subject of his wool business. He was singularly unsuccessful and soon gave up. Morel waxed enthusiastic about his plans for a ball field or tennis court for the island.

I recognized a few more of the people from the museum. On Faustine's left was a woman—Dora?—with blond curly hair; she smiled frequently, and her large head leaned forward slightly, making me think of a spirited horse. On Faustine's other side there was a dark young man, with bright eyes, bushy hair, and an intense look. Next to him sat a tall, flat-chested, extremely long-armed girl with an expression of disgust. Her name is Irene. On her other side was the woman who said, "This is not the proper time for ghost stories," that night when I was up on the hill. I cannot remember the others.

When I was a little boy, I used to play a game with the pictures in my books: I looked at them for a long time and new objects would keep appearing in an endless succession. Now as I stood there, feeling thwarted, I stared at the panels by Foujita with pictures of women, tigers, or cats.

The people filed into the assembly hall. I left the balcony, feeling terrified, for I knew my enemies were everywhere, including the basement (the servants). I went down the service stairs to the door that was concealed by a screen. The first thing I saw was a woman knitting by one of the alabaster urns and then the woman named Irene,

41

talking to a friend. I looked again, risking the possibility of being seen, and caught a glimpse of Morel at a table with five other people, playing cards. Faustine was sitting there with her back to me. The table was small, their feet were close together, and I stood there for several minutes, perhaps longer than I realized, oblivious to the danger of being observed as I tried to see whether Morel's feet and Faustine's were touching. Then this lamentable pursuit came to an abrupt end; for I saw a red-faced, astonished servant standing there watching me. He turned and went into the assembly hall. I heard footsteps. I hurried away. I hid between the first and second rows of alabaster columns in the round room where the floor was an aquarium. Fish were swimming about beneath my feet; they were identical counterparts of the dead ones I had removed shortly after I arrived on the island.

When I regained my composure, I moved toward the door. Faustine, Dora—her dinner companion—and Alec were coming up the stairs. Faustine walked slowly, with measured steps. As I looked at her I reflected that I was risking everything—my own peace of mind, the Universe, memories, my intense anxiety, the pleasure of learning about the tides and about more than one inoffensive root—for that ample body, those long, slender legs, that ridiculous sensuality.

I followed them. They turned abruptly and entered a room. Across the hall I saw an open door that revealed a lighted, empty room. I entered it cautiously. Apparently the person who had been there had forgotten to turn out the light. The neatness of the bed and of the dressing table, the absence of books and clothes, and the perfect order told me that no one was living in it.

I was uneasy when the other occupants of the museum went to their rooms. I heard their footsteps on the stairs and tried to turn out my light, but it was impossible: the switch did not work. I did not try to fix it, for it occurred to me that a light going off in an empty room would attract attention.

If it had not been for that broken switch perhaps I would have gone to sleep immediately, because I was so tired, and because I saw the lights go out, one by one, through the cracks in the doors down the hall. (I found it reassuring to know that Dora was in Faustine's room!) I could imagine that if anyone happened to walk through the hall he would come into my room to turn out the light (the rest of the museum was in total darkness). Perhaps it was inevitable that someone would enter, but I would not be in any real danger. When he saw that the switch was broken, the person would simply go away to avoid disturbing the others. I would have to hide for only a moment.

I was thinking about this when Dora's head appeared in the doorway. Her eyes looked through me. She went away, without trying to turn out the light.

I felt terrified. Now, my position compromised, I began to explore the building in my imagination, to find a safe hiding place. I did not want to leave that room, for as long as I was there I could guard Faustine's door. I sat down on the bed, leaned back, and went to sleep. Soon afterward I saw Faustine in a dream. She entered the room. She came very close to me. I woke up. The light was out. I tried not to move; I tried to begin to see in the darkness, but I could not control my breathing and my terror.

I got up, went out into the hall, and heard the silence that had followed the storm: nothing interrupted it.

I started to walk down the hall, feeling that a door would open suddenly and a pair of rough hands would reach out and grab me, a mocking voice would taunt me. The strange world I had been living in, my conjectures and anxieties, Faustine—they all seemed like an invisible path that was leading me straight to prison and death. I went downstairs, moving cautiously through the darkness. I came to a door and tried to open it, but I could not budge it—I could not even move the latch. (I have seen latches that were stuck before; but I do not understand the windows: they have no locks and yet it is impossible to open them.) I was becoming convinced that I would never be able to get out of there, I was growing more nervous and—perhaps because of this and because of my helplessness in the dark—it seemed that even the doors in the interior of the building were impossible to open. Some footsteps on the service stairs made me hurry. I did not know how to get out of the room. I felt my way along a wall, until I came to one of the enormous alabaster urns; with considerable effort and danger, I slid inside of it.

For a long time I huddled nervously against the slippery alabaster surface and the fragile lamp. I wondered if Faustine had stayed alone with Alec, or if he or she had gone out with Dora when the latter left the room.

This morning I was awakened by the sound of voices (I was very weak and too sleepy to hear what they were saying). Then everything was quiet.

I wanted to get away from the museum. I started to stand up, afraid that I would fall and break the enormous light bulb, or that someone would see my head as it emerged from the urn. Very slowly, laboriously, I climbed out. I hid behind the curtains for a moment. I was so weak that I could not move them; they seemed to be rigid and heavy, like the stone curtains carved on a tomb. I could visualize, painfully, the fancy pastries and other foods that civilization had to offer: I was sure I would find such things in the pantry. I had fainting spells, the urge to laugh out loud; then I walked boldly toward the staircase. The door was open. No one was inside. I went into the pantry—my courage made me proud. I heard footsteps. I tried to open a door to the outside, and again I encountered one of those inexorable latches. Someone was coming down the service stairs. I ran to the entrance to the pantry. Through the open door I could see part of a wicker chair and a pair of crossed legs. I turned toward the main stairway; I heard more footsteps. There were people in the dining room. I went into the assembly hall, noticed an open window, and, almost at the same time, I saw Irene and the woman who had spoken of ghosts, and the young man with the bushy hair; he walked toward me with an open book, reciting French poetry. I stopped short. Then I threaded my way stiffly between those people, almost touching them as I passed; I jumped out of the window and, in spite of the pain that racked my legs (it is about fifteen feet from the window to the ground below), I ran down through the ravine, stumbling and falling as I went, not daring to look back.

I found some food, and began to wolf it down. Suddenly I stopped, for I had lost my appetite.

Now my pain is almost gone. I am more serene. I think, although I know it seems absurd, that perhaps they did not see me in the museum. The whole day has gone by and no one has come to get me. It is frightening to accept so much good fortune!

Here is some evidence that can help my readers establish the date of the intruders' second appearance here: the following day two moons and two suns were visible, possibly only a local phenomenon; but probably they are a kind of mirage, caused by the moon or the sun, the sea and the air, and are surely visible from Rabaul and throughout this whole area. I noticed that the second sun—perhaps a reflection of the other—is much more intense. It seems that the temperature has risen infernally during the past two days, as if the new sun brought with it an unbearably hot summer. The nights are very white: there is a kind of polar glare in the air. But I imagine that the two moons and two suns hold no special interest now, for they must have been noted everywhere, either in the sky itself or in detailed and scholarly reports. I am not mentioning them because of any poetic attachment, or because of their rarity, but rather to give my readers, who receive newspapers and celebrate birthdays, a way to date these pages.

As far as I know, these are the first nights when two moons have been observed. But two suns were seen once before. Cicero speaks of them in *De Natura Deorum:* "Tum sole quod ut e patre audivi Tuditano et Aquilio consulibus evenerat."

I believe that is the correct version of the quotation.[3] At the Miranda Institute, M. Lobre made us memorize the first five pages of the Second Book and the last three pages of the Third Book. That is all I know about *The Nature of the Gods*.

The intruders did not come to get me. I can see them come and go on the hillside. Perhaps some imperfection in my soul (and the infinite numbers of mosquitoes) caused me to long for last night, when I had lost all hope of finding Faustine, and I did not feel this bitter anguish. Now I miss that moment when I thought I was settled once again in the museum, the undisputed master of my solitude.

---

[3] He is mistaken. He omits the most important word: *geminato* (from *geminatus:* "coupled, duplicated, repeated, reiterated"). The phrase is: ". . . tum sole geminato, quod, ut e patre audivi, Tuditano et Aquilio consulibus evenerat; quo quidem anno P. Africanus sol alter extinctus est." Translation: The two suns that, as I heard from my father, were seen in the Consulate of Tuditanus and Aquilius, in the year (183 B.C.) when the sun of Publius Africanus was extinguished. (Editor's Note.)

I remember what it was I was thinking about the night before last, in that insistently lighted room: About the nature of the intruders, about my relationship with them.

I tried several explanations.

I may have the famous disease that is associated with this island; it may have caused me to imagine the people, the music, Faustine; perhaps my body has developed horrible lesions, the signs of approaching death, which the other effects keep me from noticing.

The polluted air of the lowlands and my improper diet may have made me invisible. The intruders did not see me. (Else they have a superhuman discipline. I discarded secretly, with the certainty that I am right, my suspicion that this is a plot organized by the police to capture me.) Objection: I am not invisible to the birds, the lizards, the rats, the mosquitoes.

It occurred to me (precariously) that these could be beings from another planet, whose nature is different from ours, with eyes that are not used for seeing, with ears that do not hear. I remembered that they spoke correct French. I enlarged the foregoing monstrosity: this language may be a parallel attribute of our worlds, but the words may have different meanings!

I arrived at the fourth theory because of my mad impulse to relate my dreams. This is what I dreamed last night:

I was in an insane asylum. After a long consultation with a doctor (the trial?), my family had me taken there. Morel was the director of the asylum. Sometimes I knew I was on the island; sometimes I thought I was in the insane asylum; sometimes I was the director of the insane asylum.

I do not believe that a dream should necessarily be taken for reality, or reality for madness.

Fifth hypothesis: the intruders are a group of dead friends, and I am a traveler, like Dante or Swedenborg, or some other dead man of another sort, at a different phase of his metamorphosis; this island may be the purgatory or the heaven of those dead people (the possibility of several heavens has already been suggested; if only one existed, and if everyone went there and found a happy marriage and literary meetings on Wednesdays, many of us would have stopped dying).

Now I understand why novelists write about ghosts that weep and wail. The dead remain in the midst of the living. It is hard for them, after all, to change their habits—to give up smoking, or the prestige of being great lovers. I was horrified by the thought that I was invisible; horrified that Faustine, who was so close to me, actually might be on another planet (the sound of her name made me sad); but I am dead, I am out of reach, I thought; and I shall see Faustine, I shall see her go away, but my gestures, my pleas, my efforts will have no effect on her. And I knew that those horrible solutions were nothing but frustrated hopes.

Thinking about these ideas left me in a state of euphoria. I had proof that my relationship with the intruders was a relationship between beings on different planes. There could have been some catastrophe on the island that was imperceptible for its dead (I and the animals), after which the intruders arrived.

So I was dead! The thought delighted me. (I felt proud, I felt as if I were a character in a novel!)

I thought about my life. My unexciting childhood, the afternoons I spent on Paradise Street in Caracas; the days before my arrest—it seemed as if someone else had lived them; my long escape from justice; the months I have been living on this island. On two occasions I very nearly died. Once, when I was in my room at the fetid rose-colored boardinghouse at 11 West Street, during the days before the police came to get me (if I had died then, the trial would have been before the definitive Judge; my escape and my travels would have been the journey to heaven, hell, or purgatory). The other time was during the boat trip. The sun was melting my cranium and, although I rowed all the way to the island, I must have lost consciousness long before I arrived. All the memories of those days are imprecise; the only things I can recall are an infernal light, a constant swaying and the sound of water, a pain far greater than all our capacity for suffering.

I had been thinking about all this for a long time, so now I was quite tired, and I continued less logically: I was not dead until the intruders arrived; when one is alone it is impossible to be dead. Now I must eliminate the witnesses before I can come back to life. That will not be difficult: I do not exist, and therefore they will not suspect their own destruction.

And I had another idea, an incredible plan for a very private seduction, which, like a dream, would exist only for me.

These vain and unjustifiable explanations came to me during moments of extreme anxiety. But men and love-making cannot endure prolonged intensity.

I think I must be in hell. The two suns are unbearable. I am not feeling well, either, because of something I ate: some very fibrous bulbs that looked like turnips.

The suns were overhead, one above the other, and suddenly (I believe I was watching the sea until that moment) a ship loomed up very close, between the reefs. It was as if I had been sleeping (even the flies move about in their sleep, under this double sun!) and had awakened, seconds or hours later, without noticing that I had been asleep or that I was awakening. The ship was a large white freighter. "The police," I thought with irritation. "They must be coming to search the island." The ship's whistle blew three times. The intruders assembled on the hillside. Some of the women waved handkerchiefs.

The sea was calm. A launch was lowered, but it took the men almost an hour to get the motor started. A man dressed as an officer—perhaps he was the captain—got off on the island. The others returned to the ship.

The man walked up the hill. I was very curious and, in spite of my pains and the indigestible bulbs I had eaten, I went up on the other side. I saw him salute respectfully. The intruders asked him about his trip, and expressed interest in knowing whether he had "obtained everything" in Rabaul. I was behind a statue of a dying phoenix, unafraid of being seen (it seemed useless to hide). Morel escorted the man to a bench, and they both sat down.

Then I understood why the ship had come. It must have belonged to them, and now it was going to take them away.

I have three choices, I thought. Either to abduct her, to go on board the ship, or to let them take her away from me.

But if I abduct her they will surely send out a search party, and sooner or later they will find us. Is there no place on this whole island where I can hide her?

It also occurred to me that I could take her out of her room at

night when everyone was sleeping, and then the two of us would go away together in the small boat. But where would we go? Would the miracle of my trip to the island be repeated? How could I know where to go? Would risking my chances with Faustine make it worth while to hazard the tremendous dangers we would surely encounter in the middle of the ocean? Or perhaps those difficulties would be only too brief: possibly we would sink a few feet from shore.

If I managed to board the ship, without doubt I would be found. Perhaps I could talk to them, ask them to call Faustine or Morel, and then explain everything. I might have time—if they reacted unfavorably to my story—to kill myself before we arrived at the first port where there was a prison.

"I have to make a decision," I thought.

A tall, robust man with a red face, an unkempt black beard, and effeminate mannerisms approached Morel and said, "It's quite late. We still have to get ready, you know."

Morel replied, "Yes, yes. Just wait a moment, please."

The captain stood up. Morel kept on talking with a sense of urgency, patting him on the back several times, and then turned toward the fat man, while the captain saluted, and asked, "Shall we go now?"

The fat man turned to the dark-haired, intense youth who was with him, and repeated, "Shall we go?"

The young man nodded assent.

The three hurried toward the museum, paying no attention to the ladies, who were grouped nearby. The captain walked over to them, smiling courteously, and slowly escorted them in the direction of the museum.

I did not know what to do. Although it was a ridiculous scene, it alarmed me. What were they getting ready for? But still I thought that if I saw them leaving with Faustine, I would not interfere with their horrible plan, but would remain as an inactive, only slightly nervous spectator.

Fortunately, though, it was not yet time. I could see Morel's beard and his thin legs in the distance. Faustine, Dora, the woman who once spoke of ghosts, Alec, and the three men who had been there a short time before were walking down to the pool, in bathing suits. I ran from one clump of plants to another, trying to get a better look. The women hurried along, smiling; the men were engaging in calisthenics, as if they were trying to keep warm—this was inconceivable with two suns overhead. I could imagine how disillusioned they would be when they saw the pool. Since I have stopped changing the water it has become impenetrable (at least for a normal person): green, opaque, slimy, with large clusters of leaves that have grown monstrously, dead birds, and—of course—live snakes and frogs.

Undressed, Faustine is infinitely beautiful. She had that rather foolish abandon people often have when they bathe in public, and she was the first one to dive into the water. I heard them laughing and splashing about gaily.

Dora and the older woman came out first. The latter, waving her arm up and down, counted, "One, two, three!"

They must have been racing. The men came out of the pool, appearing to be exhausted. Faustine stayed in the water a while longer.

In the meantime some of the ship's crew had come over to the island. Now they were walking around. I hid behind some palm trees.

I am going to relate exactly what I saw happen from yesterday afternoon to this morning, even though these events are incredible and defy reality. Now it seems that the real situation is not the one I described on the foregoing pages; the situation I am living is not what I think it is.

When the swimmers went to get dressed, I resolved to be on my guard both day and night. However, I soon decided that this would not be necessary.

I was walking away when the dark, intense young man appeared again. A minute later I took Morel by surprise; he was looking through a window, apparently spying on someone. Morel went down the garden steps. I was not far away, and I could hear the conversation.

"I did not want to say anything about this when the others were here. I have something to suggest to you and a few of the others."

"Oh, yes?"

"Not here," said Morel, staring suspiciously at the trees. "Tonight. When everyone has gone, please stay a few minutes longer."

"Even if it is very late?"

"So much the better. The later the better. But above all, be discreet. I don't want the women to find out. Hysterics annoy me. See you later!"

He hurried away. Before he went into the house, he looked back over his shoulder. The boy was going upstairs. A signal from Morel made him stop. He walked back and forth, with his hands in his pockets, whistling naively.

I tried to think about what I had just seen, but I did not want to. It unnerved me.

About fifteen minutes later another bearded man, stout and with grayish hair (I have not yet mentioned him in my diary), appeared on the stairs and stood there looking toward the horizon. He walked down to the museum, seeming to be confused.

Morel came back. They spoke together for a moment. I managed to hear Morel say: ". . . if I told you that all your words and actions are being recorded?"

"It wouldn't bother me in the slightest."

I wondered if possibly they had found my diary. I was determined to be on the alert, to avoid the temptations of fatigue and distraction, not to let myself be taken by surprise.

The stout man was alone again, and seemed to be bewildered. Morel came back with Alec (the young man with green eyes). The three of them walked away together.

Then I saw some of the men and their servants come out carrying wicker chairs, which they put in the shadow of a large, diseased breadfruit tree (I have seen trees of the same type, only smaller, on an old plantation in Los Teques). The ladies sat down in the chairs; the men sprawled on the grass at their feet. It made me think of afternoons in my own country.

Faustine walked by on her way to the rocks. My love for this woman has become annoying (and ridiculous: we have never even spoken to each other!). She was wearing a tennis dress and that

violet-colored scarf on her head. How I shall remember this scarf after Faustine has gone away!

I wanted to offer to carry her basket or her blanket. I followed her at a distance; I saw her leave her basket by a rock, put down her blanket, stand motionless contemplating the sea or the sunset, imposing her calm on both.

This was my last chance with Faustine—my last chance to kneel down, to tell her of my love, my life. But I did nothing. It did not seem right, somehow. True, women naturally welcome any sort of tribute. But in this case it would be better to let the situation develop naturally. We are suspicious of a stranger who tells us his life story, who tells us spontaneously that he has been captured, sentenced to life imprisonment, and that we are his reason for living. We are afraid that he is merely tricking us into buying a fountain pen or a bottle with a miniature sailing vessel inside.

An alternative was to speak to her as I was watching the sea, like a serious, stupid lunatic; to comment on the two suns, on our mutual liking for sunsets; to pause so that she could ask me some questions; to tell her, at least, that I am a writer who has always wanted to live on a lonely island; to confess that I was annoyed when her friends came; to explain that I have been forced to remain on the part of the island which is nearly always flooded (this would lead us into a pleasant discussion of the lowlands and their disasters); and to declare my love and my fears that she is going to leave, that the afternoons will come and go without bringing me the accustomed joy of seeing her.

She stood up. I felt very nervous (as if Faustine had heard what I was thinking and had been offended). She went to get a book from her basket on another rock about fifteen feet away, and sat down again. She opened the book, put her hand on a page, and then looked up, staring at the sunset, as if she were only half awake.

When the weaker of the two suns had set, Faustine stood up again. I followed her. I ran after her and threw myself at her feet and I said, I almost shouted, "Faustine, I love you!"

I thought that if I acted on impulse, she could not doubt my sincerity. I do not know what effect my words had on her, for I was driven away by some footsteps and a dark shadow. I hid behind a palm tree. My breathing, which was very irregular, almost deafened me.

I heard Morel telling Faustine that he had to talk to her. She replied, "All right—let's go to the museum." (I heard this clearly.)

There was an argument. Morel objected, "No, I want to make the most of this opportunity—away from the museum so our friends will not be able to see us."

I also heard him say: "I am warning you—you are a different kind of woman—you must control your nerves."

I can state categorically that Faustine stubbornly refused to go away with him.

Morel said in a commanding tone, "When everyone else has gone tonight, you are to stay a little longer."

They were walking between the palm trees and the museum. Morel was talkative, and he made many gestures. At one point he took Faustine's arm. Then they walked on in silence. When I saw them enter the museum I decided to find myself some food so I would be feeling well during the night and be able to keep watch.

"Tea for Two" and "Valencia" persisted until after dawn. In spite of my plans, I ate very little. The people who were dancing up on the hillside, the viscous leaves, the roots that tasted of the earth, the hard, fibrous bulbs—all these were enough to convince me that I should enter the museum and look for some bread and other real food.

I went in through the coalbin around midnight. There were servants in the pantry and the storeroom. I decided it would be better to hide, to wait until the people went to their rooms. Perhaps I would be able to hear what Morel was going to propose to Faustine, the bushy-haired youth, the fat man, and green-eyed Alec. Then I would steal some food and find a way to get away from there.

It did not really matter very much to me what Morel was going to say. But I was disturbed by the arrival of the ship, and Faustine's imminent, irremediable departure.

As I walked through the large assembly hall, I saw a ghost-copy of the book by Bélidor that I had taken two weeks earlier; it was on the same shelf of green marble, in exactly the same place on the shelf. I felt my pocket; I took out the book. I compared the two: they were not two copies of the same book, but the same copy twice; the light-blue ink on both was blurred, making the word *Perse* indistinct; both had a crooked tear in the lower corner. I am speaking of an external identity—I could not even touch the book on the table. I hurried away, so they would not see me (first, some of the women; then, Morel). I walked through the room with the aquarium floor and hid in the green room, behind the screen of mirrors. Through a crack I could see the room with the aquarium.

Morel was giving orders.

"Put a chair and table here."

They put the other chairs in rows, in front of the table, as if there was going to be a lecture.

When it was very late almost everyone had arrived. There was some commotion, some curiosity, a few smiles; mostly there was an air of fatigued resignation.

"No one has permission to be absent," said Morel. "I shall not begin until everyone is here."

"Jane is not here."

"Jane Gray is not here."

"What's the difference?"

"Someone will have to go and get her."

"But she's in bed!"

"She cannot be absent."

"But she's sleeping!"

"I shall not begin until I see that she is here."

"I'll go and get her," said Dora.

"I'll go with you," said the bushy-haired youth.

I tried to write down the above conversation exactly as it occurred. If it does not seem natural now, either art or my memory is to blame. It seemed natural enough then. Seeing those people, hearing them talk, no one could expect the magical occurrence or the negation of reality that came afterward (although it happened near an illuminated aquarium, on top of long-tailed fish and lichens, in a forest of black pillars!).

Morel was speaking: "You must search the whole building. I saw him enter this room some time ago."

Was he referring to me? At last I was going to find out the real reason why these people had come to the island.

"We've searched the whole house," said a naive voice.

"That doesn't matter. You must find him!" replied Morel.

I felt as if I were surrounded now. I wanted to get away, but I did not dare to move.

I remembered that halls of mirrors were famous as places of torture. I was beginning to feel uncomfortable.

Then Dora and the youth returned with an elderly lady who appeared to be drunk (I had seen her in the pool). Two men, apparently servants, offered to help; they came up to Morel, and one said, "Haven't been able to find him."

"Haynes is sleeping in Faustine's room," said Dora to Morel. "It will be hard to get him down to the meeting."

Was Haynes the one they had been speaking about before? At first I did not see any connection between Dora's remark and Morel's conversation with the men. The latter spoke about looking for someone, and I had felt panic-stricken, finding allusions or threats in everything. Now it occurs to me that these people were never concerned with me at all. Now I know they cannot look for me.

Can I be sure? A sensible man—would he believe what I heard last night, what I believe I know? Would he tell me to forget the nightmare of thinking that all this is a trap set to capture me?

And, if it is a trap, why is it such a complex one? Why do they not simply arrest me? I find this laborious method quite idiotic.

The habits of our lives make us presume that things will happen in a certain foreseeable way, that there will be a vague coherence in the world. Now reality appears to be changed, unreal. When a man awakens, or dies, he is slow to free himself from the terrors of the dream, from the worries and manias of life. Now it will be hard for me to break the habit of being afraid of these people.

Morel took a sheaf of yellow papers filled with typed copy from a wooden bowl on the table. The bowl also contained a number of letters attached to clippings of advertisements from *Yachting* and *Motor Boating*. The letters asked about prices of used boats, terms of sale, addresses where they could be seen. I saw a few of them.

"Let Haynes sleep," said Morel. "He weighs so much—if they try to bring him down, we shall never get started!"

Morel motioned for silence, and then began tentatively, "I have something important to tell you."

He smiled nervously.

"It is nothing to worry about. In the interest of accuracy I have decided to read my speech. Please listen carefully."

(He began to read the yellow pages that I am putting into this envelope. When I ran away from the museum this morning, they were on the table; I took them with me.) [4]

"You must forgive me for this rather tedious, unpleasant incident. We shall try to forget it! Thoughts of the fine week we have spent here together will make all this seem less important.

"At first, I decided not to tell you anything. That would have spared you a very natural anxiety. We would have enjoyed ourselves up to the very last instant, and there would have been no objections. But, as all of you are friends, you have a right to know."

He paused for a moment, rolling his eyes, smiling, trembling; then he continued impulsively: "My abuse consists of having photographed you without your permission. Of course, it is not like an ordinary photograph; this is my latest invention. We shall live in this photograph forever. Imagine a stage on which our life during these seven days is acted out, complete in every detail. We are the actors. All our actions have been recorded."

"How shameful!" blurted a man with a black moustache and protruding teeth.

"I hope it's just a joke," said Dora.

Faustine was not smiling. She seemed to be indignant.

Morel continued, "I could have told you when we arrived: 'We shall live for eternity.' Perhaps then we would have forced ourselves to maintain a constant gaiety, and that would have ruined everything. I thought: 'Any week we spend together, even if we do not feel obliged

---

[4] For the sake of clarity we have enclosed the material on the yellow pages in quotation marks; the marginal notes, written in pencil and in the same handwriting as the rest of the diary, are not set off by quotes. (Editor's Note.)

to use our time profitably, will be pleasant.' And wasn't it?" He paused. "Well, then, I have given you a pleasant eternity!

"To be sure, nothing created by man is perfect. Some of our friends are missing—it could not be helped. Claude has been excused; he was working on the theory, in the form of a novel with theological overtones, that man and God are at odds with one another; he thinks it will bring him immortality and therefore he does not wish to interrupt his work. For two years now Madeleine has not been going to the mountains; her health has been poor. Leclerc had already arranged to go to Florida with the Davies."

As an afterthought, he added, "Poor Charlie, of course—"

From his tone, which emphasized the word *poor*, from the mute solemnity and the changes of position and the nervous moving of chairs that occurred at once, I inferred that the man named Charlie had died; more precisely, that he had died recently.

Then, as if to reassure his audience, Morel said, "But I have him! If anyone would like to see him, I can show him to you. He was one of my first successful experiments."

He stopped talking as he appeared to perceive the change in the room. The audience had proceeded from an affable boredom to sadness, with a slight reproof for the bad taste of mentioning a deceased friend in a light-hearted recitation; now the people seemed perplexed, almost horrified.

Morel quickly turned back to his yellow papers.

"For a long time now my brain has had two principal occupations: thinking of my inventions and thinking about—" The sympathy between Morel and his audience was definitely re-established.

"For example, as I open the pages of a book, or walk, or fill my pipe, I am imagining a happy life with—"

His words were greeted with bursts of applause.

"When I finished my invention it occurred to me, first as a mere exercise for the imagination, then as an incredible plan, that I could give perpetual reality to my romantic desire.

"My belief in my own superiority and the conviction that it is easier to make a woman fall in love with me than to manufacture heavens made me choose a spontaneous approach. My hopes of making her love me have receded now; I no longer have her confidence; nor do I have the desire, the will, to face life.

"I had to employ certain tactics, make plans." (Morel changed the wording of the sentence to mitigate the serious implications.) "At first I wanted to convince her that she should come here alone with me—but that was impossible: I have not seen her alone since I told her of my love—or else to abduct her; but we would have been fighting eternally! Please note, by the way, that the word *eternally* is not an exaggeration."

There was a considerable stir in the audience. He was saying—it seemed to me—that he had planned to seduce her, and he was trying to be funny.

"Now I shall explain my invention."

Up to this point it was a repugnant and badly organized speech. Morel is a scientist, and he becomes more precise when he overlooks his personal feelings and concentrates on his own special field; then his style is still unpleasant, filled with technical words and vain attempts to achieve a certain oratorical force, but at least it is clearer. The reader can judge for himself:

"What is the purpose of radio? To supply food, as it were, for the sense of hearing: by utilizing transmitters and receivers, we can take part in a conversation with Madeleine right in this room, even though she is thousands of miles away in a suburb of Quebec. Television does the same thing for the sense of sight. By achieving slower or faster vibrations, we can apply this principle to the other senses, to all the other senses.

"Until recently, the scientific processes for the different senses were as follows:

"For sight: television, motion pictures, photography.

"For hearing: radio, the phonograph, the telephone.[5]

"Conclusion:

---

[5] The omission of the telegraph seems to be deliberate. Morel is the author of the pamphlet *Que nous envoie Dieu?* (the words of the first telegraphic message sent by Morse); and his reply to this question is: "Un peintre inutile et une invention indiscrète." Nevertheless, paintings like *Lafayette* and the *Dying Hercules* have an undisputed value. (Editor's Note.)

"Until recently science had been able to satisfy only the senses of sight and hearing, to compensate for spatial and temporal absences. The first part of my work was valuable because it interrupted an inactivity along these lines that had become traditional, and because it continued, logically and along almost parallel lines, the thought and teachings of the brilliant men who made the world a better place by the inventions I have just mentioned.

"I should like to express my gratitude to the companies that, in France (Société Clunie) and in Switzerland (Schwachter, of Saint Gallen), realized the importance of my research and put their excellent laboratories at my disposal.

"Unfortunately, I cannot say the same of my colleagues.

"When I went to Holland to consult with the distinguished electrical engineer, Jan Van Heuse, the inventor of a primitive lie-detector, I found some encouragement and, I must add, a regrettable attitude of suspicion.

"Since then I have preferred to work alone.

"I began to search for waves and vibrations that had previously been unattainable, to devise instruments to receive and transmit them. I obtained, with relative facility, the olfactory sensations; the so-called thermal and tactile ones required all my perseverance.

"It was also necessary to perfect the existing methods. My best results were a tribute to the manufacturers of phonograph records. For a long time now we have been able to state that we need have no fear of death, at least with regard to the human voice. Photography and motion pictures have made it possible to retain images, although imperfectly. I directed this part of my work toward the retention of the images that appear in mirrors.

"With my machine a person or an animal or a thing is like the station that broadcasts the concert you hear on the radio. If you turn the dial for the olfactory waves, you will smell the jasmine perfume on Madeleine's throat, without seeing her. By turning the dial of the tactile waves, you will be able to stroke her soft, invisible hair and learn, like the blind, to know things by your hands. But if you turn all the dials at once, Madeleine will be reproduced completely, and she will appear exactly as she is; you must not forget that I am speaking of images extracted from mirrors, with the sounds, tactile sensations, flavors, odors, temperatures, all synchronized perfectly. An observer will not realize that they are images. And if our images were to appear now, you yourselves would not believe me. Instead, you would find it easier to think that I had engaged a group of actors, improbable doubles for each of you!

"This is the first part of the machine; the second part makes recordings; the third is a projector. No screens or papers are needed; the projections can be received through space, and it does not matter whether it is day or night. To explain this more clearly, I shall attempt to compare the parts of my machine with the television set that shows the images from more or less distant transmitters, with the camera that takes a motion picture of the images transmitted by the television set; and with the motion-picture projector.

"I thought I would synchronize all the parts of my machine and take scenes of our lives: an afternoon with Faustine, conversations with some of you; and in that way I would be able to make an album of very durable and clear images, which would be a legacy from the present to the future; they would please your children and friends, and the coming generations whose customs will differ from our own.

"I reasoned that if the reproductions of objects would be objects—as a photograph of a house is an object that represents another object—the reproductions of animals and plants would not be animals or plants. I was certain that my images of persons would lack consciousness of themselves (like the characters in a motion picture).

"But I found, to my surprise, that when I succeeded in synchronizing the different parts of the machine, after much hard work, I obtained reconstituted persons who would disappear if I disconnected the projecting apparatus, and would live only the moments when the scene was taken; when the scene ended they would repeat these same moments again and again, like a phonograph record or a motion picture that would end and begin again; moreover, no one could distinguish them from living persons (they appear to be circulating in another world with which our own has made a chance encounter). If we grant consciousness, and all that distinguishes us from objects, to the persons who surround us, we shall have no valid reason to deny it to the persons created by my machinery.

"When all the senses are synchronized, the soul emerges. That was to be expected. When Madeleine existed for the senses of sight, hearing, taste, smell, and touch, Madeleine herself was actually there."

I have shown that Morel's style is unpleasant, with a liberal sprinkling of technical terms, and that it attempts, vainly, to achieve a certain grandiloquence. Its banality is obvious:

"Is it hard for you to accept such a mechanical and artificial system for the reproduction of life? It might help if you bear in mind that what changes the sleight-of-hand artist's movements into magic is our inability to see!

"To make living reproductions, I need living transmitters. I do not create life.

"The thing that is latent in a phonograph record, the thing that is revealed when I press a button and turn on the machine—shouldn't we call that 'life'? Shall I insist, like the mandarins of China, that every life depends on a button which an unknown being can press? And you yourselves—how many times have you wondered about mankind's destiny, or asked the old questions: 'Where are we going? Like the unheard music that lies latent in a phonograph record, where are we until God orders us to be born?' Don't you see that there is a parallelism between the destinies of men and images?

"The theory that the images have souls seems to be confirmed by the effects of my machine on persons, animals, and vegetables used as transmitters.

"Of course, I did not achieve these results until after many partial reverses. I remember that I made the first tests with employees of the Schwachter Company. With no advance warning, I turned on the machine and took them while they were working. There were still some minor defects in the receiver; it did not assemble their data evenly; in some, for example, the image did not coincide with the tactile sensations; there are times when the errors are imperceptible for unspecialized observers, but occasionally the deviation is broad."

"Can you show us those first images?" asked Stoever.

"If you wish, of course; but I warn you that some of the ghosts are slightly monstrous!" replied Morel.

"Very well," said Dora. "Show them to us. A little entertainment is always welcome."

"I want to see them," continued Stoever, "because I remember several unexplained deaths at the Schwachter Company."

"Congratulations, Morel," said Alec, bowing. "You have found yourself a believer!"

Stoever spoke seriously, "You idiot—haven't you heard? Charlie was taken by that machine, too. When Morel was in Saint Gallen, the employees of the Schwachter Company started to die. I saw the pictures in magazines. I'll recognize them."

Morel, trembling with anger, left the room. The people had begun to shout at each other.

"There, you see," said Dora. "Now you've hurt his feelings. You must go and find him."

"How could you do a thing like that to Morel!"

"Can't you see? Don't you understand?" insisted Stoever.

"Morel is a nervous man; I don't see why you had to insult him."

"You don't understand!" shouted Stoever angrily. "He took Charlie with his machine, and Charlie died; he took some of the employees at the Schwachter Company, and some of them died mysteriously. Now he says that he has taken us!"

"And we are not dead," said Irene.

"He took himself, too."

"Doesn't anyone understand that it's just a joke?"

"But why is Morel so angry? I've never seen him like this!"

"Well, anyway, Morel has behaved badly," said the man with the protruding teeth. "He should have told us beforehand."

"I'm going to go and find him," said Stoever.

"Stay here!" shouted Dora.

"I'll go," said the man with protruding teeth. "No, I'm not going to make any trouble. I'll just ask him to excuse us and to come back and continue his speech."

They all crowded around Stoever. Excitedly they tried to calm him.

After a while the man with protruding teeth returned. "He won't come," he said. "He asks us to forgive him. I couldn't get him to come back."

Faustine, Dora, and the old woman went out of the room; then some others followed.

Only Alec, the man with protruding teeth, Stoever, and Irene remained. They seemed calm, but very serious. Then they left together.

I heard some people talking in the assembly hall, and others on the stairway. The lights went out and the house was left in the livid light of dawn. I waited, on the alert. There was no noise, there was almost no light. Had they all gone to bed? Or were they lying in wait to capture me? I stayed there, for how long I do not know, trembling, and finally I began to walk (I believe I did this to hear the sound of my own footsteps and to have evidence of some life), without noticing that perhaps I was doing exactly what my supposed pursuers wanted me to do.

I went to the table, put the yellow papers in my pocket. I saw (and it made me afraid) that the room had no windows, that I would have to pass through the assembly hall in order to get out of the building. I walked very slowly; the house seemed unending. I stood still in the doorway. Finally I walked slowly, silently, toward an open window; I jumped out and then I broke into a run.

When I got to the lowlands, I reproached myself for not having gone away the first day, for wanting to find out about those mysterious people.

After Morel's explanation, it seemed that this was a plot organized by the police; I could not forgive myself for being so slow to understand.

My suspicion may seem absurd, but I believe I can justify it. Anyone would distrust a person who said, "My companions and I are illusions; we are a new kind of photograph." In my case the distrust is even more justified: I have been accused of a crime, sentenced to life imprisonment, and it is possible that my capture is still somebody's profession, his hope of bureaucratic promotion.

But I was tired, so I went to sleep at once, making vague plans to escape. This had been a very exciting day.

I dreamed of Faustine. The dream was very sad, very touching. We were saying good-bye; they were coming to get her; the ship was about to leave. Then we were alone, saying a romantic farewell. I cried during the dream and then woke up feeling miserable and desperate because Faustine was not there; my only consolation was that we had not concealed our love. I was afraid that Faustine had gone away while I was sleeping. I got up and looked around. The ship was gone. My sadness was profound: it made me decide to kill myself. But when I glanced up I saw Stoever, Dora, and some of the others on the hillside.

I did not need to see Faustine. I thought then that I was safe: it no longer mattered whether she was there.

I understood that what Morel had said several hours ago was true (but very possibly he did not say it for the first time several hours ago, but several years ago; he repeated it that night because it was part of the week, on the eternal record).

I experienced a feeling of scorn, almost disgust, for these people and their indefatigable, repetitious activity. They appeared many times up there on the edge of the hill. To be on an island inhabited by artificial ghosts was the most unbearable of nightmares; to be in love with one of those images was worse than being in love with a ghost (perhaps we always want the person we love to have the existence of a ghost).

Here are the rest of the yellow papers that Morel did not read:

"I found that my first plan was impossible—to be alone with her and to photograph a scene of my pleasure or of our mutual joy. So I conceived another one, which is, I am sure, better.

"You all know how we discovered this island. Three factors recommended it to me: (1) the tides, (2) the reefs, (3) the light.

"The regularity of the lunar tides and the frequency of the meteorological tides assure an almost constant supply of motive power. The reefs are a vast system to wall out trespassers; the only man who knows them is our captain, McGregor; I have seen to it that he will not have to risk these dangers again. The light is clear but not dazzling—and makes it possible to preserve the images with little or no waste.

"I confess that after I discovered these outstanding virtues, I did not hesitate for an instant to invest my fortune in the purchase of the island and in the construction of the museum, the church, the pool. I rented the cargo ship, which you all call the 'yacht,' so our voyage would be more comfortable.

"The word *museum*, which I use to designate this house, is a survival of the time when I was working on plans for my invention, without knowing how it would eventually turn out. At that time I thought I would build large albums or museums, both public and private, filled with these images.

"Now the time has come to make my announcement: This island, and its buildings, is our private paradise. I have taken some precautions—physical and moral ones—for its defense: I believe they will protect it adequately. Even if we left tomorrow, we would be here eternally, repeating consecutively the moments of this week, powerless to escape from the consciousness we had in each one of them—the thoughts and feelings that the machine captured. We will be able to live a life that is always new, because in each moment of the projection we shall have no memories other than those we had in the corresponding moment of the eternal record, and because the future, left behind many times, will maintain its attributes forever." [6]

They appear from time to time. Yesterday I saw Haynes on the edge of the hill; two days ago I saw Stoever and Irene; today I saw Dora and some of the other women. They make me feel impatient: if I want to live an orderly existence, I must stop looking at these images.

My favorite temptations are to destroy them, to destroy the machines that project them (they must be in the basement), or to break the mill wheel. I control myself; I do not wish to think about my island companions because they could become an obsession.

However, I do not believe there is any danger of that. I am too busy trying to stand the floods, my hunger, the food I eat.

Now I am looking for a way to construct a permanent bed; I shall not find it here in the lowlands; the trees are decayed and cannot support me. But I am determined to change all this: when the tides

[6] *Forever:* as applied to the duration of our immortality: the machine, unadorned and of carefully chosen material, is more incorruptible than the Métro in Paris. (Morel's Note.)

are high I do not sleep, and the smaller floods interrupt my rest on the other days, but always at a different hour. I cannot get used to these inundations. I find it difficult to sleep, thinking of the moment when the muddy, lukewarm water will cover my face and choke me momentarily. I do not want to be surprised by the current, but fatigue overcomes me and then the water is already there, silently forcing its way into my respiratory passages. This makes me feel painfully tired, and I tend to be irritated and discouraged by the slightest difficulty.

I was reading the yellow papers again. I find that Morel's explanation of the ways to supply certain spatial and temporal needs can lead to confusion. Perhaps it would be better to say: Methods To Achieve Sensory Perceptions, and Methods To Achieve and Retain Such Perceptions. Radio, television, the telephone are exclusively methods of achievement; motion pictures, photography, the phonograph—authentic archives—are methods of achievement and retention.

So then, all the machines that supply certain sensory needs are methods of achievement (before we have the photograph or the phonograph record, it must be taken, recorded).

It is possible that every need is basically spatial, that somewhere the image, the touch, and the voice of those who are no longer alive must still exist ("nothing is lost—").

This has given me new hope; this is why I am going down to the basement of the museum to look at the machines.

I thought of people who are no longer alive. Someday the men who channel vibrations will assemble them in the world again. I had illusions of doing something like that myself, of inventing a way to put the presences of the dead together again, perhaps. I might be able to use Morel's machine with an attachment that would keep it from receiving the waves from living transmitters (they would no doubt be stronger).

It will be possible for all souls, both those that are intact, and the ones whose elements have been dispersed, to have immortality. But unfortunately the people who have died most recently will be obstructed by the same mass of residue as those who died long ago. To make a single man (who is now disembodied) with all his elements, and without letting an extraneous part enter, one must have the patient desire of Isis when she reconstructed Osiris.

The indefinite conservation of the souls now functioning is assured. Or rather: it will be assured when men understand that they must practice and preach the doctrine of Malthus to defend their place on earth.

It is regrettable that Morel has hidden his invention on this island. I may be mistaken: perhaps Morel is a famous man. If not, I might be able to obtain a pardon from my pursuers as a reward for giving his invention to the world. But if Morel himself did not tell the world about it one of his friends probably did. And yet it is strange that no one spoke of it back in Caracas.

I have overcome the nervous repulsion I used to feel toward the images. They do not bother me now. I am living comfortably in the museum, safe from the rising waters. I sleep well, I awake refreshed, and I have recaptured the serenity that made it possible for me to outwit my pursuers and to reach this island.

I must admit that I feel slightly uncomfortable when the images brush against me (especially if I happen to be thinking about something else); but I shall overcome that, too; and the very fact that I can think of other things indicates that my life has become quite normal again.

Now I am able to view Faustine dispassionately, as a simple object. Merely out of curiosity I have been following her for about twenty days. That was not very difficult, although it is impossible to open the doors—even the unlocked ones—(because if they were closed when the scene was recorded, they must be closed when it is projected). I might be able to force them open, but I am afraid that a partial breakage may put the whole machine out of order.

When Faustine goes to her room, she closes the door. There is only one occasion when I am not able to enter without touching her: when Dora and Alec are with her. Then the latter two come out quickly. During the first week I spent that night in the corridor, with my eye at the keyhole of the closed door, but all I could see was part of a blank wall. The next week I wanted to look in from the outside, so I walked along the cornice, exposing myself to great danger, injuring my hands and knees on the rough stone, clinging to it in terror (it is about fifteen feet above the ground). But since the curtains were drawn I was unable to see anything.

The next time I shall overcome my fear and enter the room with Faustine, Dora, and Alec.

The other nights I lie on a mat on the floor, beside her bed. It touches me to have her so close to me, and yet so unaware of this habit of sleeping together that we are acquiring.

A recluse can make machines or invest his visions with reality only imperfectly, by writing about them or depicting them to others who are more fortunate than he.

I think it will be impossible for me to learn anything by looking at the machines: hermetically sealed, they will continue to obey Morel's plan. But tomorrow I shall know for sure. I was not able to go down to the basement today, for I spent the whole afternoon trying to find some food.

If one day the images should fail, it would be wrong to suppose that I have destroyed them. On the contrary, my aim is to save them by writing this diary. Invasions by the sea and invasions by the hordes of increased populations threaten them. It pains me to think that my ignorance, kept intact by the library, which does not have a single book I can use for scientific study, may threaten them too.

I shall not elaborate on the dangers that stalk this island—both the land and the men—because the prophecies of Malthus have been forgotten; and, as for the sea, I must confess that each high tide has caused me to fear that the island may be totally submerged. A fisherman at a bar in Rabaul told me that the Ellice, or Lagoon, Islands are unstable, that some disappear and others emerge from the sea. (Am I in that archipelago? The Sicilian and Ombrellieri are my authorities for believing that I am.)

It is surprising that the invention has deceived the inventor. I too thought that the images were live beings; but my position differed from his: Morel conceived all this; he witnessed and directed the work to its completion, while I saw it in the completed form, already in operation.

The case of the inventor who is duped by his own invention emphasizes our need for circumspection. But I may be generalizing about the peculiarities of one man, moralizing about a characteristic that applies only to Morel.

I approve of the direction he gave, no doubt unconsciously, to his efforts to perpetuate man: but he has preserved nothing but sensations; and, although his invention was incomplete, he at least foreshadowed the truth: man will one day create human life. His work seems to confirm my old axiom: it is useless to try to keep the whole body alive.

Logical reasons induce us to reject Morel's hopes. The images are not alive. But since his invention has blazed the trail, as it were, another machine should be invented to find out whether the images think and feel (or at least if they have the thoughts and the feelings that the people themselves had when the picture was made; of course, the relationship between their consciousness and these thoughts and feelings cannot be determined). The machine would be very similar to the one Morel invented and would be aimed at the thoughts and sensations of the transmitter; at any distance away from Faustine we should be able to have her thoughts and sensations (visual, auditory, tactile, olfactory, gustatory).

And someday there will be a more complete machine. One's thoughts or feelings during life—or while the machine is recording—will be like an alphabet with which the image will continue to comprehend all experience (as we can form all the words in our language with the letters of the alphabet). Then life will be a repository for death. But even then the image will not be alive; objects that are essentially new will not exist for it. It will know only what it has already thought or felt, or the possible transpositions of those thoughts or feelings.

The fact that we cannot understand anything outside of time and space may perhaps suggest that our life is not appreciably different from the survival to be obtained by this machine.

When minds of greater refinement than Morel's begin to work on the invention, man will select a lonely, pleasant place, will go there with the persons he loves most, and will endure in an intimate paradise. A single garden, if the scenes to be eternalized are recorded at different moments, will contain innumerable paradises, and each group of inhabitants, unaware of the others, will move about simultaneously, almost in the same places, without colliding. But unfortunately these will be vulnerable paradises because the images will not be able to see men; and, if men do not heed the advice of Malthus, someday they will need the land of even the smallest paradise, and will destroy its defenseless inhabitants or will exile them by disconnecting their machines.[7]

I watched them for seventeen days. Not even a man who was in love would have found anything suspect about the conduct of Morel and Faustine.

I do not believe he was referring to her in his speech (although she was the only one who did not laugh at that part). But even though Morel may be in love with Faustine, why should it be assumed that Faustine returns his love?

We can always find a cause for suspicion if we look for it. On one afternoon of the eternal week they walk arm in arm near the palm groves and the museum—but surely there is nothing amiss in that casual stroll.

Because I was determined to live up to my motto, *Ostinato rigore*, I can now say with pride that my vigilance was complete; I considered neither my own comfort nor decorum: I observed what went on under the tables as well as in the open.

One night in the dining room, and another night in the assembly hall, their legs touch. If I attribute that contact to malicious intent, why do I reject the possibility of pure accident?

I repeat: there is no conclusive proof that Faustine feels any love for Morel. Perhaps my own egotism made me suspect that she did. I love Faustine: she is the reason for everything. I am afraid that she

---

[7] Under the epigraph

> Come, Malthus, and in Ciceronian prose
> Show what a rutting Population grows,
> Until the produce of the Soil is spent,
> And Brats expire for lack of Aliment.

the author writes a lengthy apology, with eloquence and the traditional arguments, for Thomas Robert Malthus and his *Essay on the Principle of Population*. We have omitted it due to lack of space. (Editor's Note.)

loves another man: my mission is to prove that she does not. When I thought that the police were after me, the images on this island seemed to be moving like the pieces in a chess game, following a strategy to capture me.

Morel would be furious, I am sure, if I spread the news of his invention. I do not believe that the fame he might gain would make any difference to him. His friends (including Faustine) would be indignant. But if Faustine had fallen out with Morel—she did not laugh with the others during his speech—then perhaps she would form an alliance with me.

Still it is possible that Morel is dead. If he had died one of his friends would have spread the news of his invention. Or else we should have to postulate a collective death, an epidemic or a shipwreck—which seems quite incredible. But still there is no way to explain the fact that no one knew of the invention when I left Caracas.

One explanation could be that no one believed him, that Morel was out of his mind, or (my original idea) that they were all mad, that the island was a kind of insane asylum.

But those explanations require as much imagination as do the epidemic or the shipwreck.

If I could get to Europe, America, or Asia, I would surely have a difficult time. When I began to be a famous fraud—instead of a famous inventor—Morel's accusations would reach me and then perhaps an order for my arrest would arrive from Caracas. And, worst of all, my perilous situation would have been brought about by the invention of a madman.

But I do not have to run away. It is a stroke of luck to be able to live with the images. If my pursuers should come, they will forget about me when they see these prodigious, inaccessible people. And so I shall stay here.

If I should find Faustine, how she would laugh when I told her about the many times I have talked to her image with tenderness and desperation. But I feel that I should not entertain this thought: and I have written it down merely to set a limit, to see that it holds no charm for me, to abandon it.

A rotating eternity may seem atrocious to an observer, but it is quite acceptable to those who dwell there. Free from bad news and disease, they live forever as if each thing were happening for the first time; they have no memory of anything that happened before. And the interruptions caused by the rhythm of the tides keep the repetition from being implacable.

Now that I have grown accustomed to seeing a life that is repeated, I find my own irreparably haphazard. My plans to alter the situation are useless: I have no next time, each moment is unique, different from every other moment, and many are wasted by my own indolence. Of course, there is no next time for the images either—each moment follows the pattern set when the eternal week was first recorded.

Our life may be thought of as a week of these images—one that may be repeated in adjoining worlds.

Without yielding to my weakness, I can imagine the touching moment when I arrive at Faustine's house, her interest in what I shall tell her, the bond that will be established between us. Perhaps now I am at last on the long and difficult road that leads to Faustine; I know I cannot live without her.

But where does Faustine live? I have been following her for weeks. She speaks of Canada—that is all I know. But I have another question—and it fills me with horror—is Faustine alive?

Perhaps because the idea of looking for a person whose whereabouts I do not know, a person who may not even be alive, strikes me as being so heartbreaking, so pathetic, Faustine has come to mean more to me than life itself.

How can I go to look for her? The boat is no longer in one piece. The trees are rotten. I am not a good enough carpenter to build a boat out of some other kind of wood, like chairs or doors; in fact, I am not even sure I could have made one from trees. I must wait until I see a ship passing the island. For so long I hoped that one would not come, but now I know I could not return alone. The only ship I have ever seen from this island was Morel's, and that was only the image of a ship.

And if I arrive at my journey's end, if I find Faustine, I shall be in one of the most difficult situations I have ever experienced. Arriving under mysterious circumstances, I shall ask to speak to her alone, and will arouse her suspicions since I shall be a stranger to her. When she discovers that I saw a part of her life, she will think I am trying to gain some dishonest advantage. And when she finds out that I have been sentenced to life imprisonment she will see her worst fears confirmed.

It never occurred to me before that a certain action could bring me good or bad luck. Now, at night, I repeat Faustine's name. Naturally, I like to say it anyway; and even though I am overcome by fatigue I still keep on repeating it (at times I feel nauseated and uneasy, queasy, when I sleep).

When I am less agitated I shall find a way to get away from here. But, in the meantime, writing down what has happened helps me to organize my thoughts. And if I am to die this diary will leave a record of the agony I suffered.

Yesterday there were no images. Desperate in the face of the secret, quiescent machines, I had a presentiment that I would never see Faustine again. But this morning the tide began to rise. I hurried down to the basement, before the images appeared, to try to understand the working of the machines, so I would not be at the mercy of the tides and would be able to make repairs when necessary. I thought that perhaps I might understand the machines if I could see them start, or at least I would get some hint about their structure. But that hope proved to be groundless.

I gained access to the power plant through the opening I had made in the wall, and—(but I must not let myself be carried away by emotion; I must write all this down carefully) I experienced the same surprise and the same exhilaration I felt when I first entered that room. I had the impression of walking through the azure stillness of a river's depths. I sat down to wait, turning my back on the opening I had made (it pained me to see the interruption in the deep-blue continuity of the tile).

How long I stayed there, basking in that beauty, I do not know, but suddenly the green machines lurched into motion. I compared them with the water pump and the motors that produced the light. I looked at them, I listened to them, I fingered them gingerly, but it was no use. My scrutiny was unnecessary, because I knew at once that I was unable to understand the machines. It was as if someone were looking, as if I were trying to cover up my embarrassment or my shame at having hurried to the basement, at having awaited this moment so eagerly.

In my fatigue I have again felt the rush of excitement. Unless I control it, I shall never find a way to leave this place.

This is exactly how it happened: I turned and walked away, with downcast eyes. But when I looked at the wall I was bewildered. I looked for the opening I had made. It was not there.

Thinking that this was just an interesting optical illusion, I stepped to one side to see if it persisted. As if I were blind, I held out my arms and felt all the walls. I bent down to pick up some of the pieces of tile I had knocked off the wall when I made the opening. After touching and retouching that part of the wall repeatedly, I had to accept the fact that it had been repaired.

Could I have been so fascinated by the blue splendor of the room, so interested in the working of the motors, that I did not hear a mason rebuilding the wall?

I moved closer. I felt the coolness of the tile against my ear, and heard an interminable silence, as if the other side had disappeared.

The iron bar that I had used to break the wall was on the floor where I had dropped it the first time I entered the room. "Lucky no one saw it!" I said, pathetically unaware of the situation. "If they had, they probably would have taken it away!"

Again I pressed my ear to this wall that seemed to be intact. Reassured by the silence, I looked for the spot where I had made the opening, and then I began to tap on the wall, thinking that it would be easier to break the fresh plaster. I tapped for a long time, with increasing desperation. The tile was invulnerable. The strongest, most violent blows echoed against the hardness and did not open even a superficial crack or loosen a tiny fragment of the blue glaze.

I rested for a moment and tried to control my nerves.

Then I resumed my efforts, moving to other parts of the wall. Chips fell, and, when large pieces of the wall began to come down, I kept on pounding, bleary-eyed, with an urgency that was far greater than the size of the iron bar, until the resistance of the wall (which seemed unaffected by the force of my repeated pounding) pushed me to the floor, frantic and exhausted. First I saw, then I touched, the pieces of masonry—they were smooth on one side, harsh, earthy on the other; then, in a vision so lucid it seemed ephemeral and supernatural, my eyes saw the blue continuity of the tile, the undamaged and whole wall, the closed room.

I pounded some more. In some places pieces of the wall broke off, but they did not reveal any sort of cavity. In fact, in the twinkling of an eye the wall was perfect again, achieving that invulnerable hardness I had already observed in the place where I had made the original opening.

I shouted, "Help!" I lunged at the wall several times, and it knocked me down. I had an imbecilic attack of tears. I was overcome by the horror of being in an enchanted place and by the confused realization that its vengeful magic was effective in spite of my disbelief.

Harassed by the terrible blue walls, I looked up at the skylight. I saw, first without understanding and then with fear, a cedar branch split apart and become two branches; then the two branches were fused, as docile as ghosts, to become one branch again. I said out loud or thought very clearly: "I shall never be able to get out. I am in an enchanted place." But then I felt ashamed, like a person who has carried a joke too far, and I understood:

These walls—like Faustine, Morel, the fish in the aquarium, one of the suns and one of the moons, the book by Bélidor—are projections of the machines. They coincide with the walls made by the masons (they are the same walls taken by the machines and then projected on themselves). Where I have broken or removed the first wall, the projected one remains. Since it is a projection nothing can pierce or eliminate it as long as the motors are running.

If I destroy the first wall, the machine room will be open when the motors stop running—it will no longer be a room, but the corner of a room. But when the motors begin again the wall will reappear, and it will be impenetrable.

Morel must have planned the double-wall protection to keep anyone from reaching the machines that control his immortality. But his study of the tides was deficient (it was probably made during a different solar period), and he thought that the power plant would function without any interruptions. Surely he is the one who invented the famous disease that, up to now, has protected the island very well.

My problem is to discover a way to stop the green motors. Perhaps I can find the switch that disconnects them. It took me only one day to learn to operate the light plant and the water pump. I think I shall be able to leave this place.

The skylight is, or will be, my salvation because I shall not resign myself to die of hunger in a state of utter desperation, paying my respects to those I leave behind, as did the Japanese sailor who, with virtuous and bureaucratic agony, faced asphyxiation in a submarine at the bottom of the ocean. The letter he wrote was found in the submarine and printed in the paper. As he awaited death he saluted the Emperor, the ministers, and, in hierarchical order, all the admirals he had time to enumerate. He added comments like: "Now I am bleeding from the nose," or "I feel as if my eardrums have broken."

While writing these details, I had the sensation of living through that experience. I hope I shall not end as he did.

The horrors of the day are written down in my diary. I have filled many pages: now it seems futile to try to find inevitable analogies with dying men who make plans for long futures or who see, at the instant of drowning, a detailed picture of their whole life before them. The final moment must be rapid, confused; we are always so far removed from death that we cannot imagine the shadows that must becloud it. Now I shall stop writing in order to concentrate, serenely, on finding the way to stop these motors. Then the breach will open again, as if by magic, and I shall be outside.

I have not yet been successful in my attempt to stop the motors. My head is aching. Ridiculous attacks of nerves, which I quickly control, rouse me from a progressive drowsiness.

I have the impression, undoubtedly illusory, that if I could receive a little fresh air from the outside I would soon be able to solve these problems. I have tried to break the skylight; like everything else, it is invulnerable.

I keep telling myself that the trouble does not issue from my lethargy or from the lack of air. These motors must be very different from all the others. It seems logical to suppose that Morel designed them so that no one who came to this island would be able to understand them. But the difficulty in running the green motors must stem from their basic difference from the other motors. As I do not understand any of them, this greater difficulty disappears.

Morel's eternity depends on the continued functioning of the motors. I can suppose that they are very solid. Therefore I must control my impulse to break them into pieces. That would only tire me out and use up the air. Writing helps me to control myself.

And what if Morel had thought to photograph the motors—

Finally my fear of death freed me from the irrational belief that I was incompetent. I might have seen the motors through a magnifying glass: they ceased to be a meaningless conglomeration of iron and steel; they had forms and arrangements that permitted me to understand their purpose.

I disconnected them. I went outside.

In the machine room, in addition to the water pump and the light plant (which I already mentioned), I recognized:

a) A network of power cables connected to the mill wheel in the lowlands;

b) An assortment of stationary receivers, recorders, and projectors connected to other strategically placed machines that operate throughout the whole island;

c) Three portable machines: receivers, recorders, and projectors for special showings.

Inside of what I had taken for the most important engine (instead it was only a box of tools) I found some incomplete plans that were hard to understand and gave me dubious assistance.

I did not acquire that insight until I had conquered my previous states of mind:

1. Desperation;

2. The feeling that I was playing a dual role, that of actor and spectator. I was obsessed by the idea that I was in a play, awaiting asphyxiation in a submarine at the bottom of the ocean. That state of mind lasted too long; and when I came out of the room night had fallen and it was too dark to look for edible roots.

First I turned on the portable receivers and projectors, the ones for special showings. I focused on flowers, leaves, flies, frogs. I had the thrill of seeing them reproduced in their exact likeness.

Then I committed the imprudence.

I put my left hand in front of the receiver; I turned on the projector and my hand appeared, just my hand, making the lazy movements it made when I photographed it.

Now it is like any other object in the museum.

I am keeping the projector on so that the hand will not disappear. The sight of it is not unpleasant, but rather unusual.

In a story, that hand would be a terrible threat for the protagonist. In reality—what harm can it do?

The vegetable transmitters—leaves, flowers—died after five or six hours; the frogs, after fifteen.

The copies survive; they are incorruptible.

I do not know which flies are real and which ones are artificial.

Perhaps the leaves and flowers died because they needed water. I did not give any food to the frogs; and they must have suffered from the unfamiliar surroundings, too.

I suspect that the effects on my hand are the result of my fear of the machine, not of the machine itself. I have a steady, faint burning sensation. Some of my skin has fallen off. Last night I slept fitfully. I imagined horrible changes in my hand. I dreamed that I scratched it, that I broke it into pieces easily. That must have been how I hurt it.

Another day will be intolerable.

First I was curious about a paragraph from Morel's speech. Then I was quite amused, thinking I had made a discovery. I am not sure how that discovery led to this other one, which is judicious, ominous.

I shall not kill myself immediately. When I am most lucid, I tend to postpone my death for one more day, to remain as proof of an amazing combination of ineptitude and enthusiasm (or despair). Perhaps writing down my idea will make it lose its force.

Here is the part of Morel's speech that I found unusual:

"You must forgive me for this rather tedious, unpleasant incident."

Why unpleasant? Because they were going to be told that they had been photographed in a new way, without having been warned beforehand. And naturally the knowledge that a week of one's life, with every detail, had been recorded forever—when that knowledge was imparted after the fact—would be quite a shock!

I also thought: One of these persons must have a dreadful secret; Morel is either trying to find it out or planning to reveal it.

And then I happened to remember that some people are afraid of having their images reproduced because they believe that their souls will be transferred to the images and they will die.

The thought that Morel had experienced misgivings because he had photographed his friends without their consent amused me; apparently that ancient fear still survived in the mind of my learned contemporary.

I read the sentence again:

"You must forgive me for this rather tedious, unpleasant incident. We shall try to forget it."

What did he mean? That they would soon overlook it, or that they would no longer be able to remember it?

The argument with Stoever was terrible. Stoever's suspicions are the same as mine. I do not know how I could have been so slow to understand.

Another thing: the theory that the images have souls seems to demand, as a basic condition, that the transmitters lose theirs when they are photographed by the machines. As Morel himself says, "The theory that the images have souls seems to be confirmed by the effects of my machine on persons, animals, and vegetables used as transmitters."

A person who would make this statement to his victims must have a very overbearing and audacious conscience, which could be confused with a lack of conscience; but such a monstrosity seems to be in keeping with the man who, following his own idea, organizes a collective death and determines, of his own accord, the common destiny of all his friends.

What was his purpose? To use this rendezvous with his friends to create a kind of private paradise? Or was there some other reason that

I have not yet been able to fathom? And if so it very possibly may not interest me.

Now I believe I can identify the dead crew members of the ship that was sunk by the cruiser *Namura:* Morel used his own death and the death of his friends to confirm the rumors about the disease on the island; Morel spread those rumors to protect his machinery, his immortality.

But all this, which I can now view rationally, means that Faustine is dead, that Faustine lives only in this image, for which I do not exist.

Then life is intolerable for me. How can I keep on living in the torment of seeming to be with Faustine when she is really so far away? Where can I find her? Away from this island Faustine is lost with the gestures and the dreams of an alien past.

On one of my first pages I said:

"I have the uncomfortable sensation that this paper is changing into a will. If I must resign myself to that, I shall try to make statements that can be verified so that no one, knowing that I was accused of duplicity, will doubt that I was condemned unjustly. I shall adopt the motto of Leonardo—*Ostinato rigore*—as my own,[8] and endeavor to live up to it."

Although I am doomed to misery, I shall not forget that motto.

I shall complete my diary by correcting mistakes and by explaining things I did not understand before. That will be my way of bridging the gap between the ideal of accuracy (which guided me from the start) and my original narration.

The tides: I read the little book by Bélidor (Bernard Forest de). It begins with a general description of the tides. I must confess that the tides on this island seem to follow the explanation given in the book, and not mine. Of course, I never studied tides (only in school, where no one studied), and I described them in the initial chapters of this diary, as they were just beginning to have some importance for me.

---

[8] It does not appear at the beginning of the manuscript. Is this omission due to a loss of memory? There is no way to answer that question, and so, as in every doubtful place, we have been faithful to the original. (Editor's Note.)

When I lived on the hill they were no threat. Although I found them interesting, I did not have the time to observe them in detail (there were other dangers to claim my attention then).

According to Bélidor, there are two spring tides each month, at the time of the full moon and the new moon, and two neap tides during the first and third quarters of the moon.

Sometimes a meteorological tide occurred a week after a spring tide (caused by strong winds and rainstorms): surely that was what made me think, mistakenly, that the tides of greater magnitude occur once a week.

Reason for the irregularity of the daily tides: According to Bélidor, the tides rise fifty minutes later each day during the first quarter of the moon, and fifty minutes earlier during the last quarter. But that theory is not completely applicable here: I believe that the rising of the tides must vary from fifteen to twenty minutes each day. Of course, I have no measuring device at my disposal. Perhaps scientists will one day study these tides and make their findings available to the world; then I shall understand them better.

This month there were a number of higher tides; two of them were lunar, and the others, meteorological.

The appearances and disappearances: The machines project the images. The power from the tides causes the machines to operate.

After rather lengthy periods of low tides, there was a series of tides that came up to the mill in the lowlands. The machines began to run, and the eternal record started playing again where it had broken off.

If Morel's speech was on the last night of the week, the first appearance must have occurred on the night of the third day.

Perhaps the absence of images during the long period before they first appeared was due to the change of the tides with the solar periods.

The two suns and the two moons: Since the week is repeated all through the year, some suns and moons do not coincide (and people complain of the cold when the weather on the island is warm, and swim in fetid water and dance in a thicket or during a storm). And if the whole island were submerged—except for the machines and projectors—the images, the museum, and the island itself would still be visible.

Perhaps the heat of the past few days has been so intense because the temperature of the day when the scene was photographed is superimposed on the present temperature.[9]

Trees and other plant life: The vegetation that was recorded by the machine is withered now; the plants that were not recorded—annuals (flowers, grasses) and the new trees—are luxuriant.

The light switch that did not work, the latches that were impossible to open, the stiff, immovable curtains: What I said before, about the doors, can be applied to the light switch and the latches: When the scene is projected, everything appears exactly as it was during the recording process. And the curtains are stiff for the same reason.

The person who turns out the light: The person who turns out the light in the room across from Faustine's is Morel. He comes in and stands by the bed for a moment. The reader will recall that I dreamed Faustine did this. It irks me to have confused Morel with Faustine.

Charlie. Imperfect ghosts: At first I could not find them. Now I believe I have found their records. But I shall not play them. They could easily shatter my equanimity, and might even prove disastrous for my mental outlook.

The Spaniards I saw in the pantry: They are Morel's servants.

The underground room, the screen of mirrors: I heard Morel say that they are for visual and acoustical experiments.

The French poetry that Stoever recited: I jotted it down:

> Ame, te souvient-il, au fond du paradis,
> De la gare d'Auteuil et des trains de jadis.

Stoever tells the old lady that it is by Verlaine.

And now there is nothing in my diary that has not been explained.[10]

---

[9] The theory of a superimposition of temperatures may not necessarily be false (even a small heater is unbearable on a summer day), but I believe that this is not the real reason. The author was on the island in spring; the eternal week was recorded in summer, and so, while functioning, the machines reflect the temperature of summer. (Editor's Note.)

[10] He neglected to explain one thing, the most incredible of all: the coexistence, in one space, of an object and its whole image. This fact suggests the possibility that the world is made up exclusively of sensations. (Editor's Note.)

Almost everything, in fact, does have an explanation. The remaining chapters will hold no surprises.

I should like to try to account for Morel's behavior.

Faustine tried to avoid him; then he planned the week, the death of all his friends, so that he could achieve immortality with Faustine. That was his compensation for having renounced all of life's possibilities. He realized that death would not be such a disaster for the others, because in exchange for a life of uncertain length, he would give them immortality with their best friends. And Faustine's life too was at his disposal.

But my very indignation is what makes me cautious: Perhaps the hell I ascribe to Morel is really my own. I am the one who is in love with Faustine, who is capable of murder and suicide; I am the monster. Morel may not have been referring to Faustine in his speech; he may have been in love with Irene, Dora, or the old woman.

But I am raving, I am a fool. Of course Morel had no interest in them. He loved the inaccessible Faustine. That is why he killed her, killed himself and all his friends, and invented immortality!

Faustine's beauty deserves that madness, that tribute, that crime. When I denied that, I was too jealous or too stubborn to admit that I loved her.

And now I see Morel's act as something sublime.

My life is not so atrocious. If I abandon my uneasy hopes of going to find Faustine, I can grow accustomed to the idea of spending my life in seraphic contemplation of her.

That way is open to me: to live, to be the happiest of mortals.

But my happiness, like everything human, is insecure. My contemplation of Faustine could be interrupted, although I cannot tolerate the thought of it:

If the machines should break (I do not know how to repair them);

If some doubt should ruin my paradise (certain conversations between Morel and Faustine, some of their glances, could cause persons of less fortitude than I to lose heart);

If I should die.

The real advantage of my situation is that now death becomes the condition and the pawn for my eternal contemplation of Faustine.

I am saved from the interminable minutes necessary to prepare for my death in a world without Faustine; I am saved from an interminable death without Faustine.

When I was ready, I turned on the receivers of simultaneous action. Seven days have been recorded. I performed well: a casual observer would not suspect that I am not a part of the original scene. That came about naturally as the result of my painstaking preparation: I devoted two weeks to continuous study and experiment. I rehearsed my every action tirelessly. I studied what Faustine says, her questions and answers; I often insert an appropriate sentence, so she appears to be answering me. I do not always follow her; I know her movements so well that I usually walk ahead. I hope that, generally, we give the impression of being inseparable, of understanding each other so well that we have no need of speaking.

I am obsessed by the hope of removing Morel's image from the eternal week. I know that it is impossible, and yet as I write these lines I feel the same intense desire, and the same torment. The images' dependence upon each other (especially that of Morel and Faustine) used to annoy me. Now it does not: because I know that, since I have entered that world, Faustine's image cannot be eliminated without mine disappearing too. And—this is the strangest part, the hardest to explain—it makes me happy to know that I depend on Haynes, Dora, Alec, Stoever, Irene, and the others (even on Morel!).

I arranged the records; the machine will project the new week eternally.

An oppressive self-consciousness made me appear unnatural during the first few days of the photographing; now I have overcome that, and, if my image has the same thoughts I had when it was taken, as I believe it does, then I shall spend eternity in the joyous contemplation of Faustine.

I was especially careful to keep my spirit free from worries. I have tried not to question Faustine's actions, to avoid feeling any hatred. I shall have the reward of a peaceful eternity; and I have the feeling that I am really living the week.

The night when Faustine, Dora, and Alec go into the room, I managed to control my curiosity. I did not try to find out what they were doing. Now I am a bit irritated that I left that part unsolved. But in eternity I give it no importance.

I have scarcely felt the progression of my death; it began in the tissues of my left hand; it has advanced greatly and yet it is so gradual, so continuous, that I do not notice it.

I am losing my sight. My sense of touch has gone; my skin is falling off; my sensations are ambiguous, painful; I try not to think about them.

When I stood in front of the screen of mirrors, I discovered that I have no beard, I am bald. I have no nails on my fingers or toes, and my flesh is tinged with rose. My strength is diminishing. I have an absurd impression of the pain: it seems to be increasing, but I feel it less.

My persistent, deplorable preoccupation with Morel's relationship to Faustine keeps me from paying much attention to my own destruction; that is an unexpected and beneficent result.

Unfortunately, not all my thoughts are so useful: in my imagination I am plagued by the hope that my illness is pure autosuggestion; that the machines are harmless; that Faustine is alive and that soon I shall find her; that together we shall laugh at these false signs of impending death; that I shall take her to Venezuela, to another Venezuela. For my own country, with its leaders, its troops with rented uniforms and deadly aim, threatens me with constant persecution on the roads, in the tunnels, in the factories. But I still love you, my Venezuela, and I have saluted you many times since the start of my disintegration: for you are also the days when I worked on the literary magazine—a group of men (and I, a wide-eyed, respectful boy) inspired by the poetry of Orduño—an ardent literary school that met in restaurants or on battered trolleys. My Venezuela, you are a piece of cassava bread as large as a shield and uninfested by insects. You are the flooded plains, with bulls, mares, and jaguars being carried along by the swift current. And you, Elisa, I see you standing there, you and the Chinese laundrymen who helped me, and in each memory you seem more like Faustine: you told them to take me to Colombia and we crossed the high plateau in the bitter cold; the Chinamen covered me with thick velvety leaves so I would not freeze to death; while I look at Faustine, I shall not forget you—and I thought I did not love you! I remember that when the imperious Valentín Gómez read us the declaration of independence on July 5 in the elliptical room of the Capitol we (Orduño and the others) showed our defiance by turning to stare at Tito Salas's painting of General Bolívar crossing the Colombian border. But when the band played our national anthem, we could not suppress our patriotic emotion, the emotion I cannot suppress now.

But my rigid discipline must never cease to combat those ideas, for they jeopardize my ultimate calm.

I can still see my image moving about with Faustine. I have almost forgotten that it was added later; anyone would surely believe we were in love and completely dependent on each other. Perhaps the weakness of my eyes makes the scenes appear this way. In any case, it is consoling to die while watching such satisfactory results.

My soul has not yet passed to the image; if it had, I would have died, I (perhaps) would no longer see Faustine, and would be with her in a vision that no one can ever destroy.

To the person who reads this diary and then invents a machine that can assemble disjoined presences, I make this request: Find Faustine and me, let me enter the heaven of her consciousness. It will be an act of piety.

STORIES FROM LA TRAMA CELESTE

In Memory of Pauline

I always loved Pauline. One of my earliest memories is of the day when Pauline and I were hiding under a leafy bower of laurel branches in a garden with two stone lions. Pauline said, "I like blue, I like grapes, I like ice, I like roses, I like white horses." I knew then that my happiness had begun, for in those preferences I could identify myself with Pauline. We resembled each other so miraculously that in the book about the final union of souls with the soul of the world, she wrote in the margin: "Ours have already been united." At that time *ours* meant her soul and mine.

To explain that similarity I argued that I was a hasty and imperfect copy, a rough draft of Pauline. I remember that I wrote in my notebook: "Every poem is a copy of Poetry and in each thing there is a prefiguration of God." Then I thought: My resemblance to Pauline is what saves me. I saw (and even now I see) that my identification with her was the best influence on my life, a kind of sanctuary where I would be purged of my natural defects: apathy, negligence, vanity.

Life was a pleasant habit which led us to look upon our eventual marriage as something natural and certain. Pauline's parents, unimpressed by the literary prestige that I prematurely won and lost, promised to give their consent when I received my doctorate. And many times we imagined an orderly future with enough time to work, to travel, and to love each other. We imagined it so vividly, we were convinced that it could not fail to come true.

Although we spoke of marriage, we did not regard each other as sweethearts. We had spent our whole childhood together, and we continued to treat each other with the shy reticence of children. I did not dare to play the role of a lover and tell her solemnly, "I love you." But still I did love her, I was mad about her, and my startled and scrupulous eyes were dazzled by her perfection.

Pauline liked me to entertain friends. She always made the preparations, attended to the guests, and, secretly, pretended to be the mistress of the house. But I must confess that I did not enjoy those affairs. The party we gave to introduce Julius Montero to some writers was no exception.

The night before, Montero had visited me for the first time. He came in brandishing a voluminous manuscript which he, with an air of a tyrant, read to me in its entirety, secure in his belief that an unpublished literary work conferred on its author the right to usurp as much of another person's time as he desired. Soon after he left I had already forgotten his swarthy, unshaven face. The only interesting thing about the story he read me—Montero urged me to tell him quite honestly whether it had too strong an impact—was that it seemed to be a vague attempt to imitate a number of completely different writers. The theme of the story was that if a certain melody issues from a relationship between the violin and the movements of the violinist, then the soul of each person issues from a definite relationship between movement and matter. The hero made a machine—a kind of frame, with pieces of wood and ropes—to produce souls. Then he died. There was a wake and a burial, but he was secretly alive in the frame. At the end of the story the frame appeared near a stereoscope and a Galena stone supported by a tripod in the room where a young girl had died.

When I managed to change the subject, Montero expressed a strange desire to meet some writers.

"Why don't you come over tomorrow afternoon?" I suggested. "I'll introduce you to some."

He described himself as a savage and accepted the invitation. Perhaps my pleasure in seeing him leave was what induced me to accompany him to the street floor. When we left the elevator, Montero discovered the garden out in the courtyard. Sometimes, when seen through the glass door from the hall in the thin afternoon light, that tiny garden suggests the mysterious image of a forest at the bottom of a lake. At night the glow of lilac and orange lights changes it into a horrible candyland paradise. Montero saw it at night.

"To be frank with you," he said, after taking a long look, "this is the most interesting thing I have seen here so far."

The next day Pauline arrived early. By five that afternoon she had everything ready for the party. I showed her a Chinese figurine of jade which I had bought that morning in an antique shop. It was a wild horse with raised forefeet and a flowing mane. The shopkeeper had assured me that it symbolized passion.

Putting the little horse on a shelf of the bookcase, Pauline exclaimed, "It is beautiful, like a first love affair!" When I said I wanted her to have it, she threw her arms around my neck and kissed me impulsively.

We drank a cup of tea together. I told her I had been offered a fellowship to study in London for two years. Suddenly we believed in an immediate marriage, the trip to England, our life there. We considered details of domestic economy: the almost enjoyable privations we would suffer; the distribution of hours of study, diversion, rest, and, perhaps, work; what Pauline would do while I attended classes; the clothes and books we would take. And then, after an interval of planning, we conceded that I would have to give up the scholarship. My examinations were only a week away, but already it was evident that Pauline's parents wished to postpone our marriage.

The guests began to arrive. I was not happy. I found it hard to talk to anyone, and kept inventing excuses to leave the room. I was in no mood for conversation; and I discovered that my memory was vague and unpredictable. Uneasy, futile, miserable, I moved from one group to another, wishing that people would leave, waiting for my moments alone with Pauline, while I escorted her home.

She was standing by the window, talking to Montero. When I glanced at her, she looked up and turned her perfect face toward me. I felt that her love was an inviolable refuge where we two were alone. Now I desired fervently to tell her that I adored her, and I made up my mind to abandon, that very evening, the absurd and childish reticence that had kept me, until then, from declaring my love. But if only I could communicate my thought to her without speaking! Her face wore an expression of generous, ecstatic, and surprised gratitude.

I walked over to Pauline, and she asked me the name of the poem in which a man becomes so estranged from a woman that he does not even greet her when they meet in heaven. I knew that the poem was by Browning, and I remembered some of the verses. I spent the rest of the evening looking for it in the Oxford Edition. If I could not have Pauline to myself, then I preferred to look for something she wanted instead of talking to people who did not interest me; but my mind was not functioning clearly, and I wondered if my lack of success in finding the poem was a kind of omen. When I turned toward the window again, they were gone. Louis Albert Morgan, the pianist, must have noticed my concern.

"Pauline is just showing Montero around the apartment," he said.

I shrugged my shoulders, tried to conceal my annoyance, and pretended to be interested in the Browning again. Out of the corner of my eye I caught a glimpse of Morgan entering my bedroom. I thought, "He has gone to find her." He came out, followed by Pauline and Montero.

Finally someone went home; then, slowly and deliberately, the others left. The moment came when no one was there except Pauline, Montero, and me. As I had feared, Pauline said, "It's very late. I have to go."

"I'll take you home, if I may," Montero volunteered quickly.

"So will I," I said.

I was speaking to Pauline, but I looked at Montero, and my eyes were filled with scorn and loathing.

When we came out of the elevator, I noticed that Pauline did not have the little Chinese horse I had given her.

"You've forgotten my present!" I said.

I went back to the apartment and returned with the figurine. I found them leaning against the glass door, looking at the garden. I took Pauline's arm and tried to keep Montero from walking on the other side of her. I very pointedly left him out of the conversation.

He was not offended. When we said good night to Pauline, he insisted on walking home with me. On the way he spoke of literature, probably with sincerity and with a certain fervor. I said to myself, "He is the writer. I am just a tired man who is worried about a woman." I pondered on the incongruity between his physical vigor and his literary weakness. I thought, "He is protected by a hard shell. My feelings do not reach him." I looked with aversion at his clear eyes, his hairy moustache, his bull neck.

That week I scarcely saw Pauline. I studied a great deal. After my last examination I telephoned her. She congratulated me with unnatural vehemence, and said she would come to see me later that afternoon.

I took a nap, bathed slowly, and waited for Pauline while I leafed through a book about the Fausts of Müller and Lessing.

When I saw her I exclaimed, "You've changed!"

"Yes," she said. "How well we know each other. You can tell what I am thinking even before I speak."

Enraptured, we gazed into each other's eyes.

"Thank you," I said.

Nothing had ever touched me as much as that admission, by Pauline, of the deep conformity of our souls. I basked naively in the warmth of that compliment. I do not remember when I began to wonder (incredulously) whether Pauline's words had another meaning. Before I had time to consider that possibility, she began a confused explanation.

Suddenly I heard her say, " . . . and that first afternoon we were already hopelessly in love."

I wondered what she was talking about.

"He is very jealous," Pauline continued. "He doesn't object to our friendship, but I promised that I wouldn't see you any more for a while."

I was still waiting for the impossible clarification that would reassure me. I did not know whether Pauline was joking or serious. I did not know what sort of expression was on my face. Nor did I know then the extent of my grief.

"I must go now," said Pauline. "Julius is waiting for me downstairs. He didn't want to come up."

"Who?" I asked.

Suddenly, as if nothing had happened, I was afraid Pauline had discovered that I was an impostor, and that she knew our souls were not really united after all.

"Julius Montero," she answered ingenuously.

Her reply could not have surprised me; but on that horrible afternoon nothing impressed me as much as those two words. For the first time in my life I felt that a breach had opened between us.

"Are you going to marry him?" I asked almost scornfully.

I do not remember what she said. I believe she invited me to the wedding.

Then I was alone. The whole thing was absurd. No person was more incompatible with Pauline (and with me) than Montero. Or was I mistaken? If Pauline loved that man, perhaps she and I had never been alike at all. And as I came to that realization I was aware that I had suspected the dreadful truth many times before.

I was very sad, but I do not believe I was jealous. Lying face downward on my bed, I stretched out my arm and my hand touched the book I had been reading a short while before. I flung it away in disgust.

I went out for a walk. I stopped to watch a group of children playing at the corner. That afternoon, I did not see how I could go on living.

I could not forget Pauline. As I preferred the painful moments of our separation to my subsequent loneliness, I went over them and examined them in minute detail and relived them. As a result of my brooding anxiety, I thought I discovered new interpretations for what had happened. So, for example, in Pauline's voice telling me the name of her lover I found a tenderness that moved me deeply, at first. I thought that she was sorry for me, and her kindness was as touching as her love had been before. But then, after thinking it over, I decided that her tenderness was not meant for me but for the name she pronounced.

I accepted the fellowship, and quietly started to make preparations for the voyage. But the news got out. Pauline visited me the afternoon before I sailed.

I had felt alienated from her, but the moment I saw her I fell in love all over again. I realized that her visit was a clandestine one, although she did not say it. I grasped her hands. I trembled with gratitude.

"I shall always love you," said Pauline. "Somehow, I shall always love you more than anyone else."

Perhaps she thought she had committed an act of treason. She knew that I did not doubt her loyalty to Montero, but as if it troubled her to have spoken words that implied—if not for me, for an imaginary witness—a disloyal intention, she hastened to add, "Of course, what I feel for you doesn't count now. I am in love with Julius."

Nothing else mattered, she said. The past was a desert where she had waited for Montero. Of our love, or friendship, she had no memory.

There was not much to say after that. I was very angry, and pretended that I was busy. I took her down in the elevator. When I opened the door to the street, we saw that it was raining.

"I'll get you a taxi," I said.

But in a voice full of emotion Pauline shouted, "Good-bye, Darling!"

Then she ran across the street and was gone. I turned away sadly. When I looked around, I saw a man crouching in the garden. He stood up and pressed his face and hands against the glass door. It was Montero.

Streaks of lilac and orange-colored light were outlined against a green background of dark clumps of shrubbery. Montero's face, pressed against the wet glass, looked whitish and deformed.

I thought of an aquarium, of a fish in an aquarium. Then, with futile bitterness, I told myself that Montero's face suggested other monsters: the fish misshapen by the pressure of the water, living at the bottom of the sea.

I sailed the next morning. During the crossing I scarcely left my cabin. I wrote and studied constantly.

I wanted to forget Pauline. During my two years in England I avoided anything that could remind me of her, from encounters with other Argentines to the few dispatches from Buenos Aires published by the newspapers. It is true that she appeared to me in dreams with such persuasive and vivid reality that I wondered whether my soul was counteracting by night the privations I imposed on it during the day. I eluded the memory of her obstinately. By the end of the first year I succeeded in excluding her from my nights and, almost, in forgetting her.

The afternoon of my arrival from Europe I thought about Pauline again. I wondered whether the memories at my apartment would be too intense. When I opened the door I felt some emotion, and I paused respectfully to commemorate the past and the extremes of joy and sorrow I had known. Then I had a shameful revelation. I was not moved by the secret monuments of our love, suddenly bared in the depths of my memory: I was moved by the emphatic light streaming through the window, the light of Buenos Aires.

Around four o'clock I went to the corner store and bought a pound of coffee. At the bakery the clerk recognized me. He greeted me with noisy cordiality, and told me that for a long time—six months, at least—I had not honored him with my patronage. After those amenities I asked him timidly, foolishly, for a small loaf of bread. He asked the usual question, "White or dark?"

I replied, as usual, "White."

I went home. The day was clear and very cold.

I thought about Pauline while I was making coffee. Sometimes, late in the afternoon, we would drink a cup of black coffee together.

Then, as if I were in a dream, I shifted abruptly from my affable and even-tempered indifference to the excitement, the madness that the sight of Pauline caused me to feel. When I saw her, I fell down on my knees, I buried my face in her hands and, for the first time, I gave vent to all my grief at having lost her.

It happened this way: I heard three knocks at the door. I wondered who it was; I remembered that my coffee would get cold; I opened the door with a certain irritation.

And then—I do not know how long all this took—Pauline asked me to follow her. I realized that she was correcting, by her forceful actions, the mistakes of our past relationship. It seems to me (but I tend to be inaccurate about that afternoon) that she corrected them with excessive determination. When she asked me to embrace her ("Embrace me!" she said. "Now!"), I was overjoyed. We looked into each other's eyes and, like two rivers flowing together, our souls were united. Outside the rain pelted against the windows, on the roof. I interpreted the rain, which was the resurgence of the whole world, as a panic extension of our love.

But my emotion did not keep me from discovering that Montero had contaminated Pauline's conversation. Sometimes when she spoke, I had the unpleasant impression that I was listening to my rival. I recognized the characteristic heaviness of the phrase, the candid and laborious attempts to find the right word; I recognized, painfully, the undeniable vulgarity.

With an effort, I was able to control myself. I looked at her face, her smile, her eyes. It was Pauline herself, intrinsic and perfect. Nothing had really changed her.

Then, as I contemplated her image in the shadowy recesses of the mirror, within the dark border of wreaths, garlands, and angels, she seemed different. It was as if I had discovered another version of Pauline, as if I saw her in a new way. I gave thanks for the separation that had interrupted my habit of seeing her, but had returned her to me more beautiful than ever.

"I must go," said Pauline. "Julius is waiting for me."

I perceived a strange mixture of scorn and anguish in her voice. I thought unhappily, "In the old days Pauline would not have been untrue to anyone." When I looked up she was gone.

I waited for a moment; then I called her. I called her again. I went down to the entrance and ran along the street. She was nowhere in sight. I went back into the building, shivering. I said to myself, "The shower cooled things off." But I noticed that the street was dry.

Returning to my apartment, I saw that it was nine o'clock. I did not feel like going out for dinner; I was afraid of meeting someone I knew. I made some coffee. I drank two or three cups and ate part of a piece of bread.

I did not even know when Pauline and I would see each other again. I wanted to talk to her. I wanted to ask her to clear up some of my doubts (doubts were tormenting me, but I knew she could clear them up easily). Suddenly my ingratitude startled me. Fate was offering me every happiness and I was not satisfied. That afternoon had been the culmination of both our lives. That was what it meant to Pauline, and to me. That was the reason why I had not asked for any explanation. (To speak, to ask questions would have been, somehow, to differentiate ourselves.)

But waiting until the next day to see Pauline seemed impossible. With an intense feeling of relief I resolved to go to Montero's house that very evening. Immediately afterward I changed my mind. I could not do that without first speaking to Pauline. I decided to look for a friend—Louis Albert Morgan seemed to be the logical one—and ask him to tell me what he knew about Pauline's life during my absence from Buenos Aires.

Then it occurred to me that the best thing would be simply to go to bed and sleep. When I had rested I would see everything more clearly. And, besides, I was not in the mood to hear anyone speak disparagingly of Pauline. Going to bed was like being put into a torture chamber (perhaps I remembered my nights of insomnia, when merely to stay in bed was a way to pretend not to be awake). I turned out the light.

I would not dwell on Pauline's actions any longer. I knew too little to understand the situation. Since I was unable to empty my mind and to stop thinking, I would take refuge in the memory of that afternoon.

I would continue to love Pauline's face even if I had found something strange and unnatural in her behavior. Her face was the same as always, the pure and marvelous face that had loved me before Montero made his abominable appearance in our lives. I said to myself, "There is a fidelity in faces that souls perhaps do not share."

Or had I been mistaken all along? Was I in love with a blind projection of my preferences and dislikes? Had I never really known Pauline?

I selected one image from that afternoon—Pauline standing in front of the dark, smooth depths of the mirror—and tried to evoke it. When I could see the image, I had a sudden revelation: my doubts were caused by the fact that I was forgetting Pauline. I had tried to concentrate on the contemplation of her image. But imagination and memory are capricious faculties: I could see her tousled hair, a fold of her dress, the vague semidarkness around her, but not Pauline.

Many images, animated by spontaneous energy, passed before my closed eyes. And then I made a discovery. The small horse of jade could be seen on Pauline's right, in a corner of the mirror, like something on the dark edge of an abyss.

At first I was not surprised; but after a few minutes I remembered that the figurine was not in my apartment. I had given it to Pauline two years ago.

I told myself that it was simply a superimposition of anachronous memories (the older one, of the horse; the more recent one, of Pauline). That explained it; my fears evaporated, and I should have gone to sleep. But then I had an outrageous, and in the light of what I was to learn later, a pathetic thought. "If I don't go to sleep soon," I reflected, "I'll look haggard tomorrow and Pauline won't find me interesting."

Soon I realized that my memory of the figurine in the bedroom mirror was completely inaccurate. I had never put it in the bedroom. The only place in my apartment it had ever been was in the living room (on the bookshelf or in Pauline's hands or in my own).

Terrified, I tried to conjure up those memories again. The mirror reappeared, outlined by angels and garlands of wood, with Pauline in the center and the little horse at the right side. I was not sure whether it reflected the room. Perhaps it did, but in a vague and summary way. On the other hand, the little horse was rearing splendidly on the shelf of the bookcase, which filled the whole background. A new person was hovering in the darkness at one side; I did not recognize him immediately. Then, with only slight interest, I noticed that I was that person.

I saw Pauline's face, in its totality. It seemed to be projected to me by the extreme intensity of her beauty and her despair. When I awoke I was crying.

It was impossible to judge how long I had been sleeping. But my dream was no invention. It was an unconscious continuation of my imaginings, and reproduced the scenes of the afternoon faithfully.

I looked at my watch. It was five o'clock. I would get up early and, even at the risk of making Pauline angry, go to her house. That decision, however, did not relieve my anguish perceptibly.

I got up at seven-thirty, took a long bath, and dressed slowly.

I did not know where Pauline lived. The janitor at my building let me borrow his telephone book and city directory. Neither listed Montero's address. I looked for Pauline's name; it was not listed either. Then I discovered that someone else was living at Montero's former residence. I thought I would ask Pauline's parents for the address.

I had not seen them for a long time, not since I found out that Pauline loved Montero. Now, to explain, I would have to tell them how much I had suffered. I did not have the courage.

I decided to talk to Louis Albert Morgan. I could not go to his house before eleven. I wandered through the streets in a daze, pausing to speculate on the shape of a molding, or pondering on the meaning of a word heard at random. I remember that at Independence Square a woman, with her shoes in one hand and a book in the other, was walking up and down on the damp grass in her bare feet.

Morgan received me in bed, drinking from an enormous bowl which he held with both hands. I caught a glimpse of a whitish liquid with a piece of bread floating on the surface.

"Where does Montero live?" I asked.

He had finished drinking the milk, and was fishing bits of bread from the bottom of the cup.

"Montero is in jail," he replied.

I could not conceal my amazement.

"What?" Morgan continued. "Didn't you know?"

He undoubtedly imagined that I knew everything except that one detail, but because he liked to talk he told me the whole story. I thought that I was going to faint, that I had fallen suddenly into a pit; and there, too, I heard the ceremonious, implacable, and precise voice that related incomprehensible facts with the monstrous and unquestioning conviction that they were already known to me.

This is what Morgan told me: Suspecting that Pauline would come to visit me the day before I left for Europe, Montero hid in the garden. He saw her come out; he followed her; he overtook her in the street. When a crowd began to gather, he forced her to get into a taxi. They drove around all night along the shore and out by the lakes, and early the next morning he shot her to death in a hotel in the suburbs. That had not happened yesterday; it had happened the night before I left for Europe; it had happened two years ago.

In life's most terrible moments we tend to fall into a kind of protective irresponsibility. Instead of thinking about what is happening to us, we focus our attention on trivialities.

At that moment I asked Morgan, "Do you remember the last party I gave before I went to Europe?"

Morgan said that he did.

"When you noticed I was concerned, and you went to my bedroom to call Pauline, what was Montero doing?" I asked.

"Nothing," replied Morgan briskly. "Nothing. Oh, now I remember. He was looking at himself in the mirror."

I went back to my apartment. In the entrance hall I met the janitor. Affecting indifference, I asked if he knew that Miss Pauline had died.

"Why, of course!" he said. "It was in all the papers. The police even came here to question me." The man looked at me curiously. "Are you all right? Do you want me to help you upstairs?" he asked.

I said no, and hurried up to my apartment. I have a vague memory of struggling with the key; of picking up some letters under the door; and of throwing myself face down on my bed.

Later, I was standing in front of the mirror thinking, "I am sure that Pauline visited me last night. She died knowing that her marriage to Montero had been a mistake—an atrocious mistake—and that we were the truth. She came back from death to complete her destiny, our destiny." I remembered a sentence that Pauline had written in a book years ago: "Ours have already been united." I kept thinking, "Last night it finally happened, at the moment when I made love to her." Then I told myself, "I am unworthy of her. I have doubted, I have been jealous. She came back from death to love me."

Pauline had pardoned me. Never before had we loved each other so much. Never before had we been so close to each other.

I was still under the spell of that sad and triumphant intoxication of love when I wondered—or rather, when my brain, accustomed to the habit of proposing alternatives, wondered—whether there was another explanation for the visit of the previous night. Then, like a thunderbolt, the truth came to me.

Now I wish I could find that I am mistaken again. Unfortunately, as always happens when the truth comes out, my horrible explanation clarifies the things that seemed mysterious. They, in turn, confirm the truth.

Our wretched love did not draw Pauline from her grave. There was no ghost of Pauline. What I embraced was a monstrous ghost of my rival's jealousy.

The key to it all is found in Pauline's visit to me the night before I sailed for Europe. Montero followed her and waited for her in the garden. He quarreled with her all night long, and because he did not believe her explanations—but how could he have doubted her integrity?—he killed her the next morning.

I imagined him in jail, brooding about her visit to me, picturing it to himself with the cruel obstinacy of his jealousy.

The image that entered my apartment was a projection of Montero's hideous imagination. The reason I did not discover it then was that I was so touched and happy that I desired only to follow Pauline's bidding. And yet there were several clues. One was the rain. During the visit of the real Pauline—the night before I sailed—I did not hear the rain. Montero, in the garden, felt it directly on his body. When he imagined us, he thought that we had heard it. That is why I heard the rain last night. And then I found that the street was dry.

The figurine is another clue. I had it in my apartment for just one day: the day of my party. But for Montero it was like a symbol of the place. That is why it appeared last night.

I did not recognize myself in the mirror because Montero did not imagine me clearly. Nor did he imagine the bedroom with precision. He did not really know Pauline. The image projected by Montero behaved in a way that was unlike Pauline and, what is more, it even talked like him.

The fantasy Montero invented is his torment. My torment is more real. It is the certainty that Pauline did not come back to me because she was disenchanted in her love. It is the certainty that she never really loved me at all. It is the certainty that Montero knew about aspects of her life that I have heard others mention obliquely. It is the certainty that when I embraced her—in the supposed moment of the union of our souls—I obeyed a request from Pauline that she never made to me, one that my rival had heard many times.

The Future Kings

Perhaps this story should begin with the memory of a circus performance held in 1918. That was when my dazzled eyes first beheld—in antics that, although admittedly humble, seemed prodigious to me then—the animals that deserve our deepest respect: seals. As for the feeling of joy I unconsciously associate with those memories—now I attribute it (but let us not forget that in these unhappy times we are subject to obsessions) to the noble, blissful intoxication of victory; but when I try to relive my feelings of that time with greater exactitude I am aware that at the root of my happiness, like symbols of future mysteries, were the enormous flag-bedecked circus tent and three children—Helen, Mark, and I—hand in hand on an ominous threshold.

When the seals had finished their performance, Mark left our box. A chimpanzee was riding a bicycle around the red circumference of the ring. The animal was not looking at his narrow path; his eyes were riveted on Helen. Suddenly things began to happen. Helen cried;

Mark came back and said that he had obtained permission for us to visit the seals and the other animals; Helen implored and threatened: she said that if I went she would never speak to me again; I followed Mark.

Even then Mark was the secret and indomitable agent who organized everything in our lives. He was very intelligent, very strong, very rich. Much of our childhood we spent together at his homes: the town house or the large country estate of Saint Remi.

Only Helen seemed to resist his influence. With a calm and spontaneous insistence that somehow had the power to thwart him, Helen continued to prefer me, to believe in me and not in him.

After we finished college I entered law school. I attended classes regularly for four years. When I heard about students who had graduated in one or two years, I was skeptical.

"What good can you possibly derive," I would ask, "from reading hundreds of pages in such a short time?"

Mark did not study. He read for his own enjoyment and directed our reading. Under his guidance I made a frivolous and profitable inquiry into the history of the quadrature of the circle, the progress made by Arab navigators, the possibilities of logistics, the nature and multiplication of chromosomes, the works of Resta on comparative cosmographies.

Later Mark became a student at the School of Natural Science. As a friend remarked, that seemed to confirm the fact that he did not take life seriously. Even so, the course is long and difficult. Mark graduated in a year.

"I have decided to devote my life to study," he told me one night. "I shall live in seclusion at Saint Remi. I need a companion, an intelligent girl, to live with me and be my assistant."

Inexplicably I felt alarmed. I realized that I was to find that girl for him. Against my will, uncertainly, I began to search for her in a mental cataloguing of the women I knew. Very soon I abandoned the search.

Helen went with Mark. I withdrew from law practice and went to Australia. There were no good-byes. Helen and Mark were already ensconced at the villa; I did not have time to visit them, or even call.

In Australia I was the assistant administrator, then the administrator, of a ranch. Sometimes, in the afternoons, I would count the orange-colored flagstones of the patio, and each stone would represent one of the women in my life. Two memories stood out more poignantly than the rest: one, very sad, was of Helen; the other was of Louise, the grocer's daughter, who lived across from Saint Remi. We used to play with her each afternoon, and she was a pleasant, but no longer vivid, memory of that time. I wondered what had become of her. We had shared a part of our childhood, and then I had forgotten her. What vestige of her was left to me? Only the metal pencil I am writing with (she gave it to me once for a birthday present and I always carry it with me) and a desperate, tender reproach that seems to haunt me.

To dispel the boredom of my afternoons I wrote novels about espionage. Under the pseudonym of Speculator I published six or seven books in Melbourne. They ran to several editions, but the critics were not enthusiastic.

I spent nine years among the dunghills and the sheepfolds, until war was declared and I returned to my country. They said I was too old for the front and so, to my own surprise, I became a counterspy. Perhaps my novels made them think I was qualified for such work.

One afternoon I learned from conversation with a friend that the office had become suspicious of the people who lived at Saint Remi. I spoke to my chief about it. He suspected that enemy planes were being directed from the villa to bomb that section of the city. I convinced him that I was the man to head the investigation.

II

Early the next morning I left my quarters and crossed the noisy street. A pure sky was overhead as I descended into the cavernous recesses of the subway. I had to wait on the platform until the people who had taken shelter there during the night came out of the tunnels with their bags and mattresses. It was ten o'clock before the trains started running again. I rode to the end of the line and then emerged, by means of a labyrinthine iron stairway, into the quiet suburb darkened by trees. There, amid a conglomeration of indifferent materialized memories, were the garage adorned with medallions (it was formerly the stable), the picnic grounds, the tennis courts. I looked in vain for a taxi, or even a horse and carriage, to take me to the villa. I began to feel tired as I walked down an avenue of very tall and leafy trees with dark trunks, lustrous foliage, and orange-colored flowers, which did not coincide exactly with my memories. When I passed the trees I began to recognize the place. I had the impression that the area had been badly hit by the bombings (but the attack that is going on at this moment must be the worst one of all). I walked on, past undamaged houses, streets without perforations. Then I came to the wall that surrounds the estate of Saint Remi; it was in a ruinous condition. From the outside I could not determine whether the house had been hit by the bombings. I skirted the wall, feeling that I was in a dream of endless fatigue.

The neighborhood had changed, but the store that had belonged to Louise's parents was still standing directly opposite the main gate of Saint Remi. I entered the store. As my feet touched the smooth planks of oak that had once been a part of the dining room at Saint Remi, I felt a sensation of love, the first I had experienced in many years, pervade my soul. In the dark room a man and woman I did not recognize stood waiting to serve me. I took them for the new owners of the store, and asked if I could buy something to eat.

"We don't have very much," said the grocer. He was a disheveled man with a sallow complexion.

"Well, we have just as much as other places," said the woman vaguely. She went to prepare lunch for me.

I spoke of the bombings, the food shortages, high prices, the black market, man's descent from the monkey, our need to be indulgent with the government, how the sacrifice of the war had affected all of us, the winners of last Sunday's game, and, finally, the country estate of Saint Remi.

"We've often wondered what goes on there," said the man. "Especially lately!"

I heard the woman's voice from the back room, "People are talking!"

"The people who live at Saint Remi never go out," explained the man. "And no one ever goes in."

"Why worry," said the woman. "I guess you'll find eccentrics in every neighborhood."

"We don't know what goes on behind that wall," said the man darkly. After a pause he continued, "And we haven't known for a long time!"

"What difference does it make?" supplied the woman.

She placed a voluminous plate of cabbage on the counter and invited me to sit down. Then she brought a small glass of sour wine and a piece of bread.

I summoned courage and asked, "Who knows about the goings-on at the villa?"

"Not a soul," whispered the woman, squinting.

"The man who delivers the fish knows," said the man.

He was due to pass the store at one o'clock, or thereabouts, and was the only person who ever went near the villa.

"You mean he goes in the house every day?" I inquired.

"No, never," said the woman with a smile.

"He leaves the fish at the door," explained the man.

The fish peddler came along after one-thirty, in a horse-drawn cart.

"Do you deliver fish to Saint Remi?" I asked.

"Sure thing," he said. "Been doing it for years."

"Do you ever see the man who lives there?"

"Every day."

"Are you the only person who makes deliveries to the villa?"

"Naturally. Fish is all they eat. They eat more fish than an army. Because of them I was able to get my wagon, and now I have a horse too!"

I decided not to go to Saint Remi until evening. I asked the grocer if it would be possible to rest in one of the upstairs rooms. He took me up to the top floor, to a room that was long and narrow, with a door at each end.

I fell asleep, and then awoke with the sensation of having slept for a long time. I looked at my watch and saw that it was ten to five. I was afraid I had slept all day, all night, and that it was the morning of the next day. Bemused by sleep, I went to the door to call the man. I chose the wrong door; I opened it—Instead of the rickety stairway I expected to find, there was an orderly room with pictures, bookcases, lamps, draperies, rugs. A girl was seated at a desk. She raised her head and looked at me with kind and honest eyes. It was Louise. She pronounced my name.

"But—your parents?" I asked.

She told me that her parents had sold the store to some relatives and had gone to live in the country. She rented the room from them. I believe she was as touched and happy as I was.

Perhaps because it all seemed like a dream, I dared to tell her I had thought about her many times.

She interrupted me with a sudden anxious question, "Promise you won't go into the villa?"

We heard steps on the stairway.

"We mustn't be seen together. I don't want anyone to know who I am," I whispered. "I'll be back around eight-thirty."

I closed the door. The grocer was standing at the other door, asking if he might have a word with me.

"I know about your mission," he said. "I want to help you."

"My mission?"

"The bombings," he replied. "They have leveled the whole area, but this is an island."

"Have any bombs fallen here?"

"Lately, yes. A few. They were dropped by mistake or on purpose by some green planes flying at a very high altitude."

"All right," I replied. "And what can you tell me about the people who live at the villa?"

"You will hear that the owner of the villa has kidnapped the lady. Don't believe it!"

"Then the lady has not been kidnapped?"

"They have both been kidnapped."

As we went downstairs, I asked, "And who are the kidnappers?"

"I suspect no one knows. People give the most fantastic explanations."

"But do they all live in the villa?"

"Yes. They all live there."

He spoke some more without explaining anything. I conjectured that a sudden secret prefiguring of my ineptitude for this adventure or the ineffable or atrocious nature of his confidences had convinced him that it was useless to talk to me. I did not insist too much with my questions: it was not advisable to show eagerness. We said good-bye to each other, and I asked him not to tell anyone about our conversation.

I walked away from the store, trying to stay out of sight of a possible observer at the upstairs window. About ten minutes later I came to a place where the wall was almost totally disintegrated. I looked around to make certain that no one was watching; then I climbed over the crumbled remains of the wall and jumped down onto the grounds of the estate.

The degree to which that noble and beautiful garden had been neglected impressed me profoundly. I do not mean that the garden in that condition—with insects and plants allowed to develop freely, as if it were a jungle—seemed less noble or less beautiful. A partially destroyed summerhouse; a tree with ashen foliage, which disappeared in the summer sky beyond the brilliant leaves of the creeping vine that was choking it to death; a fallen statue of Diana; a dry fountain; a bush covered with fragrant yellow flowers, embedded in a monstrous ant hill; benches along the solitary pathways that seemed to be waiting for persons from another age; very tall trees with no leaves on their uppermost branches; precarious walls with windows edged in gray, green or blue—Now, in the light of what I have learned, I see in that combination of abundance and decrepitude, in that infinitely pathetic beauty, a symbol of the transitory reign of men.

I glanced at my watch. I had three hours of daylight left for my investigation, and then I would see Louise. I knew where to find her. There was—I thought—no reason for me to feel so impatient.

From my vantage point the house was not visible. I advanced cautiously, hiding behind the trees. Except for a continuous buzzing of bees and, now and then, a gust of wind that shook the leaves, the silence was almost complete. Feeling that I was being observed, I crouched down by a bust of Phaedrus. I looked around. No one was there. I wanted to run, but I did not have the necessary strength. I had the impression that I was moving, hiding in the presence of invisible eyes; I was terrified, but I thought I knew—and this will seem like an indication of my unbalanced mental state—that there was no malevolence in those secret eyes.

(I know that this story is confused. I am writing automatically; in spite of my fatigue and my suffering, the habit of literary composition is writing these lines. They say that we remember our whole life at the moment of drowning. But it is one thing to remember; another, to write.)

I fell to the ground. An attack was just beginning; it did not seem far away. I remember thinking that I should take advantage of the bombing to enter the house. Some green planes flew overhead at an excessive altitude; then I peered out through the foliage of a tree and saw the villa in all its vastness at the end of the path. I don't know how long I stayed there. I remember thinking that the building sprawling between the trees reminded me of a huge antediluvian animal. Trying to protect myself, dragging myself over the ground, running when I lost control of my nerves, I reached the porch. I peered through the window at what had been, in former days, the children's dining room. Everything was exactly as I remembered it, but covered with a layer of dust and cobwebs. I pushed the window open and climbed through. The pictures of wild horses were still hanging on the wall; seeing them reassured me somewhat. I walked down the hall; I went through the guest wing; I tried to enter the game room. It was filled with small mounds of earth that looked like wasp nests, and infinite numbers of black ants were crawling on the floor. On the walls and the furniture of the ballroom I saw some white caterpillars that looked like very large silkworms; they had white skin and almost-human faces, and their round, greenish eyes stared at me with attentive immobility. I fled up the stairs. Night had fallen and the moon's splendor was filtering through the cracks in the ceiling; through the cracks in the floor I saw the music room with its dark furniture covered with yellow damask. I saw that walls no longer separated the music room, the dining room, the ballroom, and the small red room. Where the red room should have been, I saw a kind of swamp or lake with rushes growing in it and some viscous forms swimming in the dark water; I saw, or thought I saw, a mermaid on the muddy bank.

I heard footsteps approaching. I went down the stairs, out to the winter garden, and hid behind a blue porcelain urn. Someone was walking heavily in the music room. If I crawled to the door, I would be able to see who it was. I heard splashing noises, the sound of churning water, and then a long silence intervened; then I heard the steps again. I peeked out cautiously. At first I saw nothing strange: my eyes, glancing over the yellow damask furniture, the imitation of Netscher's *Henrietta*, the tapestry with the two figures of Eridanus, the harmonium, the bronze statue of Mercury, finally came to the water. There I saw a seal (it was what I had taken for a mermaid a few moments before); and then I saw a group of seals, eagerly devouring fish. The footsteps were drawing near again. A ragged woman came in—Helen, in rags, looking old and dirty—carrying a net filled with fish.

She let the heavy load fall to the floor. We looked into each other's eyes. I said, "Let me take you away from all this."

I said it out of loyalty to my former feelings, the feelings that had become a habit through the years. But I thought with rancor, "She owes all this to Mark"—not "I owe all this to Mark," as I used to think. "Mark has degraded her like this."

A door opened. Mark came in, in tatters, looking as old and dirty as Helen. Feeling genuinely sorry for him, I held out my hands in a gesture of friendship. His raucous gaiety and the look of relief and interest with which he greeted me denoted (I am sure of it now) a hidden meaning.

"What's going on here?" I asked.

"Nothing," said Mark.

"We were expecting you," said Helen. "We've always been expecting you."

"I've come to take you away," I said.

Mark turned to Helen. "Take the fish," he ordered.

"We must get away from here," I said.

As if he had not heard me, Mark placed the heavy burden on her back. Helen staggered away with it.

"Where is she going?" I asked.

"To take the fish to the seals."

"Why do you make her work like that?"

"I don't make her do anything," he replied vaguely.

I looked at my watch. I had the impression that it stopped at that instant.

"It is nine o'clock," I thought. "It's time for me to go. Louise is waiting."

I found myself thinking the prayer: "I must go because Louise is waiting" in algebraic terms. I was gratified to observe that I had mastered symbolic logic. I wanted to continue my mental gymnastics. And then I found myself in my habitual poverty, feeling (as I always feel after a dream) that by a vehement effort of my memory I would be able to recuperate the lost treasures. I was alone.

I experienced an intimate heaviness in my arms and legs. I groped my way in the dark, as if I could not see. My hands were trembling. I came to a hall covered with mosaic tile; there were skylights on the ceiling and paintings from the Flemish school on the walls. Mark stood at the end of the hall, in the moonlight. I called to him. I asked him where he was going.

"To bring in another load of fish," he replied.

"You and Helen have become the servants of the seals," I observed bitterly.

He gave me a long smile. Then he said, "We could ask for nothing better."

"Perhaps not—but at least think of Helen—" Then I added imploringly, "We must get away from this place!"

"No," he said slowly. "No. And now you are going to stay here too."

At that moment the sirens wailed three times, announcing the approach of enemy aircraft. Unaccountably I felt relieved.

"Are you going to force me to stay here?" I asked.

"You will want to stay of your own accord. We have accomplished some interesting things, and now the seals will carry on our work. I am sure you will want to be here to observe it. Do you recall how enthusiastic we were when I discovered Darwin? The infinite number of books on evolution that I read in a few days? The evolution wrought on a species by the blind action of nature takes thousands of years to accomplish. I wanted to achieve the same result in a shorter time by means of a definite plan. Man is a provisional result on one evolutionary path. But there are other ways: those of other mammals, birds, fish, the amphibians, the insects— I conquered the gregarious instinct of the ants: now they build individual anthills. But the seals are our masterpiece. We have tortured the young to find out what could be done with a vigilance that was ever alert; we have worked on cells and embryos; we have made a comparative study of the chromosomes of the frozen fossils from Siberia. But it was not enough to work on individual animals; we had to establish genetic patterns."

"And have you taught your seals how to talk?" I asked ironically.

"There is no need for them to talk. They communicate with their thoughts. They reproach me for not having changed their flippers into hands. But they are infinitely kind, and they bear no grudges. They are interested in man's evolutionary possibilities; they did not wish to force Helen and me to do anything, because that would have meant that one of us would have had to operate on the other, and they know how much we love each other. All these years they have kept repeating, 'Wait until someone from the outside world comes!' "

"And now I am here," I thought uneasily. Immediately I found myself thinking that the seals, assisted by Mark and Helen, had produced radical changes on the white caterpillars in the ballroom. The caterpillars were almost unreal creatures, bereft of the indispensable defenses required by an active life. Now they lived in a world like the one dreamed about by idealists, where reality consisted of the clear, precise ideas they had the ability to project.

The bombs began to fall; they seemed to be very close. Mark ran to the music room.

I heard an explosion. I felt a sharp pain in my back. I coughed, I choked. I was lying on the ground—I was sobbing. Some dust—perhaps from pieces of shattered plaster—was floating in the air.

Outside my line of vision, something that seemed to be animated with a life of its own was disintegrating.

Mark was standing beside me. "I'm going to give you an injection," he said.

I could not resist. My legs seemed to be paralyzed. The pain was intolerable. More bombs fell. I thought that the whole villa was about to collapse. There was a smell of mud, a smell of fish.

"The green planes are flying so high that the seals cannot drive them away," I thought.

I turned around. Mark was not at my side. Perhaps everyone in the house had been killed. I tried to remember Helen. I recaptured the image of Louise asking me if I planned to go into the villa, Louise telling me she rented that room, Louise smiling at me sadly when I left.

I felt the effect of the injection almost immediately. The pain stopped. I was afraid that I was bleeding to death. Struggling, I managed to look, to touch myself. There was no blood.

"I won't have time to see Louise tonight," I thought.

Then it occurred to me that I might not ever see her again, that I might be an invalid for the rest of my life.

I lay there feeling perplexed, trying very hard to control my breathing, resigning myself to the inevitable, fortifying my soul. I remembered that the pencil Louise had given me and my notebook were both in my pocket. I decided to write everything down before the effect of the anesthetic wore off.

I wrote with extraordinary rapidity, as if a superior will impelled me and helped me.

The bombing has just begun again. I am growing weaker—And now my solitude is all-encompassing.

The Idol

I have just drunk a cup of coffee. I have the illusion that my mind is clear, and I feel vaguely unwell. My present state is preferable to the dangers that await me when I sleep: the figures that emerge, one from another, as if from an invisible fountain. I pause in rapt contemplation of the infinite whiteness of the Meissen porcelain. The small figure of Horus, the god of libraries, which was sent me from Cairo by my correspondent, the Coptic merchant Paphnuti, projects a definite and severe shadow on the wall. From time to time I hear the antique bronze clock, and I am aware that at three o'clock this morning the three nymphs will appear to the solemn, triple, and joyous melody. I regard the wood of the table, the leather of the chair, the fabric of my clothes, the nails on my fingers. The presence of material objects never seemed as intense to me as it does tonight. I recall enviously that a certain famous novelist used to drink tea and work on the book he was writing whenever he suffered from insomnia. My task, a more personal one, is merely to tell a story; but for me and (perhaps) for one of my readers that story may be of the utmost importance. One beginning seems as good as another; I propose this one:

My professional relationship with Martín Garmendia dates from 1929, when I furnished and decorated his apartment on Bulnes Street. Our mutual friend, Mrs. Riso, suggested me for the job and I believe I completed it satisfactorily. Since that time Mr. Garmendia has honored me with his business and, what is more significant, with his friendship.

How hard I worked in those days! Burdened with heavy lamps, velvets, and figurines I traversed the five hundred yards between his apartment and my house on Alvear Avenue innumerable times. It is not presumptuous to say that the problems presented by the decoration of three or four rooms for Mr. Garmendia would have overwhelmed a less agile taste than my own. For example, there was the problem of the living room. It is a square room, and the window and doors are arranged asymmetrically. Very well, I admit it: in an anxious moment I was afraid that the table, the sofa, the rug, the book collection—like Kant's, composed exclusively of books dedicated by friends and admirers—would never fit in well together. But I must not let myself digress on artistic reminiscences. I am writing as a man now, not as an interior designer. I should merely like to point out that the objects I touch acquire a life, vigor, and perhaps a charm of their own.

A few days after I finished the work, Garmendia came to my house. I did not attend to him at once, but let him wander through the rooms to soothe his spirit with the beauty, less profuse than authentic, of my collections. Then I asked if he wished to make a complaint. He said that he did. I closed my eyes, sharpening my wits to prepare for any reproach. My friend did not speak. Finally I half opened my eyes, and saw that he was indicating a tea set of white, blue, black, and gold porcelain in a showcase. Garmendia had fallen in love with the set, and was complaining that I had never offered it to him. He asked me how much it cost and where it was from. If the first question, for a collector like Garmendia, is unimportant, the second is fundamental. I improvised a price for each piece. I looked at the mark on a cup, searched through my papers, and, not without some agitation, realized that I did not know the origin of the set at that moment. Why should

I deny it? I was horrified. The situation was dangerous. In my work such ignorance can be fatal. Under the circumstances I could scarcely be blamed for assuring my friend that his tea set was from Ludwigsburg. I never had an opportunity to correct the error. Garmendia made an exhaustive study of the history of the city, the castle, the porcelain and its distinguishing characteristics; the genealogy of the dukes and kings; the sentimental biography of Fräulein von Grävenitz. For those of us who met at tea time in the dense interior of the apartment on Bulnes Street, the "Ludwigsburg" was not simply a tactile and visual delight; it was also a pretext for our host to relate his pertinent set of anecdotes.

No sooner had some of my kindly acts and time—above all, time—begun to soothe my conscience when a devilish improvisation was my undoing once again. I sold Garmendia three very rare pieces—a teapot, a cream pitcher, and a sugar bowl—of blanc de chine. I should have described them as fraudulent Te-hua (today those imitations are as much in demand as the entirely improbable originals); I described them irrevocably as Vieux Canton. My secret debt to Garmendia, like a wound, was opened again.

And, therefore, on the last of my periodic trips to Europe in 1930, my desire to acquire objects that could interest Garmendia influenced more than one of my purchases.

The urge to provide my clientele with a continuous injection of beauty sent me to the most famous antique markets of Spain, Belgium, and Holland; then brought me to the Via del Babbuíno in Rome, and the Hotel Drouot in Paris; and led me, finally, to isolated places like Gulniac, in Brittany. I arrived there two weeks before the auction sale at the castle. On the advice of a friend I took a room at the pension of Madame Belardeau, a widow who always wore black and flaunted a maternal air. The only other guest was a rheumatic Englishman named Thompson who spent the whole day submerged (probably naked) in a tub of sand which had been placed, for his convenience, in the dining room.

I asked them about the people who lived in the castle. The lady assured me that the last of the Gulniacs (like the libertine in plays, who always arrives at the third act in a wheel chair) had lost his money and his health in orgies. I asked who participated in the orgies.

Were they from the town? (She appeared to be insulted.) Or were they from Paris and other places? (She expressed disbelief.) For a moment I lost my patience.

"All right," I snapped. "I give up. If you won't talk about the people, tell me about the orgies. What were they like?"

"Diabolical."

"Aha!" I said, half closing my eyes and savoring the unfailing flight of my imagination. "Gulniac is a retired colonial official. I can guess what his atrocious sprees are like. Alone, locked in his room, he gets drunk."

"Gulniac never touches alcohol," the lady assured me. "As for your statement that he was a colonial official, that is too monstrous for words."

"Please don't be angry," I said. "But about those orgies—they must have been quite wild to make Gulniac lose his health."

"His sight, which is more important," she interrupted.

"Is he blind?"

"All the men in his family become blind before they die. It must be a hereditary affliction. There is an anonymous poem from the fifteenth century about the blindness of the Gulniacs. Would you like to hear it?"

She recited it, I wrote it down, I translated it. It not only mentioned blindness: it alluded to the cult of the dog, the frenzy of the rites of initiation, the cruelty of the priestesses (girls who were as fresh and wholesome as the country air). She abounded in anecdotes and long, irrelevant, confused digressions. Until yesterday, I remembered very little of the original; and only this one stanza of the translation:

> Perfect and cruel are your nights,
> Though stars reflect in water blue
> And Heaven's hound still watches you
> With eyes of all his proselytes.

Yesterday, in a dream, I retrieved the original; this is the French version of the stanza I quoted:

> Ah, tu ne vois pas la nuit cruelle
> Qui brille; cet invisible temple
> D'où le céleste chien te contemple
> Avec les yeux morts de ses fidèles.

From the tub Thompson remarked, "I see the old bard did not forget his Shelley, who speaks of 'Heaven's winged hound' in the *Prometheus*."

I asked if it would be possible to visit the castle.

"Visitors will not be tolerated until two or three days before the auction," said the lady.

My room faced a deep and tremulous wood; in the distance I could see the castle tower through the autumnal gold of the elms. I gazed at it, burning with the most impatient curiosity. How could I wait a week, I asked myself, when to wait even for a few minutes was such exquisite torture? And so it happened that one afternoon, after consuming a stimulating *champagne nature* at lunch, I wandered through the wood, and at length came face to face with an insignificant, rust-consumed door. I pulled the bell rope, and the remnants of my courage abandoned me. Lacking the strength to run away, I waited with stoic resignation for the dogs and the insults of the last of the Gulniacs. The door was opened instead by three charming young ladies, one of whom (the other two remained silent and appeared to be her servants) apologized for the disorderly condition of the castle and claimed for herself the honor of being my guide. She led me through halls and underground passages, cellars and towers, showing me some treasures, some beauty, much history. She gave me an animated summary of the background of each foot of architecture and each inch of ornamentation, and finally brought the tour to a close by serving toast and hot chocolate, which she and her servants had prepared.

Needless to say, such a reception surprised me, for I had been afraid that around each corner, behind every door, the master of the house would be lurking, virulent and autocratic.

Refreshed by the nourishment, I ventured to ask, "And Monsieur Gulniac?"

"He never leaves his room," they replied.

"He is blind, I believe?"

"Yes, almost completely."

I thought that it would be indiscreet to ask for explanations.

At the auction I acquired several curios, and then regretted what I had bought and what I did not buy, as I always do.

At a really favorable price I purchased the enormous sword that Alain Barbetorte used when he killed the Saxon giant. It still interrupts the delicate harmony of my rooms, as it waits for an unlikely buyer. I also bought an ancient Celtic idol: a wooden statue not quite twenty inches high of an enthroned god with a dog's head. I suspect that it is a Breton version of Anubis. In the Egyptian form the god has a finer head, more like a jackal's. Here it was the head of a coarse watchdog.

But what caused me to select those objects? Why did I look for the documented piece, and reject the *potiche*? Why did I prefer the fallacious charm of history to the genuine charm of form? Why did I, a connoisseur, buy the St. Cyril and refuse the pitcher and washbowl I found in the untidy squalor of a servant's room? Such discoveries—the chairs from Vienna and Las Flores; the purple glass vase, shaped like a hand with a ring on one finger, from Luján; the crockery *mate* cups from Tapalqué—had contributed greatly to my prestige. I was no doubt misled by the search for authenticity, Garmendia's criterion.

What induced me to buy the idol, for example? The corrupt and odious expression I noticed on its face the very first moment I saw it? Its legend?

We followed a dark narrow corridor down to the chamber of the dog. An oblique ray of light from a side window fell directly on the god. Beneath the throne, there was a long stone couch. Behind it, nailed to the wall, were two stone tablets. Two eyes were carved on one, and a door was carved on the other. The god was completely covered with nails. My little guide told me the legends that explained it. According to the best-known legend in Gulniac—the statue is quite famous—each nail represented a soul won for the god. Another version of questionable validity, preferred by certain erudite historians, maintained that an early bishop of Brittany, alarmed by the wide diffusion of the superstition, ordered the idol's body to be covered with nails. That did not seem credible (and my charming guide was of the same opinion). For if the bishop was really sincere, why did he protect the idol with an armor of nail heads instead of simply destroying it outright? Why did he leave its vicious face uncovered? I studied it carefully. Then I understood why the statue stared with that atrocious, vacant expression: it had no eyes.

"They made it without eyes to show that it has no soul," said the girl.

At the auction I also bought a statue of St. Cyril (it had once been the property of Chateaubriand), Charette's autograph, and the manuscript of Hardouin's *Chronologie*.

When I returned to Buenos Aires I allowed Garmendia to be the first to view the things I had acquired during my journey. He was interested in the St. Cyril. I sold him the dog. Following my exact instructions, he placed it in a corner of his living room. Eureka! The dog did not look the least bit awesome by the Aubusson, by the silver candelabra, and by the glass, ebony, and damask of his showcases. What was even more extraordinary, it did not seem to be out of place.

One beautiful morning at the end of August—one of those mornings when the approach of spring is betrayed by a certain warmth in the air, a special vehemence of the verdure, an easing of respiratory congestion—I was arranging the shelf of antique maps (or was it the antique clocks?) when the ringing of the doorbell startled me. Fearing that it was some inopportune buyer, I ran to open the door. A young girl with a suitcase walked confidently into the room. Something about her—the cheap and frowzy clothing, her lean, angular body, and her long, muscular arms—reminded me of the male college student disguised as a woman in the varsity show. But my portrait of Geneviève Estermaria would be quite unfaithful if I did not add that her face was very beautiful. Her hair was black, her skin white, with rosy patches on her cheeks. The formation of her head, the placement of her eyes, suggested a cat; there was an unexpected vigor in her thick neck; her body had no curves. She was wearing a dress that was extremely green, and long, flat shoes.

The girl looked into my eyes and smiled innocently. Then she asked me in a harsh French accent if I knew who she was. I was still thinking about the maps; I was planning a new arrangement for the Persian miniatures and weighing the advantages and risks of appropriating the screen that belonged to Coromandel, the old boarder in the backroom, and claiming it as one of my latest acquisitions from the Hotel Drouot; and so, quite frankly, the enigma she proposed did not interest me very much. Grasping my flannel cloth firmly, I began to clean the English clock of William Beckford. Geneviève modified her question—I believe she changed it to "Don't you remember me?"—then she put her valise on the floor, and handed me the clocks one by one so I could clean them. We left the shelf in perfect order. When we turned to the Persian miniatures, I learned that my exasperating helper was one of the silent servant girls I had seen during my first visit to the castle of Gulniac.

"It appears," I said with an irony that was eclipsed by my limited knowledge of French, "that you left your enviable gift of silence in Brittany."

She replied that she hoped to find a good home where she could work as a maid. She possessed only a few francs and had placed all her hopes in me.

"I don't know anyone in this country," said Geneviève Estermaria naively.

Silently, with awkward, dangerous hands, with grim determination and a candid and anxious expression, she helped me to put my rooms in order. I admit that I began to worry about her immediate destiny. Although I told myself that her plight was no concern of mine, I was not able to put it out of my mind. I was sure that if I sent her away—even though I made a pretense at the most ridiculous courtesies, such as "Come again soon!" and the like, she would burst into tears. In truth I would be abandoning her in a strange city. It did not occur to me to wonder whether the girl had had ulterior motives in arriving alone, or whether her apparent lack of guile was only a pose.

"I'll see what I can do for you," I said. She looked so disconsolate that I added (against my better judgment), "But for now go upstairs and try not to let any of my clients see you."

"Very well, sir," she replied uncomprehendingly.

"On the second floor there are many empty rooms," I continued. "Stay in one until I call you. Or if you wish," I added, revealing my weakness and my incoherence, "go down to the basement—the kitchen is there—and prepare something for lunch."

I do not recall whether I mentioned that my display occupies a *pavillon de chasse* on Alvear Avenue, a little Louis XV villa faced with imitation stone. My economy is (was) perfect. A cleaning woman—old and painted—would come each morning (she was ill the day Geneviève arrived). I am responsible to no one but myself; it occurred to me that I might have a job for Geneviève, especially if she would be willing to work for her room and board. But would she attain the standard of efficiency I naturally demand? My brief experience with her that morning had unnerved me: she did not distinguish between the size of objects that were smaller than her hand, nor could she tell the difference between the front and the back of the miniatures. With brazen assurance she found whimsical similarities between my face and the head of an amusing Venetian carving of an elephant.

But to return to my house: the kitchen, as I said before, is in the basement, where, in addition to a collection of empty boxes, I keep enough supplies to prepare simple meals in case of emergency. My display is on the first and second floors. On the latter, not far from an antiquated bathroom, there is a small storage room that I use for a bedroom. The top floor, the attic, has servants' quarters; they are vacant, provide no income, and are unfurnished. I sent the girl up to one of those comfortable but empty rooms. Imagine my surprise when I found that she was in the kitchen, when I heard her invite me to sit down at the table, when I consumed a luncheon that was superlative—not for the combination of dishes, but for each one alone, worthy of Foyot and the best years of Paillard. First, there was a memorable golden omelet, baptized with mock pomposity by my capricious *chef-maître d'hotel: omelette à la mère* something-or-other. That was followed by beans and meat with tomato sauce, onion, and pepper. I decided that the banquet should be complete, so I uncorked a *demi-bouteille* of St. Emilion Claret. After my second glass Geneviève seemed infused with a deep inner radiance. By comparison (I reflected) the young ladies of our country are drab, shallow, tiresome. By dessert—crepes suzette—Geneviève and I had become rather good friends (the way you befriend the stray dog that follows you in the street). But I still had a problem to solve: Geneviève's immediate destiny. The girl could not stay with me permanently. She was not suitable as a salesperson, but perhaps she could be my cook— But I must confess I was terrified by the thought of gaining excess weight. One week of Breton cuisine and I would have to appeal to those unpleasant masseurs known as gymnastics and hiking. And so it seemed that I had to find a way to get that girl, that veritable devil, out of my house.

To overcome my feeling of having eaten too much, I went out for a walk. I decided to visit Garmendia, and sample his candied fruits, enjoy a *chartreuse*, and smoke a cigar (his sweets and his liqueurs are on a par with his tobacco). Fortunately I met the concierge as I entered the building. Before it was too late I learned from her turbulent outburst that Garmendia was in bed with influenza. I did not go up to his apartment: I detest annoying anyone who is sick, and I always fear contagion. I also learned that the woman, in spite of her asseverations of good will, would be unable to care for Mr. Garmendia, who had a very high fever, without neglecting her regular work. The hour for great decisions had come. We could not wait for Garmendia to resolve the impasse, I said. That very afternoon I would bring a reliable young lady who would be both a nurse and a servant during his illness. If the concierge wished to tell Mr. Garmendia, she had my permission; but my decision, once made, could not be altered.

Feeling relieved, I walked back to Alvear Avenue with a lighter step. But soon afterward depression overtook me again. It would not be easy to tell Geneviève of my decision. First I would have to lay the groundwork, then wheedle and cajole.

I was turning my key in the lock when Geneviève opened the door unexpectedly. My key ring broke, scattering the keys in every direction. My annoyance gave me the courage to tell her about my plan.

"I have a sick friend," I explained in a French that was more fluent than correct. "I want a reliable person to take care of him."

When she realized what I wanted her to do, Geneviève expressed no objection, no emotion. Singing—her voice was as fresh and spontaneous as a waterfall—she went to get her things and, still singing, came down carrying her straw valise. I escorted her to my friend's apartment building and left her in the hands of the astonished concierge.

Some days later I visited my friend. At six-thirty, Geneviève entered the room adorned with trays, porcelain, and food. In her uniform—the prescribed black dress with starched white cap and apron, the excessively white gloves—she was an animated and lovely woman.

"She has become very popular in the neighborhood," declared Garmendia with mysterious pride. "Even though she knows very little Spanish, she is everyone's friend. And she can hold her own at the market. No one would dare to overcharge her—they respect her too much!"

He added that he would not say one word against Geneviève. During his illness the girl had taken care of him like a mother, and he would always be grateful.

That same afternoon Garmendia gave me his most recent published work, a small book entitled *Mates, Bombillas, Containers for Yerba Mate, Sugar Bowls, and Other Relics from the Days of Mama Inés*. With pride I showed Geneviève the copy he had inscribed to me in his own hand.

"Is that all he has written?" she asked.

"What do you mean—is that all?" I repeated sarcastically. "All that!"

I waved before her astonished eyes the fifteen copies sent by the printer.

Looking distraught, Geneviève finally removed the tea service and one of us, I don't remember whether it was Garmendia or I—remarked on how maddening it would be to fall in love with a girl like her. We were joking about the possibility when Garmendia suddenly recalled a dream he had had the night before.

"It was grotesque," he said, and I would almost swear that he blushed.

He had dreamed that he was madly in love with Geneviève and she refused him.

"I shall give you my hand on one condition," Geneviève had said. In the dream those words connoted surrender, not just the offer of her hand. As for the condition, Garmendia could not remember it.

My work—or more precisely the decoration of a *maison de plaisance* in Glew—took me away from Buenos Aires for a long week. When I returned I found Garmendia tired and nervous.

"I know it's absurd," he exclaimed, "but this woman is destroying me. I dream of her every night. I have foolish, romantic dreams that disgust me when I awake. When I sleep I love her with a chaste and intrepid passion."

"And is Geneviève chaste too?" I asked, burning with the inevitable vulgarity that lies within every man.

"Yes. Perhaps that is why the obsession persists."

"Then you will have to solve your problem during the daytime."

"I prefer to continue with my dreams," he replied solemnly. After a pause he added, "What I am going to tell you is ridiculous. Perhaps you will despise me for it. But these dreams have shattered my peace of mind."

I did not know whether I had heard the whole problem or merely an introduction.

"Perhaps," proceeded Garmendia, "if I do not see her during the daytime, I shall forget her at night. Please don't be offended—I don't mean this as a reproach, but you know about this matter, and I thought you might be able to help me."

I told him I did not understand. Without stopping, he went on, "Would you find another job for Geneviève? I must get her away from here."

Business was not going at all badly, although more than one object I had acquired on my last trip was slow to sell; and my cleaning woman, on the pretext that she had married, no longer worked for me; so I considered the possibility of hiring Geneviève in her place. When I make a decision, I act promptly without deliberations or misgivings. That same evening I went to fetch my little French girl.

I spent the weekend at the beautiful country estate of some friends at Aldo Bozzini. I returned home with a basket filled to overflowing with fresh vegetables, a trophy that the artist, the health faddist, and the perennial nature lover would have viewed with equal envy. My thoughts were of Geneviève, and of how pleased and grateful she would be to prepare those idyllic products of the soil.

But as I was about to cross the threshold of my house, I thought of Garmendia, his delicate health, his aversion to canned food—"devitaminized," as he calls it—the many favors he had done for me and, without further ado, I decided to take my basket to him.

I found him in a state of agitation that verged on anger. My gift, however, caused him to shed his animus. He spoke about his dreams—they had not ceased—and about Geneviève, with some remorse, some nostalgia. He confessed that in each dream his love became more extravagant. In one of the most recent dreams he had given Geneviève a beautiful ruby ring that once belonged to his mother.

Then he told me about the origin of the dreams.

"I was very ill," he explained. "I still had some fever, but was beginning to feel better. Geneviève came in to cheer me up. She told me that the son of the warehouse foreman had also had influenza. To celebrate his recovery, his parents had given him a little shaggy dog. Then I dozed off, and as I slept the dog underwent alarming alterations and I began to fall in love with Geneviève."

"And now?" I asked.

"Now it is horrible," he said, and covered his eyes.

"What do you plan to do?"

"If I only knew—" he said. "Perhaps you should take the dog." He was not referring to the shaggy dog of the foreman's son, but to the idol. "Geneviève's departure has not been enough."

I pondered on my friend's ideas about dreams. What he needed to do, I reflected, was to remove things from his mind, not from his house. And yet I did as he suggested. As I took the idol away, I had an insight. When I returned to Garmendia's living room, I had to admit that the absence of the dog had destroyed the magic harmony of the room. I tried all kinds of capricious arrangements of furniture and bric-a-brac, but the result was always the same: something was lacking. Then I ventured to reveal my plan.

"No more appeasement!" I said with amazing composure. "In the end this feckless policy will get you nowhere. First Geneviève; then the dog; and who knows where it will end? It would be wiser to make a complete change. You need a totally different atmosphere."

I observed Garmendia in silence. His irksome face bore traces of torpor and surprise.

Undismayed, I continued, "In these rooms, a man who has suffered an obsession is trapped like a prisoner. Why, the very atmosphere is obsessive, diabolical, nightmarish."

"What do you suggest?" he asked.

I detected the lack of interest in his tone. It was clear that Garmendia's dreams had changed him. He was no longer the trusting, enthusiastic friend I had known in better days, and the change saddened me.

"What do I suggest? Nothing could be simpler. Substitute an ascetic, modern atmosphere for this rococo and *fin de siècle*—in short, sick—one. Now, I happen to have some really sedative paintings by Juan Gris, and perhaps a Braque; I have chairs and, by a stroke of luck, some screens made from designs by Man Ray; and some ceramics decorated with long poems by Tsara and Breton."

My friend looked at me impassively. One maxim I never forget is that a salesman never gets discouraged.

"To make the change as painless as possible," I added, "I shall accept all these objects on consignment."

Once again I had occasion to congratulate myself on the flair with which I handle my affairs and persuade clients and friends to see things my way.

For Garmendia answered shortly, "As you wish."

I perceived, however, that he seemed unhappy, I might even say utterly disenchanted. The painful truth is that from that moment on, Garmendia was cool, even rude to me.

The delicacy of my reply gave me reason to be proud. "Unless you show a little more enthusiasm, I shall do nothing, absolutely nothing."

As soon as I returned home, I began to assemble the modern furniture. The next day the movers came early. *A tout seigneur, tout honneur:* the poor devils worked like animals. Before long they had removed everything from the apartment on Bulnes Street. Without stopping to rest, they quickly filled the living room with the new pieces, all wide and very comfortable. When the workmen left, the artist took over. With good taste and a hammer I had the truly herculean task of getting order out of that chaos. Scrupulous as usual, I refused to enlist Geneviève's valuable cooperation; who knows what atrocious repercussions her return might have had on Garmendia's dreams.

When I have a job to do, time means nothing to me. I spent a whole week on Bulnes Street. My friend stayed out of sight. There were some fleeting but bitter moments when I felt certain that he was angry and deliberately avoided me.

Meanwhile, Geneviève was weaving the black web of perfidy. She told me that a client, that *rara avis*, had visited my showrooms during my absence. Instead of running to Bulnes Street to find me, or at least selling him something (but since when, *s'il vous plaît*, does Mademoiselle Geneviève understand my price code?), she chatted with him and even arranged, behind my back, to work as a maid at his bachelor apartment. What an unfortunate turn of events! (She told me about it one night when I came home after a hard day's work, expecting to get some desperately needed rest.) I reproached her for her appalling conduct. She assured me that she would do whatever I ordered; she resorted to all kinds of subterfuges and evasions, and tried to change the subject by telling me that a sheepdog had been lost.

"What sheepdog?" I asked.

"The one that lives in the dark garden at the corner of Colonel Díaz Street," she replied quickly.

Alas! My worst fears were soon confirmed. I took my hat, gloves, and walking stick, and hurried to the corner she had mentioned. After peering through the fence into the empty garden, I rang the doorbell. I asked the concierge whether a dog had been lost. He said that no one in the building kept a dog.

Faced with my solitude and my anxiety, I exhausted my body but found no peace for my soul walking through the streets of the section of town that used to be known as Tierra del Fuego.

An even greater disappointment awaited me on my return home. Geneviève had gone out, leaving no explanation. Tormented by anger, depression, and despair, I could imagine her scrubbing floors in the disreputable residence of my unknown client. First I decided to wait up until she returned. It was my melancholy, very transitory, consolation to invent sarcastic innuendoes, to imagine her humiliation and her remorse when I hurled them at her. Then I knew that my complacence was only a deceptive snare that would embroil me in further torments of my own making.

The wait could be a long one, and my nerves were in no condition to stand it, so I undressed and went to bed. That night was atrocious.

I should have known better than to try to sleep. I tossed and turned for hours, and finally, in the pallid early morning hours, I found oblivion as sleep engulfed me. I dreamed that I was strolling through the dark garden at the corner of Colonel Díaz Street; I was about to enter the house when I awoke. It was nine o'clock in the morning and I felt rested and refreshed. When my memory became more acute, I had the impression of scarcely having slept at all during the course of that brief dream.

My anxiety of the previous night seemed impossible to explain. I thought about it calmly, as if it were something apart from me and quite amusing; almost as if it were a sort of madness that had been completely cured. Without ascertaining whether Geneviève was at home—my indifference caused me to miss breakfast—I went to Bulnes Street with the pathetic hope of receiving payment in part or in full for the new furniture.

Garmendia received me coldly. The poor man could not conceal his feelings: he was really annoyed. There were moments when I worried about the ceramic vase inscribed with verses by André Breton, which seemed destined to come crashing against my head.

His description of the objects I had arranged in his apartment left me feeling crushed; it is almost a sacrilege to reproduce his words:

"These are the worst examples of foolishness, ineptitude, and dishonesty I have ever seen!"

He proffered other enormities, then interrupted himself, shouting melodramatically, "And, furthermore, I shall never forgive you for having taken Geneviève away from me!"

"I don't understand you," I replied honestly; and at that very moment I began to have doubts about his sanity.

"You understand me perfectly," he declared.

As if I had not heard him, I continued, "If you want the girl back, you can have her. I can't send her this afternoon because she made arrangements—without consulting me, to be sure—to work at another man's apartment. I'll speak to him about it today or tomorrow and—you have my word—there will be no difficulty whatever."

He listened to my noble and persuasive speech with lowered eyes, without encouraging me even once with words or gestures of assent. His cold and bitter reply left me stupefied.

"Allow me," he said, "allow me to say that your word means absolutely nothing."

I left my friend's house forthwith, feeling that our relationship had entered a critical, unpromising phase. Perhaps that change was due to a sudden attack of distrust and parsimony, the chronic afflictions of the rich. To conceal those despicable feelings, he had pretended to be jealous.

It rather frightens me to think about Garmendia's reaction: discarding the confidence he owed to me as a friend, he ascribed my desire to change his décor—the cause of his madness—to pecuniary motives. If I had any reason other than to dispel his obsession, it was simply to exercise my taste and artistic talent at a time when business was virtually paralyzed. But to consider my assistance as a business transaction was quite ridiculous. I have sold very few of the articles he gave me on consignment, and I have not received one cent—and probably never will—for the furnishings in his apartment.

When I came home, I found Geneviève reclining gracefully beside the Celtic idol and conversing affably with a repulsive potbellied individual. He had a long black moustache, a black suit, and black gloves. I realized at once that he was the fellow who wanted her to work for him.

In spite of my agitation I saw (I am sure of this) that the girl was wearing the beautiful ruby ring that had belonged to Garmendia's mother. I am also sure that Geneviève noticed my astonished glance.

I stammered a peremptory demand for explanations, but Geneviève, pretending not to understand, pointed vaguely in the direction of the man and then fled from the room.

With exquisite urbanity I asked him what he wished.

"Well," he said, struggling with respiratory difficulties, "I've—uh—I've come for the young lady, the French girl, who works here—or used to, anyway."

"Do you want me to call her?" I asked.

"No—it's not necessary—or, all right, if you wish," he replied. "I've let my maid go, and I just wanted to find out when this girl would be able to report for work."

I felt as if salt had been sprinkled on an open wound.

"You just wanted to know when Geneviève would be able to report for work? Very well. But there is one difficulty."

The man raised his eyebrows and thrust his enormous face and moustache forward expectantly, expressing a candor that may have been genuine, may have been false, but in any case was decidedly odious.

"Arrangements have already been made," I continued, "for the girl to work at the home of a very close friend of mine."

"Well, then," said the man, "I might as well be going. We have nothing else to discuss."

"Oh, but we do!" I said. "I haven't finished yet! Listen to me carefully: Geneviève is not leaving this house. I don't care about friends or previous arrangements, and I shall not permit anyone to speak to her behind my back."

The man opened his eyes wide, pulled his hat down over his ears, and went out puffing like an antiquated and pompous locomotive.

That little incident must have affected me. At night I dreamed of Geneviève. I would swear that I dreamed of her, although I never actually saw her in my dreams, not once. She appeared to me in symbols: she was the impassioned penumbra of the shadows and the secret meaning of all my actions. I dreamed that I entered the house at the corner of Colonel Díaz Street. But the house was very old and very vast, and I was lost in an interminable succession of drawing rooms filled with portraits and tapestries. Tremulous with relief and gratitude, I found a dark, narrow corridor. I followed it, and in the distance I perceived an oblique shaft of light. My fear and my disgust were so vehement that they caused me to awaken.

Nothing of note happened the next day. It is true that there was one small episode that revealed Geneviève's unsuspected depths. That alone would be enough to explain my conduct, which certainly needs no justification. My duty is clear: I must see that Geneviève does not get any new victims. Once and for all I must put an end to her hereditary, blind, and stubborn depravity. That is why I shall never let her go.

When she brought my breakfast, I asked her about the ruby ring. She looked down at her hands innocently. The ring was not on her finger. Not to be intimidated by her cunning evasion, I repeated the question. First she denied the existence of any ring; then she admitted having found it in a gutter, puddle, or indefinite location on the street; she said that it was only a cheap piece of costume jewelry; and added that she had lost it at nightfall. My repeated questions were useless: they produced tears, but not confessions. Possibly she was telling the truth—a false blush and a genuine one are almost identical—to unnerve me.

Trembling I descended the staircase, opened the balcony door, and looked out. I have no recollection of having seen anything: neither the sun nor the cars nor the people nor the houses nor the trees. The world had died for me. Soon afterward I found myself polishing the nails on the idol with a flannel cloth. The metal was very old, and my halfhearted efforts were to no avail. I was not able to bring out the luster of a single nail; the idol did not lose its ancient and terrifying look.

Last night, with singular candor, I slept again. Inevitably I found myself back in the dark, narrow corridor, not far from the room with the oblique shaft of light. I felt that I should stay away from that room; that I should turn back and, before it was too late, escape; but I also had the intolerable certainty that Geneviève and Garmendia were there. It seemed preferable to die than to live with that doubt, so I took a step forward. From the corridor I could see only the part of the room that was directly opposite the door; but the secret mechanics of dreams let me see what I feared. Garmendia was lying on the stone couch; the girl, wearing a thin white tunic, which in my dream denoted a priestess, was kneeling by the couch, gazing at him ecstatically. There were some nails and a hammer on the floor. With infinite slowness Geneviève took a nail, lifted the hammer, and then I covered my eyes. A moment later she was smiling and saying, "Don't worry," and, as if to reassure me, she indicated two new nails glittering on the idol's body. I felt the urge to escape. The girl recited the long poem of the Gulniacs. As I watched her intently, I experienced something like love. She called to me gaily. Then her words began to change consistency and meaning, until the change was sudden and total, like a captive fish threshing noisily on the surface of the water, when it had been swimming in the quiet depths moments before. That was what woke me: Geneviève, standing by my bed, was repeating some words in a ritualistic fashion and staring at me.

"Garmendia's concierge wishes to see you," she was saying. "Shall I have her come in?"

"Certainly not!" I replied indignantly. "How can I see her now?"

The dream must have impressed me, for I changed my mind immediately.

"Very well," I said. "Show her in, show her in."

I hastily reached for the brilliantine on my night table and restored my unruly hair to a semblance of order.

The woman, escorted by Geneviève, entered my bedroom. I could see that she was willing, even determined, to burst into tears.

"What is the matter now?" I asked with resignation.

"You must come at once," she replied.

"What is the matter?" I insisted.

"Mr. Garmendia is ill, very ill," she screamed, on the verge of hysteria.

"Go back and stay with him," I said. "I'll be right over."

I had a prefiguring of an imminent eruption of words, tears, hiccups. I motioned to Geneviève to show the concierge out.

The woman was waiting at the door when I arrived at Bulnes Street. She clasped her hands, shook her head, and tried to speak.

"Upstairs!" I said briskly. "Come on!"

We went up. The woman opened the door. I stood on the threshold. The apartment appeared to be in total darkness.

"Garmendia," I said. "Garmendia!"

There was no reply. After a brief hesitation I decided to enter the room. I took a step, and shouted, "Garmendia!"

My friend's voice, as if a mortal indifference had drained it of all feeling, spoke softly: "What do you want?"

"Why are you in the dark?" I asked, relieved that he had spoken at last.

I opened the windows.

Garmendia was sitting on a metal chair in that almost abstract gray, white, and yellow room. For some mysterious reason I felt sorry for him.

I held out my hand to touch his shoulder, but something—his

strange immobility, the fixity of his glance, which never wavered from an imaginary object in the air—deterred me.

"What is the matter?"

"What difference does it make to you?" he replied. "You have stolen Geneviève. Geneviève has stolen my soul."

"No one has stolen anything," I objected vigorously. "Anyway, this is no time for speeches."

"I am not making speeches," he said. "I am blind."

I waved my hand in front of his eyes. He closed them.

"If you think you're blind," I remarked, "you're crazy!"

Those words, spoken with spontaneous vulgarity, were the last I ever uttered in the presence of my friend. In my attempt at humor I had stumbled onto the exact and atrocious diagnosis. Garmendia was not blind: he thought he was blind because he had gone mad.

I gave some vague instructions to the concierge and, feeling apprehensive, went home. I got through the morning as well as I could. I dusted and arranged showcases, put the rooms in order (removing a desk here, adding a chair there)—mechanical work, more appropriate for a robot than for an artistic man like myself. I ate lunch and then went to my study to smoke the last cigar Garmendia had given me. While I contemplated the melancholy smoke rings, I recalled my dream of the previous night and I had a sudden insight. As if I were obeying a will that was no longer my own, I stood up, I walked. Like a person in a faint who glimpses a light and then begins to regain consciousness, I conceived a hope: the hope that I was mistaken. Terrified, I looked at the tremendous Celtic idol.

I was not mistaken. Two new nails glittered on its body.

"Geneviève! Geneviève!" I shouted.

The girl hurried into the room looking alarmed. At first her blue eyes and her virtuous braids almost convinced me of her innocence. But I overcame the temptation to forget everything that had happened, to believe in her apparent ingenuousness.

"What about these new nails?" I asked.

"I don't know anything about it," she said.

"What do you mean? *I* certainly didn't put them there!"

The expression of alarm disappeared from Geneviève's face.

"Neither did I," she said placidly. She paused, and added, "Remember, you keep the hammer and nails under lock and key!"

That was the truth. I have not yet lost my mind completely, and I do not permit incompetent hands to tamper with nails that are no longer being imported or to touch my old English hammer. At first I was naturally indignant, really angry. Then I realized that if the new nails on the dog had not been put there by Geneviève or by me, there was a difficult problem to be solved. I considered the most implausible explanations—for example, that Geneviève's ghost, the Geneviève dreamed by me and also, alas! by Garmendia, had placed those nails on the idol's body. As I considered that absurd idea, I began to feel drowsy; I leaned back in my comfortable chair, half-closed my eyes— Then I jumped up, aware of the danger. I walked around the room, trying to stay awake. I felt that the dog was watching me with his awful eyeless face. In desperation I remembered that it was I who had brought him back from Bulnes Street. I realized that I should not make the same mistake Garmendia made; the mere removal of the girl and the dog from my house would not save me from them. But was there any hope that I could save myself? When I thought of what had happened to Garmendia, I believed that there was. It seemed impossible that I would have to endure this dreadful fate. But when I remembered my dreams and my inevitable progress toward the chamber of the dog, I was less certain. Until I find a way out of this situation, I thought, until I find whether there is a way out, I must not let myself sleep. That escape would be too atrocious.

I remembered the dreams and perhaps I slept. I was in the dark, narrow corridor, I walked slowly down it. When I was about to enter the chamber, I made an involuntary movement of terror (as if my whole consciousness were not completely submerged in sleep, as if I were a drowning man in a shipwreck reaching up to grasp the part of the ship that was still above water). I awoke. I found myself sitting in my easy-chair, but I did not recall having sat down. I regarded its monstrous leather arms with disgust. I stood up. Instinctively I ran to the center of the room. I felt horrified by all the objects, all the manifestations of the matter that was ambushing me and pursuing me like an infallible hunter. I discovered (or thought I discovered) that to be alive is to flee, in an ephemeral and paradoxical way, from matter; and that the fear that assailed me then was the fear of death.

I would go outside, I would go away, I would walk for many miles. Impetuously, I imagined immediate changes of location. Then I realized the futility of my plan. I would be like a bird that flew away with its cage attached to its back. It would be better simply to stay home quietly, without moving a muscle. Fatigue could be dangerous: it could cause me to sleep.

The evening has slipped by rapidly. I have not slept, but from time to time I have memories that come (I am certain) from a dream. How can I explain that recurrent phenomenon? Do I close my eyes, dream for an instant, and then awaken? But that cannot be, for I have not closed my eyes once all day. If I had, I would remember the moment of awakening; my eyelids would not feel so heavy. But, if I have not been dreaming, where did I see, only a short while ago, the corridor that descends to the chamber of the dog? Where did I see Garmendia's eyes carved on a stone tablet, and where did I see him open a door carved on another tablet beside it? Where did I see Geneviève reclining on a stone couch, calling to me? Where did I kneel down, and where did someone set a condition for me to fulfill, a condition I cannot remember now? And was I awake or dreaming when I saw the man who tried to take Geneviève away from me pacing up and down in front of my house? Was I dreaming or was I awake when I heard, from my balcony, a conversation between that man and Geneviève, at my front door? Was I awake or was I dreaming when I heard Geneviève say good-bye and call, "I'll see you tomorrow"?

If I had not begun to write, my dreams would have led me, inevitably, to depression and madness. Early this morning, when I started to write, I found salvation. There were times when I wrote with genuine pleasure. Near the end I became very drowsy—I suppose that is only too apparent. Now and then I was aroused by my nightmares, or by the bronze clock with its hourly melody and its nymphs and shepherds, or by the sound of Geneviève cleaning in the basement. As if she did not wish to go to bed before her master, she has been working all night long. I can hear her moving about beneath my room. If I did not know it was she, I would swear there was an animal down there. The agitation in the basement is almost continuous. Occasionally I manage to forget it.

Geneviève and her mysterious task do not worry me. I am not afraid. When I reach the end of this page I shall write, very carefully, very firmly, the words *The End*; then, with the relief of a man who returns to his beloved after a painful attempt at separation, I shall submit to the tender, cold, and chaste embrace of my bed, and I shall lapse into a beatific slumber. And what a rest I shall have! My ordeal has led me to the truth at last. A long series of coincidences that can be explained easily—or can be left unexplained, like life, like each one of us—suggested to me a fantastic story in which I am both the victim and the hero.

There is no such story. I shall sleep without fear. Geneviève will not make me blind. Geneviève will not steal my soul. (Is there anything more stupid than the myth of Faust?) It is possible to steal a person's soul only if he has already lost it. Mine, when I am happy, is more than adequate.

Geneviève has just interrupted me. She came into my room and, with singular solicitude, with a gentle reproach, she said that it is morning now, that I must go to bed, that I must rest, that I must sleep.

The Celestial Plot

When Captain Ireneus Morris and Dr. Charles Albert Servian disappeared from Buenos Aires one 20 December, the newspapers made only a passing mention of the fact. It was hinted that an investigation was being made, since the case had certain suspicious aspects. Further, it was believed that, since the plane used by the fugitives had a limited flight range, they could not be very far away. At about that time I received a package containing three large volumes (the complete works of Louis Auguste Blanqui); a ring of slight value (an aquamarine carved with the image of a horse-headed goddess); and a typed manuscript entitled "The Adventures of Captain Morris," signed C. A. S., which I am transcribing below.

THE ADVENTURES OF CAPTAIN MORRIS

This story could begin with some Celtic legend about the journey of a hero to a land at the bottom of a well, or an inviolable prison made of living branches, or a ring that makes its wearer invisible, or a magic cloud, or a young girl deep within a mirror that is held by the knight who is destined to save her, or the interminable and fruitless search for the tomb of King Arthur:

> This is the tomb of March and this the tomb of Gwythyir;
> This is the tomb of Gwgawn Gleddyffreidd;
> But the tomb of Arthur is unknown.

It could also begin with the news, which I heard with some surprise and a certain indifference, that the military tribunal was accusing Captain Morris of treason. Or with the negation of astronomy. Or with a theory of those movements called "passes" that are used to make spirits appear or disappear.

I shall select a less exciting beginning. If it lacks the charm of magic, at least it will be methodical. This does not imply a repudiation of the supernatural; even less does it imply a repudiation of the allusions or invocations of my first paragraph.

My name is Charles Albert Servian, and I was born in Rauch. I am of Armenian descent. My country has not existed for eight centuries, but there is a solidarity among my people, and all our descendants will hate the Turks. The old saying "Once an Armenian, always an Armenian" is still true today. We are like a secret society, a clan; although we are dispersed on different continents, our mysterious blood, the distinctive eyes and noses of our people, our way of understanding and enjoying the earth, our talents, our intrigues, our unique excesses, and the passionate beauty of our women unite us.

I am a bachelor and, like Don Quixote, I live (or rather, lived) with my niece: a pleasant and diligent young girl. I would add another adjective—serene—but that word would not characterize her accurately now. My niece liked to play at being my secretary, and so I let her answer my telephone, organize my vast filing system, and write out medical histories from the notes I took while my patients described their ailments. She had another, equally innocent occupation—she accompanied me to the cinema every Friday afternoon. The day when all this began happened to be a Friday.

I was in my office, and suddenly the door burst open and a young soldier rushed into the room. My niece was to my right, behind the desk. Without changing her expression, she handed me a sheet of paper on which to write his complaints. The young officer introduced himself—his name was Lieutenant Kramer—stared brazenly at my secretary, and then asked if he might have a word with me. Of course I assented.

"Captain Ireneus Morris would like to see you," he said. "He is a patient at the Military Hospital."

Perhaps contaminated by the martial bearing of my interlocutor, I replied briskly, "Yes, sir!"

"When can you come to see him?"

"Right away. If Morris can have visitors now—"

"He can," said Kramer, and with noisy, gymnastic movements he saluted smartly and left.

I looked at my niece; her expression had altered. I felt angry, and asked her what was the matter.

"Do you know that there's only one person you're interested in?" she asked.

Ingenuously, I turned as she pointed: I saw myself in the mirror. My niece ran out of the room.

For some time she had been growing more and more impatient with me. And now she was saying that I was selfish! I attributed her accusation in part to my bookplates. The words *Know thyself* are printed on them in Greek, Latin, and Spanish (I never suspected the effect that maxim would have on my life), and there is a small sketch of me looking through a magnifying glass at my reflection in a mirror. My niece had attached thousands of those bookplates to thousands of volumes in my versatile library. But there was another reason why she said that I was selfish: I am a methodical person, and methodical men (those of us who postpone involvement with women because we are engaged in serious occupations) appear to be either madmen or fools or egotists.

I examined my next two patients automatically, and then hurried off to the Military Hospital.

The clock was just striking six as I reached the old building on Pozos Street. I sat alone in the waiting room, and then submitted to a brief interrogation. After that some attendants escorted me to Morris's room. A sentinel with fixed bayonet stood at the door.

Inside the room two men were playing dominoes near Morris's bed. They did not acknowledge my presence.

Morris and I have known each other for years; we have never been friends. I was very fond of his father. He was a fine old fellow, with a round close-cropped white head and excessively hard, alert blue eyes. He possessed an irrepressible Welsh patriotism and an uncontrollable urge to relate Celtic legends. For many years (the happiest of my life) he was my teacher. I studied with him every afternoon. I listened while he told about the adventures of the Mabinogion, and then we drank *yerba mate* together. At such times Ireneus would be playing outdoors; he caught birds and rats and then created heterogeneous cadavers with a penknife, a needle, and thread. Old Morris said that his son was going to be a doctor. I was going to be an inventor because I hated Ireneus's experiments, and once I had designed an interplanetary missile that would make extensive journeys to other parts of the universe, and a hydraulic motor capable of perpetual motion. Ireneus and I were alienated by a mutual and conscious antipathy. Now when we meet we experience a feeling of intense joy, a flowering of nostalgia and cordiality; we repeat a brief dialogue with fervent allusions to an imaginary friendship and an imaginary past, and then we have nothing else to say to each other.

The tenacious Celtic strain from Wales ended in his father. Ireneus is completely Argentine, and neither understands nor respects foreigners. Even his appearance is typically Argentine: he is short, slender, fine-boned, with carefully combed, shiny black hair and a knowing look about him.

He seemed very touched that I had come (I had never seen him like that, not even on the night his father died).

"Let me shake your hand," he said, speaking loudly enough for the men who were playing dominoes to hear. "At this crucial time, you have been my only friend."

It seemed like a rather extravagant way to thank me for my visit.

"We have a lot to talk about," continued Morris, "but you must realize that in the presence of a couple of circumstances like these"—he nodded gravely in the direction of the two men—"I prefer to say nothing. Anyway, I shall be home in a few days—you must look in on me then."

I thought he was saying good-bye. Morris added that I should stay a bit longer, if I had time.

"Oh, I almost forgot," he said. "Thank you for the books."

I mumbled something, feeling confused. I did not know what books he was talking about. I have made mistakes in my life, but I have never sent any books to Ireneus.

He spoke of airplane accidents; he denied that there were places—Palomar Air Base in Buenos Aires, the Valley of the Kings in Egypt—where such accidents could be caused by air currents.

It seemed incredible to hear him say "the Valley of the Kings." I inquired how he happened to know about that.

"That is Father Moreau's theory," Morris replied. "Others maintain that our pilots are not well trained, that discipline is contrary to the idiosyncrasy of our people, if you follow me. Actually, the Argentine flyer has a feeling of pride in his plane. If you don't believe me, remember the feats of Mira, with his 'Swallow,' a tin can tied together with wires—"

I asked him how he felt, and what sort of treatment he was receiving. Then it was my turn to speak loudly enough so that the domino players would hear.

"Don't let them give you any injections. No injections! Don't let them poison your blood. Take a purgative and then an Arnica 10,000. You're a typical Arnica case. Remember: nothing but infinitesimal doses."

I went away with the impression of having won a small victory. During the ensuing three weeks life at home seemed the same as ever. Now, looking back, I think that my niece was more polite than usual, and less cordial. Following our usual custom we went to the cinema together the next two Fridays. But on the third Friday, when I went to call her, she was not there. She had gone out; she had forgotten that it was our afternoon for the cinema.

Then I received a message from Morris. He said he was home and wanted me to come to see him some afternoon. I decided to go immediately.

He was in the study, and I could see that he was much better. Some people tend so invincibly toward an equilibrium of health that not even the worst poisons invented by allopathy can daunt them.

As I entered the room I had the sensation of receding in time. I was almost surprised not to see old Morris there (he died ten years ago), polished and benign, calmly administering the *mate* "ceremony." Nothing was changed. The same books were on the shelves; the same busts of Lloyd George and William Morris that had contemplated my carefree youth contemplated me now; and the horrible painting that had startled my first attacks of insomnia was still hanging on the wall: *The Death of Griffith ap Rhys,* who was known as the light and the power and the pride of the men from the South.

I tried to steer the conversation to the subject that interested him. He said he merely had a few details to add to the information he had given me in his letter. I did not know what to say: I had not received a letter from Ireneus. With sudden decision I asked him to tell me the story from the beginning, if it would not tire him too much.

And then Ireneus Morris told me his mysterious story.

Until the past 23 June he had been a test pilot for military planes, first at the military installation at Córdoba, and later at Palomar Air Base.

He assured me that a test pilot enjoyed considerable prestige. He had made more flights than any other American pilot (South and Central). His resistance was extraordinary.

He had made so many flights that automatically, inevitably, he reduced them all to one single flight.

He took a notebook from his pocket and drew a series of lines in a zigzag pattern on a blank page. He carefully wrote down numbers (distances, altitudes, the degrees of angles). Then he tore out the page and gave it to me. He said that I possessed his "classic flight plan."

Around the middle of June they notified him that he would be testing a new Breguet—the 309—a one-place combat plane, which had been built according to a French patent of two or three years before. The test was to be classified top-secret. Morris went home, picked up a notebook—"as I did here, a minute ago," he said—and drew the flight plan, "like the one I just gave you." Then he tried to make it a bit more complicated; "in this same study where we spent so many happy hours together," he thought about the lines he had added, he memorized them.

The morning of 23 June, the dawn of a beautiful and terrible adventure, was gray and rainy. When Morris arrived at the airport the plane was in the hangar, and he had to wait for them to take it out. He walked up and down to keep from feeling the cold; his feet were soaking wet. Finally the Breguet appeared. It was a low-winged monoplane, "nothing otherworldly, I can assure you." He gave it a cursory examination.

Morris leaned forward, and whispered in a confidential tone, "The seat was narrow, extremely uncomfortable." He remembered that the fuel-gauge indicator pointed to "full," and that there were no insignia on the wings of the plane. He said that he waved his hand, and immediately afterward the gesture seemed false. He taxied about five hundred yards, and took off. He began to execute his new test-flight plan.

He was the strongest test pilot in the country. Purely a matter of physical strength, he assured me. And I had never known him to exaggerate unduly. Although I found it hard to believe, he said that suddenly he experienced a darkening of vision. Morris, recounting the adventure, grew loquacious, excited, and I became engrossed in his story: soon after taking off in the new plane, he experienced a darkening of vision, he told himself guiltily that he was going to faint, he collided with a vast dark mass (perhaps a cloud), he had a fleeting, ecstatic glimpse of something like the glimpse of a radiant paradise— He was scarcely able to get the plane back on course when he was about to touch the landing field.

He regained consciousness. He was stretched out painfully on a white bed in a high-ceilinged room with bare white walls. A bumblebee was buzzing; for a few seconds he thought he was somewhere out in the country, and that he had awakened from a nap. Then he realized that he had been injured, that he was a patient in the Military Hospital. He was not particularly surprised, but he did not yet remember the accident. And when he did the real surprise came, for he did not understand how he could have fainted. Actually, he had not fainted at all— But I shall say more about that later.

The person at his side was a woman. He looked at her. She was a nurse.

Dogmatic and critical, he spoke to me about women in general. He was rather bitter. He said that there was one type of woman, and even one certain woman, destined to satisfy each man's physical needs, and he added something to the effect that it was better not to find her, because if he did a man sensed that she was a decisive element in his life and he treated her with fear or clumsiness, preparing the way for a future of anxiety and monotonous frustration. The other women in the world would present no noticeable differences or dangers for a respectable sort of man, he said. I asked him if the nurse was his type of woman. He said no, and explained, "She is a placid, maternal type—pretty enough, I guess."

He went on with his story.

Some officers came in (he enumerated their ranks). A soldier brought a table and chair, and a typewriter. He sat down and began to type. When he stopped, the officer asked Morris, "Your name?"

That did not surprise him. He thought, "Just a routine question." He told them his name, and perceived the first indication of the horrible plot in which, unaccountably, he had become involved. All the officers laughed. Morris had never thought that there was anything amusing about his name, and he was irritated.

"You might have invented something less incredible," another officer said. "Write it down, anyway," he said, turning to the soldier at the typewriter.

"Nationality?"

"Argentine," he said without hesitation.

"Are you in the Army?"

"Well, I had the accident, but anyone would think you did!" he said, with an attempt at irony.

They laughed a little (among themselves, as if Morris were not there).

"I belong to the Army, with the rank of captain, 7th Regiment, 121st Squadron," continued Morris.

"Based at Montevideo?" asked one of the officers sarcastically.

"No, at Palomar," replied Morris.

He gave his address: 971 Bolívar Street. The group left, and came back the next day with several different officers. When Morris realized that they doubted, or pretended to doubt, his nationality, he wanted to get out of bed and fight them. His injury and the gentle pressure of the nurse restrained him. The officers returned the next afternoon, and the following morning. The weather was very hot; his whole body ached. He told me that he would have confessed to anything in order to be left in peace.

What were they trying to do? Why did they not know who he was? Why did they insult him, why did they pretend that he was not an Argentine? He was perplexed and infuriated. One night the nurse took his hand, and told him that he was not defending himself very cleverly. He said that he had no reason to defend himself at all. He stayed awake that whole night, feeling alternately waves of anger, a determination to face the situation calmly, and then violent reactions that made him swear to refuse "to play this absurd game any longer." In the morning he wanted to apologize to the nurse for the way he had treated her. He knew she only meant to help him—"and she is not ugly, if you know what I mean"—but, as he did not know how to make apologies, he asked her irritably what she would advise him to do. The nurse suggested that he call some responsible person to testify on his behalf.

When the officers returned he told them that he was a friend of Lieutenant Kramer and Lieutenant Viera, Captain Faverio, Lieutenant Colonel Margaride, and Lieutenant Colonel Navarro.

Around five o'clock Lieutenant Kramer, his lifelong friend, came in with the officers. Morris admitted that the sight of Kramer brought tears to his eyes. (To cover his embarrassment, he added, "After a shock, a man is not himself!") He remembered that he sat bolt upright in bed and held out his hand, shouting "Come in, old man!"

Kramer stood there eyeing him coldly.

"Lieutenant Kramer, do you know this man?" asked one of the officers. His voice was insidious.

Morris said that he expected Kramer, with a sudden exclamation of cordiality, to reveal that his attitude was part of a joke.

"I have never seen him before," replied Kramer too vehemently, as if he was afraid they would not believe him. "I give you my word that I have never seen him before!"

They believed him at once, and the tension that had existed for a few seconds was broken. They went away. Morris heard the laughter of the officers, and Kramer's frank laugh and the voice of an officer saying, "I'm not a bit surprised. Believe me, I'm not a bit surprised. What a colossal nerve he has!"

Essentially the same thing happened with Viera and Margaride, but there was more violence. A book—one of the books allegedly sent by me—was on the bed, within Morris's reach, and he threw it at Viera when the lieutenant pretended not to know him. Morris gave me a detailed description of the incident, which I did not find completely credible. I did not doubt his anger, but I could not believe that his injury would have permitted him to move so quickly. The officers thought there was no need to call Faverio, who was in Mendoza. Then Morris had an inspiration: threats might have changed the young men into traitors, but they would have no effect on General Huet, an old friend of his family, who had always been like a father, or a very strict stepfather, to him.

They told him drily that there was no general with such a ridiculous name in the Argentine Army, nor had there ever been.

Morris was not afraid. Perhaps if he had known some fear, he could have handled the situation better. His inherent interest in women stood him in good stead—"and you know how they like to exaggerate danger, how hypercritical they are," he said.

Once before, the nurse had taken his hand to try to convince him of the danger he was facing; now Morris looked into her eyes, and asked the meaning of the plot against him. The nurse told him what she had heard: his statement that he had tested the Breguet on 23 June was false; no one had tested planes at Palomar Air Base that afternoon. The Breguet had recently been adopted by the Argentine Army, but the numeration of Morris's plane did not correspond to the system currently in use.

"Do they think I am a spy?" he asked with incredulity. Again he felt anger rising within him.

"They think you have come from some neighboring country," ventured the nurse timidly.

Morris swore to her as an Argentine that he was an Argentine, that he was not a spy. She seemed quite touched, and then continued in the same tone of voice: "Your uniform resembles ours, but they have discovered that the seams are made differently." When she added, "Didn't it occur to you that they would notice?" Morris realized that she did not believe him either. He felt that rage was choking him. To conceal it, he kissed her on the mouth, and held her in his arms.

A few days later the nurse said, "They found out that you gave a false address."

Morris's protests were useless; the woman produced documentary evidence showing that a Mr. Charles Grimaldi lived at Bolívar 971. Morris experienced a brief sensation of memory, of amnesia. The name Charles Grimaldi seemed to be linked to some past experience; he was unable to identify it more precisely.

The nurse told him that his case had caused people to take opposing sides: those who believed he was a foreigner, and those who believed he was an Argentine. In other words, some wanted to exile him; others, to execute him.

"By insisting that you are an Argentine," said the woman, "you are helping the cause of those who are demanding your execution."

Morris confessed that for the first time he had felt in his own country "the desolation of those who travel abroad." And still he was not afraid.

The woman pleaded with him tearfully, and at last he promised to do whatever she asked.

"I don't know why, but I wanted to make her happy."

The woman begged him to admit that he was not an Argentine.

"It was a terrible shock, as if someone had suddenly pushed me under a cold shower. But I promised to do it, even though I had no intention of keeping my promise."

He explained his objections to her. "If I say I am from a certain country, they will investigate and find out that it's not true."

"That doesn't matter," said the nurse. "No country would admit that it sent spies to another country. But if you make that statement, and if I can persuade some influential person to help you, the group in favor of exile may win, if it is not too late."

The next day an officer came to take his statement. They were alone. "Your case has already been decided," the man said. "They will sign the death warrant within a week."

Morris interpreted the situation for me: "I had nothing to lose." And so, to see what would happen, he told the officer, "I confess that I am an Uruguayan."

That afternoon the nurse explained that it had been a trick; she had been afraid that he would not keep his promise; the officer was a friend of hers, and had instructions to obtain his confession.

"If it had been any other woman, I think I would have beaten her," said Morris shortly.

His confession had not arrived in time; the situation was growing worse. His last remaining hope was to be helped by a man whom the nurse knew, whose identity she could not reveal. The man wanted to see Morris before he would agree to do anything for him.

"She told me frankly," said Morris, "that she had tried to avoid the interview. She was afraid I would make a bad impression. But the man wanted to see me and he was our only hope. She advised me to be prepared to compromise."

"The man will not come to the hospital," said the nurse.

"Then there's no use," replied Morris with a sense of relief.

"The first night we can trust the sentinels you must go to see him," the nurse continued. "You are well now; you can go alone."

She took a ring from her finger and gave it to him.

"I put it on my little finger," said Morris. "I am not sure about the stone—it may be valuable or only a piece of glass. The head of a horse is carved on the underside of it. I was to wear it with the stone turned toward the inside of my hand, and the sentinels would let me come and go as if they did not see me."

The nurse gave him instructions. He was to leave at twelve-thirty and return before three-fifteen A.M. The nurse wrote the man's address on a piece of paper.

"Do you still have it?" I asked.

"Yes, I think so," he replied, and looked in his wallet. He handed me the paper somewhat peevishly.

It was a slip of blue paper. The address—6890 Márquez—was written in a firm, feminine hand (with unexpected insight Morris said that the handwriting revealed a Sacred Heart education).

"What is the nurse's name?" I asked out of simple curiosity.

Morris appeared to be annoyed.

"They call her Idibal," he said finally. "I don't know whether it is her first name or her last."

He continued the story:

155

On the prearranged night Idibal did not come. He did not know what to do. At twelve-thirty he decided to go.

It seemed futile to show the ring to the sentinel at the door of his room. The man raised his bayonet. Morris showed the ring; he was allowed to pass freely. He backed up against a door: in the distance, at the end of the corridor, he had seen a corporal. Then, following Idibal's instructions, he went down a service stairway, and came to a door leading to the street. He showed the ring and went out.

He hailed a taxicab; he gave the driver the address on the paper. They drove for half an hour or so. Near Juan B. Justo and Gaona Streets they circled the railroad yards, and drove down a tree-lined avenue near the city limits. After five or six blocks they stopped in front of a church with many columns and domes, which loomed white in the darkness above the low neighborhood houses.

He thought there had been a mistake; he consulted the paper; the number it gave was the number of the church.

"Were you to go in, or wait outside?" I asked.

He said he had been uncertain, but he went inside. No one was there.

"What was the church like?" I asked.

"Oh, just like all the others," he replied.

Then he told me that he waited by a fountain with three jets of water—some fish were swimming in it—and soon a priest appeared. He asked if Morris was looking for someone. Morris said no. The priest went away; then he came back again. He did that three or four times. Morris was surprised at the man's curiosity, and had about decided to ask for his help when the man inquired if he had "the ring of the brotherhood."

"The ring—of what?" asked Morris. To me he added, "How could I have known that he was referring to the ring Idibal gave me?"

The man looked at his hands intently and insisted, "Show me the ring!"

Morris shuddered with nervous repulsion; then he showed the ring.

The man took him to the sacristy, and asked for an explanation. He listened to Morris's story passively, "as if he took it for a rather astute, but false, explanation. He seemed to be sure that he would hear, eventually, the true version, my confession."

When he was convinced that Morris would say nothing more, he displayed signs of exasperation and brought the interview to a close. He said he would try to do something for him.

As Morris went out, he looked for Rivadavia Street. Before him were the outlines of two towers that looked like the entrance to a castle or an ancient city; actually they were the entrance to an interminable void in the darkness. He had the impression of being in a supernatural and sinister Buenos Aires. After a few blocks he began to feel tired. When he came to Rivadavia Street, he took a taxi and gave the driver his own address: 971 Bolívar Street.

He got out at the corner of Independence and Bolívar. He walked up to the door of his house. It was not yet two in the morning. There was still time.

He tried to insert his key in the lock; it did not fit. He rang the doorbell. He stood there for ten minutes, but no one came to the door. It made him furious to find that the maid had taken advantage of his absence—his misfortune—to spend the night elsewhere. He rang the bell again, as vigorously as he could. He heard sounds that seemed to come from the remote interior of the house; then a series of rhythmical thuds that kept growing louder. A human figure appeared; it looked enormous. Morris pulled down the brim of his hat, and moved back into the shadows. Immediately he recognized the sleepy and indignant man, and he had the impression that he, Morris, was the one who was dreaming. He said to himself, "Yes, it's Grimaldi. The old cripple, Charles Grimaldi himself!" Then, as he remembered that name, incredibly he was standing face to face with the man who had been living in the house when his father bought it more than fifteen years ago.

"What do you want?" bellowed Grimaldi.

Morris recalled how the man had stubbornly refused to move, and how his father had sent gifts to induce him to leave the premises after fruitlessly threatening to evict him.

"Is Miss Carmen Soares in?" asked Morris, stalling for time.

Grimaldi swore, slammed the door, turned out the light. In the darkness Morris heard the uneven footsteps growing fainter; then, with a commotion of glass and steel, a streetcar clanged by; and there was silence again.

"He didn't recognize me!" thought Morris triumphantly.

Immediately afterward he experienced shame, surprise, rage. He wanted to kick down the door, and drag the intruder out. As if he were drunk, he shouted, "I'm going to report you to the police!" He wondered about the meaning of the multiple and overwhelming offensive his friends had launched against him. He decided to consult me.

If he found me at home, he would have time to explain the facts to me. He hailed a taxi, and told the driver to take him to Owen Way. The man had never heard of that street. Morris asked him sardonically how he had been able to get a job as a taxicab driver. He cursed the police, who allowed interlopers to move into our homes, and foreigners, who never learned to find their way about our cities. The driver suggested he take another cab. Morris ordered him to drive out Vélez Sársfield until he crossed the railroad tracks.

The crossing was barricaded; interminable gray trains were maneuvering back and forth. Morris ordered him to drive around Solá Station on Toll Street. He got out at the corner of Australia and Luzuriaga. The driver said that Morris would have to pay him because he could not wait, and that there was no such street as Owen Way. Morris did not answer; he walked confidently down the street, turning south on Luzuriaga. The cab driver followed, shouting insults. Morris realized that both he and the driver would spend the night in jail if a policeman happened to come along at that moment.

"And then they would find out that you had run away from the hospital," I said. "Perhaps the nurse and the others who helped you would be implicated, too."

"That was the least of my worries," replied Morris, and he continued the story:

He walked to the end of the block, but did not find Owen Way. He walked another block, and still another. The driver kept protesting; his voice became lower, his tone more sarcastic. Morris retraced his steps; he turned down Alvarado, and came to Pereyra Park, at Rochadale Street. He went down Rochadale. In the middle of the block, on his right, there should have been an opening between the houses where Owen Way intersected it. Morris began to feel sick to his stomach. There was no intersection. He walked to the end of the block and came to Australia Street. He looked up and saw the tank of the International Company on Luzuriaga Street silhouetted against a background of nocturnal clouds. Owen Way should have been opposite, but it was not.

He glanced at his watch; he had scarcely twenty minutes left.

He walked faster, but soon he stopped again. Standing with his feet buried in thick, slippery mud in front of a dismal row of identical houses, he realized that he was lost. He wanted to return to Pereyra Park; he could not find it. He was afraid that the cab driver would discover that he was lost. He saw a man approaching; he asked him where Owen Way was. The man did not know; he said he was from a different section of the city. With growing exasperation, Morris kept on walking. Another man appeared. Morris walked up to him, and the cab driver jumped out of the taxi and followed. Morris and the driver, shouting, asked if he knew where Owen Way was. The man looked frightened, as if he thought they had some evil intent, and said he had never heard of that street. He was about to say something else, but Morris gave him a menacing look and he hurried away.

It was 3:15 A.M. Morris told the cab driver to take him to Caseros and Entre Ríos.

There was a different sentinel on duty at the hospital. Morris walked up and down in front of the door two or three times without daring to enter. He decided to try his luck; he showed the ring. The sentinel let him pass.

The nurse came late the following afternoon.

"You did not make a good impression on the man at the church," she said. "Naturally, he was impressed by the way you told the story—he is always telling the members of the brotherhood about the importance of deception—but he was offended by your refusal to confide in him."

It was doubtful that the man would help Morris now.

The situation had grown worse. The hope that he could pass for a foreigner was gone, and his life was in immediate danger. He wrote a detailed account of what had happened and sent it to me. Then, to justify his act, he said that the woman's fear was getting on his nerves. Perhaps at last he was beginning to be afraid himself.

Idibal went to see the man again. As a favor to her—"not to the odious spy"—he promised that certain influential persons would intervene on his behalf. The plan was to have Morris try a realistic repetition of the flight he had made before. They would give him an airplane and let him repeat the test he said he had made on the day of the accident.

In spite of the influence exerted in his favor, it developed that the test plane would be a two-place aircraft. That made the second part of the plan—Morris's escape to Uruguay—somewhat more difficult. Morris said he would be able to dispose of the other man. Then the intermediaries insisted that the plane should be identical to the one he was flying at the time of the accident.

After a week in which she overwhelmed him with hopes and anxieties, Idibal came in looking radiant, and said that everything had been arranged. The test was to take place in five days, on the following Friday, and he was to make it alone.

"I'll wait for you at Colonia, Uruguay," she said, with a look of tenderness. "As soon as you take off, head straight for Uruguay. Do you promise?"

He promised. Then he turned over in bed, pretending to sleep.

"I felt I was being forced into marriage and it made me furious," he said.

He did not know then that they were really saying good-bye.

They took him to the barracks the very next day, as he was now completely recovered.

"Those were happy times," he said. "There was nothing to do but drink *mate* and play poker with the guards."

"But you don't play poker!" I said. It was just a sudden inspiration. Actually, I did not know whether he played it or not.

"Oh, well, some card game or other," he replied, unruffled.

I was very surprised. I had always thought that chance, or circumstances, had made Morris an archetypal sort of person; it never occurred to me that he, like other men, could enjoy simple pleasures.

"You will probably call me a poor devil," he continued, "but I spent my time thinking about the woman. I was so frantic, I began to believe I had forgotten her—"

"You mean you tried to imagine what she looked like, but couldn't?" I supplied.

"How did you know?" But without waiting for me to answer, he went on with the story:

One rainy morning they drove him to Palomar Air Base in an old open car. A solemn assembly of military men and officials greeted him there.

"It looked like a wake," said Morris. "A wake or an execution."

Several mechanics opened the hangar and pushed out a Dewotine, a very ancient pursuit plane.

Morris started the engine. He saw that there was not enough fuel for ten minutes of flight, and that it would be impossible to reach Uruguay. For a moment he was disappointed; then he told himself gloomily that perhaps it would be better after all to die than to live like a slave. The plan had failed; it was no use to fly now; he felt an urge to say, "Very well, gentlemen. Have it your way!" Out of apathy he let events take their course. He decided to try his new test-flight plan again.

He taxied for about five hundred yards and then took off. He completed the first part of the plan, but when he started to make the other maneuvers he felt a recurrence of the old nausea; he fainted, and heard himself utter an angry protest because he was fainting. Just before touching the landing field, he managed to set the plane right again.

When he regained consciousness, he was stretched out painfully on a white bed in a high-ceilinged room with bare white walls. He realized that he had been injured, that he was a patient in the Military Hospital. He wondered if it was merely a dream.

"A dream you had at the moment of waking," I said, completing his thought.

He learned that the crash had occurred on 31 August. He lost his sense of time. Three or four days passed. He was glad that Idibal was in Colonia; he felt ashamed of having had that second accident. Besides, he knew that she would reproach him for not having flown directly to Uruguay.

"When she hears about the accident, she will come back," he thought. "It will be only two or three days until I see her again."

A different nurse was on duty now. She and Morris spent the afternoons holding hands.

Idibal did not return. Morris began to worry. One night his anxiety reached a fever pitch.

"You will think I am mad," he said, "for wanting to see her so much. But I thought she had come back and had found out about the other nurse, and that was why she didn't want to see me."

He asked an intern to call Idibal. The man went away and did not come back. Much later (but actually that same night; it seemed incredible to Morris that one night could last so long) he returned; he told Morris that no one named Idibal worked in the hospital. Morris insisted that the man should find out when she had stopped working there. The intern came early the next morning and said that the office was closed.

Morris dreamed of Idibal. He thought about her during the day. He began to dream that he could not find her. Finally he could no longer imagine what she looked like, or even dream about her.

They told him that no one named Idibal "worked or had worked for the organization."

The new nurse suggested he might try to do some reading. They brought him the newspapers. But nothing interested him—not even the sports and racing section.

"I was desperate—so I asked for the books you sent me."

They told him that no one had sent any books.

(I almost committed an indiscretion; I almost admitted that I had not sent him anything.)

He thought they had found out about his escape plan and about Idibal's part in it; that was why she did not come. He looked at his hands: the ring was not on his finger. He asked for it. They told him it was too late, that the main office (where it had been placed for safekeeping) was closed. He endured an atrocious and very long night, thinking that they would never give the ring back to him.

"Thinking," I added, "that if they did not return the ring, you would have no trace of Idibal."

"I did not think of that," he replied honestly. "But I spent the night feeling as if I had gone mad. The next day they brought me the ring."

"Do you still have it?" I asked, surprised by my own incredulity.

"Yes," he answered. "I keep it in a safe place."

He opened a desk drawer and took out the ring. The stone was bright and clear, but it lacked fire. At its depth there was the bust of a woman with the head of a horse, carved in high relief; I suspected that it was the effigy of some ancient divinity. I know very little about jewelry, but I could see that the ring was valuable.

One morning some officers came into his room, followed by a soldier who brought in a table and chair, and a typewriter. He sat down and began to type as an officer dictated: "Name: Ireneus Morris; Nationality: Argentine; Regiment: 3rd; Squadron: 121st; Base: Palomar."

He thought it was natural that they dispensed with formalities and did not ask his name for that was, after all, his second statement.

"I noticed," said Morris, "that they had made some progress."

Now they accepted the fact that he was an Argentine, that he was in the Argentine Army, stationed at Palomar Air Base. But their return to sanity did not last long. They asked his whereabouts since 23 June (the date of the first accident) and where he had left the Breguet 304.

("The number was not 304," Morris explained, "it was 309.")

He was surprised that they had made such a foolish mistake.

They asked where he had obtained the old Dewotine. When he said that the Breguet was surely somewhere in the vicinity since the crash on 23 June had occurred near Palomar, and that they should know how he had obtained the Dewotine since they themselves had provided it for a repetition of the test of 23 June, they pretended not to believe him.

But they no longer pretended that he was a foreigner or a spy. They accused him of having been in another country since 23 June. They were accusing him—when he realized it he began to grow angry again—of having sold military secrets to another country. The undecipherable conspiracy continued; but now his accusers had changed their plan of attack.

Gesticulatory and cordial, Lieutenant Viera walked into the room. Morris insulted him. Viera feigned astonishment; then he grew hostile.

"Things seemed to be improving," said Morris. "The traitors were acting like friends again."

General Huet visited him. Even Kramer paid him a visit. Morris was taken off his guard, and did not have a chance to react properly.

"I don't believe a word of the accusations, old man," said Kramer effusively.

They embraced warmly. Some day, Morris thought, I shall know what this is all about. He asked Kramer to go to my office.

"Tell me, Morris," I ventured, "do you remember what books I sent you?"

"No, I don't," he said gravely. "But you mentioned them in your note, you know."

I had not written Morris a note.

I took his arm and helped him walk to the bedroom. He opened the drawer of his night table and took out a letter written on stationery I did not recognize. He handed it to me.

The writing looked like a bad imitation of my own. My capital *T*'s and *E*'s are like block letters; the ones in the note were made with elaborate flourishes. I read:

I acknowledge receipt of your favor of the 16th, which reached me after some delay, due no doubt to an error in the address. I do not live on "Owen" Way, but on Miranda Street in the section of town known as Nazca. I assure you that I read your story with great interest. I am not able to visit you at this time; I am not well; but solicitous feminine hands are caring for me and before long I shall be better; then I shall have the pleasure of seeing you.

As a token of sympathy, I am sending you these books by Blanqui, and I recommend that you read the poem beginning on page 281 of Volume III.

I said good-bye to Morris. I promised to return the following week. The whole affair interested me and left me baffled. I did not doubt Morris's sincerity; but I had not written him that letter; I had never sent him any books; I was not acquainted with the works of Blanqui.

And here let me make several observations about "my letter":

1) The writer addresses Morris in a formal way. Since Morris is somewhat untutored in literary matters, he did not notice that and

accordingly he was not offended; but I have always spoken to him familiarly.

2) I swear that I am innocent of the phrase "I acknowledge receipt of your favor."

3) The quotation marks around the *Owen* surprised me, and I should like the reader to take particular note of that.

My ignorance of Blanqui's works is due, perhaps, to my reading plan. From my early youth I have been aware of the importance of organizing my reading to keep from being overwhelmed by the inordinately large production of literary works and to achieve, even superficially, an encyclopedic culture. That plan has guided my life: first I concentrated on philosophy, then on French literature, then on the natural sciences, and later on ancient Celtic literature, especially from the land of the Cymry (due to the influence of Morris's father). Of course, medicine has occupied an important place throughout, but it has never interrupted the plan.

A few days before Lieutenant Kramer came to my office, I had finished the books on the occult sciences. I completed a study of the works of Papus, Richet, Lhomond, Stanislas de Guaita, Labougle, the Bishop of La Rochelle, Lodge, Hogden, and Albert the Great. I was especially interested in conjuration, appearances and disappearances. With regard to the latter, I shall always remember the case of Sir Daniel Sludge Home, who, at the request of the Society for Psychical Research of London, and before an assembly composed exclusively of baronets, made some of the passes used to cause the disappearance of ghosts—and immediately dropped dead! But I must express my doubts about the new Elijahs who reputedly vanish without leaving traces or corpses.

The "mystery" of the letter induced me to read the works of Blanqui. I found him in the encyclopedia, and learned that he wrote on political subjects. Happily that was not incompatible with my plan: occult sciences are followed by politics and sociology. I observe such transitions to avoid mental stagnation.

Early the next morning I went to a book store on Corrientes Street. No one was there except a doddering old man, the clerk, who shuffled about inefficiently and pretended not to notice my presence. I rummaged around and finally found a dusty bundle of books bound in dark leather with gold titles and fillets: the complete works of Blanqui. I bought the lot for fifteen pesos.

There is no poetry on page 281 of my edition. Although I have not read the whole work, I believe that the passage in question is "L' Eternité par les Astres," a prose poem; in my edition it begins on page 307 of Volume II.

I found the explanation for Morris's adventure in that poem or essay.

I went to the western part of the city, to the section known as Nazca. I spoke to the storekeepers; there is no one living on Miranda Street who has the same name as I.

I went to Márquez Street. There is no such number as 6890; there are no churches. There was—that afternoon—a poetic light that made the grass of the lawns look very green, very clear, and the trees seem lilac-colored and transparent. The street is not near the railroad yards. It is near the Noria Bridge.

I went to the railroad yards. I found it difficult to cross the tracks near Juan B. Justo and Gaona Streets. I inquired how I could get to the other side of the yards.

"Go down Rivadavia," they said, "until you come to Cuzco Street. Then cross the tracks."

Naturally, there is no Márquez Street in that vicinity; the street that Morris calls Márquez must be Bynnon. Neither at 6890, nor anywhere else on the street, are there any churches. The Saint Cajetan Church is not far from there, on Cuzco Street; that is of no importance: Saint Cajetan is not the right church. The fact that there are no churches on Bynnon Street does not invalidate my theory that it is the street mentioned by Morris— But I shall explain that more fully later.

I also found the towers that my friend thought he saw in an open, isolated spot: they are at the entrance to the Vélez Sársfield Athletic Club, at Fragueiro and Barragán Streets.

I did not have to pay a special visit to Owen Way: I live there. When Morris was lost, I suspect that he was in front of the dreary row of identical houses in the Monsignor Espinosa section, a modest neighborhood, and that his feet were buried in the white clay of Pedriel Street.

I went to see Morris again. I asked him whether he remembered having passed a street named Hamilcar or Hannibal on his memorable nocturnal expedition. He said that he did not. I asked him if there was some symbol near the cross in the church he visited. He looked at me quizzically, as if he thought I was joking.

"You can't expect me to remember a thing like that!" he said finally.

"But it might be important," I said. "Try to remember." And then, "Try to recall if there was something next to the cross," I insisted.

"Perhaps there was," he murmured. "Perhaps a—"

"A trapezoid?" I suggested.

"Yes, a trapezoid," he said without conviction.

"Was there a line through it?"

"How do you know?" he exclaimed. "Were you on Márquez Street?" Then he brightened perceptibly. "But wait—now I remember: Yes! There was a cross—and a trapezoid with a line through it—a kind of arrow." He seemed to be quite excited.

"And did you notice a statue of a saint?"

"Wait a minute, old friend," he said, trying to control his impatience, "I didn't make an inventory!"

"All right. Forget it," I said.

When his irritation had diminished, I asked him to show me the ring and to tell me the nurse's name again.

I went home feeling quite optimistic. I heard sounds in my niece's room; I presumed that she was putting her things in order. I did not tell her I was there, for I did not want any interruptions. I took the book by Blanqui, put it under my arm, and went out.

I sat down on a bench in Pereyra Park. Once again I read this paragraph:

There are probably infinite identical worlds, infinite worlds with slight variations, infinite different worlds. What I am writing now in this jail at Fort Toro, I have already written before and I shall write throughout eternity, on a table, on a paper, in a jail, that are all quite similar. In infinite worlds my situation will be the same, but perhaps the reason for my incarceration may gradually lose its nobility, until it becomes sordid, and perhaps my words may have, in other worlds, the undeniable superiority of the *mot juste*.

On 23 June Morris crashed with his Breguet in the Buenos Aires of a world that was almost identical to this one. The confusion that followed the accident kept him from noticing the obvious differences; to notice the less obvious ones would have required a perspicacity and education that Morris did not possess.

He took off one gray and rainy morning; he crashed on an extremely bright one. The bumblebee in the hospital suggests summer; the "very hot weather" that overwhelmed him during the interrogation confirms it.[1]

In his story Morris gives some distinct characteristics of the world he visited. In that world, for example, there is no Wales: streets with Welsh names do not exist in that Buenos Aires: Bynnon becomes Márquez and Morris, in the labyrinths of night and his own obfuscation, looks in vain for Owen Way. Viera, Kramer, Margaride, Faverio, and I exist there because we are not of Welsh origin; General Huet and Ireneus Morris himself, both of Welsh descent, do not exist (he merely came there by accident). The Charles Albert Servian of that world, in his letter, encloses the word *Owen* in quotation marks because it seems strange to him; and for the same reason the officers laughed when Morris said his name.

Grimaldi is still living at 971 Bolívar Street since no person named Morris existed in that Buenos Aires.

Morris's story reveals that Carthage was not destroyed in that other world. That was why I asked my foolish questions about streets named Hannibal and Hamilcar.

Someone may ask how the Spanish language can exist if Carthage did not disappear. Shall I remind you that between victory and annihilation there can be intermediate degrees?

The ring that I have in my possession is a double proof. It is proof that Morris was in another world: no expert, of the many I have consulted, recognized the stone. It is proof of the existence (in that other world) of Carthage: the horse is a Carthaginian symbol. I am sure that many people have seen similar rings in the Musée Lavigerie.

Further, the nurse's name—Idibal, or Iddibal—is Carthaginian; the font with ritual fish and the trapezoid with a kind of arrow are

---

[1] In Buenos Aires the seasons are reversed, and therefore June would be the beginning of winter. (Translator's Note.)

Carthaginian; finally—*horresco referens*—there are the brotherhoods or *circuli,* as Carthaginian and malevolent as the insatiable Moloch. I denounce those groups of Carthaginians as the iniquitous precursors of the syndicate, the communist cell, and the secret societies formed by the individuals of some groups to undermine our civilization.

But to resume my theorizing, I wonder whether I bought the works of Blanqui because they were mentioned in the letter Morris showed me, or because the histories of these two worlds are parallel. Since there are no people named Morris in the other one, Celtic legends were not included in the other reading plan. The other Charles Albert Servian was able to advance more rapidly than I; he naturally reached political science before I did.

I am proud of him: with the few facts at his disposal, he explained the mysterious appearance of Morris. And so that Morris would understand too, he told him to read "L'Eternité par les Astres." But I cannot understand why he would choose to live in the undesirable Nazca section!

Morris went to that other world and returned. He did not have recourse to my interplanetary missile or to the other vehicles that men have designed to help them transcend an incredible astronomy. How did he make his journeys? I opened Kent's dictionary; after the word *pass,* I read: "A complicated series of movements made with the hands, by means of which appearances and disappearances are effected." I thought that perhaps the hands were not indispensable, that the movements could be made with other objects—for example, with airplanes.

My theory is that the "new test-flight plan" coincides with some pass (on both occasions Morris seems to faint, and then changes worlds).

In that other world they thought he was a spy from another country; here, they explain his absence by saying that he flew to a foreign country to sell military information. He knows nothing of this, and thinks he is the victim of a heinous plot.

When I returned home I found a note from my niece on my desk. She said that she had eloped with that reformed traitor, Lieutenant Kramer.

"I find solace in the knowledge that you will not be sorry to see me go, since you never had any interest in me," she said cruelly. Then, revealing the depth of her rancor, she added, "Kramer loves me; I am happy."

I felt very depressed. I did not see any patients or leave the house for about three weeks. I thought somewhat enviously about my astral self, who also was confined to his home, but who was being cared for by "solicitous feminine hands." I believe I know the touch of those hands; I believe I know what hands he meant.

Then I went to see Morris. I tried to talk to him about my niece (it seems I cannot keep from talking, incessantly, about her).

"Is she the maternal type?"

I said that she was not. I heard him say something about the nurse.

The possibility of meeting a new version of myself is not what would induce me to travel to that other Buenos Aires. The idea of seeing a reflection of myself, like the picture on my bookplates, or of knowing myself, like the motto inscribed on them—these things do not interest me. But I am intrigued, perhaps, by the possibility of being able to enjoy an experience that the other Servian, fortunately, has not yet had.

But these are personal problems. I am also worried about Morris. Everyone here knows him and has tried to be patient with him; but his denials have become monotonous and his refusal to talk has angered his superiors. He is surely facing loss of rank or even the firing squad.

If I had asked him for the ring, he never would have given it to me. He is stubborn, and would never have agreed to let me have this proof of the existence of other worlds. And besides, Morris had become insanely attached to that ring! Perhaps a gentleman (the infallible alias of the *cambrioleur*) would not condone my act; but the compassionate conscience will, I am sure. I am happy to say that all this has had an unexpected result: after losing the ring, Morris has been more willing to listen to my plan of escape.

We, the Armenians, are united. Within our society, we form an indestructible nucleus. I have good friends in the Army. Morris will be able to attempt a repetition of his accident. And this time I shall go with him!

C. A. S.

Charles Albert Servian's story seemed utterly fantastic. I am not unfamiliar with the legend of Morgan's chariot; the passenger tells where he wishes to go, and the chariot takes him there; but that is a legend. And, even if Captain Ireneus Morris had fallen into another world, it was unlikely that he would fall into that same world again.

I suspected that all along. Subsequent events confirmed that I was right.

Some friends and I planned and postponed, year after year, a trip to the Uruguay-Brazil border. Finally we felt we could not put it off any longer, so we made the trip this year.

On 3 April we were lunching at a country restaurant; afterward we planned to visit a very interesting *fazenda*.

An interminable Cadillac drove up, followed by a cloud of dust; a sort of jockey got out. It was Captain Morris.

He paid for our lunch and had a drink with us. I found out later that he was the secretary, or flunky, of a man engaged in contraband activities.

I did not go with my friends to visit the *fazenda*. Instead I stayed behind to talk to Morris. He told me about his adventures: skirmishes with the police; tricks to outwit justice and ruin his rivals; escapes made across rivers while clutching a horse's tail; drunken orgies and women— Undoubtedly he exaggerated his cunning and his courage. I cannot exaggerate his monotony.

All of a sudden, I thought I had made a discovery. I asked questions; when Morris went away, I continued my investigation.

I found proof that Morris had arrived around the middle of June of the previous year, and that *he was seen in the area many times between the beginning of September and the end of December*. On 8 September he rode in the horse races at Yaguarão; then he spent several days in bed after falling off a horse.

Nevertheless, during that same part of September, Captain Morris was hospitalized at the Military Hospital in Buenos Aires; the military authorities, his fellow Army officers, childhood friends—Dr. Servian and the now Captain Kramer—and General Huet, his old family friend—all of them swear to it.

The explanation is obvious:

In several almost identical worlds, several Captain Morrises went out one day (here it was 23 June) to test airplanes. Our Morris, deciding to flee, escaped to Uruguay or Brazil. Another Morris, who left from another Buenos Aires, made some "passes" with his plane and found himself in the Buenos Aires of another world (where Wales did not exist and where Carthage did exist; where Idibal is waiting now). That Ireneus Morris then took off in the Dewotine, again made the "passes," and crashed in this Buenos Aires. As he looked exactly like the other Morris, even close friends were deceived. But he was not the same man. Our Morris (the one who is in Brazil) took off on 23 June in the Breguet 304; the other one knew perfectly well that he had tested the Breguet 309. Then, with Dr. Servian, he tries the passes again, and disappears. They may have reached another world; but it is less probable that they will find Servian's niece and the Carthaginian girl.

Perhaps Servian was correct in quoting Blanqui's theory of the plurality of worlds; having a more limited background, I should have preferred to propose the authority of a classic: ". . . according to Democritus, there are infinite worlds, some of which are not only similar but perfectly identical" (Cicero, *Academica*, II, XVII); or: "Here we are in Bauli, near Pozzuoli; do you think that now, in an infinite number of exactly identical places, there may be people who have the same names as we, who have received the same honors, who have experienced the same things, and in mind, age, and appearance are identical to ourselves, who are discussing this same subject together, just as we are doing now?" (*Id.*, II, XL).

Finally, for readers who are accustomed to the old notion of planetary and spherical worlds, the journeys between the Buenos Aires of different worlds will seem incredible. They will wonder why the travelers always arrive at Buenos Aires and not other places, like oceans or deserts. My only reply to such a question is that perhaps these worlds are like bundles of parallel spaces and times.

The Other Labyrinth

PART ONE

dissimulare velis, te liquet esse meum.
Ovid, *Tristia*, III, III, 18.

Somewhat unjustly Anthal Horvath thought, "It is as if time had stopped, or as if I had never been away. Before I left for Paris he was speaking of this, and now he still speaks of it. He is brooding on this incident from the past, he is forgetting the present."

But not even Horvath suspected the terrible adventure that lay before them. He reread Istvan Banyay's note:

"In 1604 a dead man was found in one of the rooms of the Tunnel Inn. No one had seen him arrive. No one knew him. The Ottoman authorities displayed the corpse in the market place by the citadel in the Gellertheggy, and for three days and nights the people of Buda filed by it in a long procession that was like a river of silence amid the turmoil of the fair. No one recognized the dead man, who was wearing a dark cape, narrow trousers, and leather sandals, and who appeared to be of a low rank, as he had neither a wig nor a sword.

"There were no signs of violence on the ample but not obese body. The only door to the room was bolted from the inside; the window was closed; there was no other access to the room. The authorities declared that the man had not been murdered, but the people, although they did not agree with that declaration (the dead man appeared to be a Hungarian and several officials of the Ottoman administration lived at the same Inn), were grateful for it, because they were always held responsible for a crime when the real culprit was not apprehended, and were punished with impartial butchery.

"A manuscript was found in a pocket of the dead man's cape: the authorities said that the incredible and uninteresting document was the victim's biography. But the authorities were Turkish and, as they themselves said, the document was written in an unidentified Hungarian dialect. The fact that the language used was not Osmanli or even Latin confirmed their belief that the writer's cultural background was decidedly mediocre. They made precise observations about the physical aspect of the document: it consisted of twenty-four sheets of paper with writing on only one side of each page, and some of the lines crossed others at right angles; the paper was smooth and glossy, and the ink was mysterious (although the manuscript seemed to have been written in ink, there was no trace of ink on the paper; the ink blended into the paper without appearing to be superimposed on it). It was rumored that those twenty-four pages had been sent to Constantinople to be examined by a commission of physicians and poets.

"Nothing else is known about the manuscript, which is thought to be lost to the West, although an occasional scholar still appears with the romantic hope of finding it."

Anthal Horvath stood in front of the mirror. He rubbed his hand over his clean-shaven face and thought, "At twilight or at dawn, in dark rooms or with nearsighted women, I shall be successful." He was tall and thin, and the benign expression on his face caused men to relegate him to insignificance, or even obscurity.

He was living in the ancient building that, until the middle of the eighteenth century, had been the Tunnel Inn. It was part of the vast estate that belonged to Istvan Banyay (or, more exactly, to Banyay's parents), and was situated in the garden on Logody Street, about fifty yards from the main house. It was a two-story building; the carriage house was on the ground floor, and there were two large rooms and some offices above. Always closed was the door to a room called "the museum," which contained the innumerable objects that an ancestor of the Banyay family had accumulated during his laborious life as an implacable collector. Piled high in the darkness were clocks that resembled miniature villages, with figurines and houses; ebony harmoniums, decorated by eighteenth-century artists, which produced shrill, splintery sounds at the slightest touch; crude instruments of optics, astronomy, and torture, including a Turkish version of the demoiselle; a chess set on a board that, by means of symbols, told all the known stories and legends about the origin of the game; one of the twenty-four life-size porcelain gorillas that the Prussian government obliged Moses Mendelssohn to buy on his wedding day; a Russian doll with the inscription "Stuttgart, 1785," on which were superimposed twelve avatars of the Wandering Jew (proving that the legend was known before the nineteenth century); a billiard table with miniature figures that played first at one end and then at the other, made by Philip the Englishman, the "clockmaker of Hume"; copies of the wooden dove and the bronze fly made by Regiomontanus; a porcelain tea set that illustrated the history of Genghis Khan of the Golden Horde—

The sight of the room caused Anthal Horvath to feel a wistful sadness, as if the whole past were there, as if all the hopes, all the frustrations and all the modest follies of men were skulking there in the darkness. Banyay's room was next to the "museum"; it was his bedroom, his study, his living room, his library. With his parents away (they were vacationing at one of the summer resorts at Nyiregyhaza or Nagy-Banya), Banyay had moved to the main building and had invited Anthal Horvath, his lifelong friend, to occupy his room in the garden pavilion. After an extended stay in Paris, Horvath had returned to his own country, almost famous and totally discredited.

Anthal thought about the note Banyay had left for him. "We all have a curious tendency to ascribe importance to the things that concern us," he reflected. "A confused idea, if it is our own, seems like an interesting argument; an ancestor, if he is our own, seems distinguished. All his life Istvan has been obsessed by the death that occurred three hundred years ago, simply because it took place in his house. But Madeleine is right: it is a mania, and we who are his friends must help him overcome it. Istvan can't understand why I don't write a mystery novel based on the incident. But he doesn't know the rules: the action has to take place in that incomparable Paris of the Second Empire or, at least, in a London fog; and the *sûreté* must be featured importantly. Istvan, although he can do only one thing at a time and cannot establish relationships and make comparisons, is not stupid; he is capable, with guidance, of doing work that requires subtle and even profound intelligence; and, without anyone's help, he has supernatural powers."

Anthal Horvath was pompous and dignified when he remembered to be. Conscious of his poverty, unsure of his physical appearance, he aspired only to intellectual superiority. Unscrupulously, perhaps even crudely, he tried to display it. He believed that his inability to formulate rapid, clever phrases in conversation was only a minor shortcoming.

He had just arrived from Paris with some prestige as a novelist, with an excess of pride, with a determination to belittle the Hungarian writers, both young and old; to defend the school of Fortuné de Boisgobey and to revile Émile Gaboriau; to accede, with veiled eagerness, to the numerous demands for novels he received from publishers who were famous for not paying their writers; to bestow on Banyay, as always, a generous intellectual protection and to tolerate Banyay's economic assistance; to remember Madeleine.

In Paris he had been the humble and frugal secretary of Count Banyay, Istvan's tutelary uncle. That modest position had continued for three years until suddenly, mysteriously, and irremissibly the Count's administrators decided to dispense with his services. It was therefore a grave offense to his family for Istvan to have invited Horvath into his parents' home.

Horvath cleaned his razor, dried it. He murmured, "It's too warm in here." He walked to the window, then hesitated. "Fresh air, in a building, is dangerous," he said. A confused feeling of impatience made him want to go outside.

He remembered the verses of Janos Arany:

> Seek not the Garden of Paradise:
> The abyss is burning now within your heart
> Or peace, your soul's instructor, flowers there.

Horvath thought, "He is fighting the Austrians. He is fighting the Magyars. I shall not let them surround me. I shall never yield to those passions again. I shall not condescend to die for those provincial phantasmagorias. My friends, who act as if they were possessed, who are the irresponsible masqueraders of this local nightmare, will not extinguish the fire in my heart—" Shouting the words, he recited:

Or Paris, your soul's instructor, flowers there!

Just then the door opened. Silent and enormous, Istvan Banyay came into the room. Controlling his anger, Anthal Horvath reflected that for the first time his friend had taken him by surprise in a ridiculous situation.

Banyay eyed him anxiously, began to rock gently back and forth as if to summon courage, and finally said, "The note."

He had left it four days earlier; now he wanted it back. Horvath realized that Istvan had changed his mind and no longer wanted him to write about the mysterious stranger who had been found dead at the Tunnel Inn.

"I can't use that plot," said Horvath affecting harshness; and then, more cordially, "I am already considering several others."

"Sorry," said Banyay. "I'm sure you would have produced a magnificent piece of work."

"I specialize in international themes," said Horvath. "You know the sort of thing: the gentleman *cambrioleur*, the *wagon-lit*, the Riviera. I find a national background quite suffocating. Perhaps you may be able—"

"Perhaps," Banyay conceded reluctantly. "But I have some good news for you: I have the lost manuscript, the biography of the man who was found at the Tunnel Inn! I haven't had a chance to study it carefully, but I suspect it is interesting. I'm thinking of doing a critical edition of it—do you think I would be capable?"

"Who found the manuscript?" asked Horvath.

Banyay opened his eyes wide; his expression was kind and candid and his usually halting voice sounded fluent. "Professor Liptay found it accidentally in the University archives."

Horvath appeared to be relieved. "I want to hear about your work for the *Hungarian Encyclopedia*," he said vehemently. "I want to talk about France. I want to tell you about Madeleine. A French girl—do you understand why I'm not interested in any of the local females?

Think, Istvan: a French girl, in France. But let's go out some place. I can't breathe in this room."

"All right," replied Banyay, lying down on the sofa. He held his enormous round head with his left hand, and lowered his enormous round eyes. His expression revealed sad, benign, and unsuppressed anxiety. With amazement Horvath surveyed the extraordinary length, the extraordinary verticality, of that horizontal body.

"I'm writing biographies of seventeenth-century Hungarians for the *Encyclopedia*," Banyay continued. "Mostly politicians and military men, with a generous assortment of the clergy. I know the period well—in fact, it's the only one that seems real to me. Antiquity is fantastic, the Middle Ages shabby, the eighteenth century crassly modern. The seventeenth century seems like the natural era of human life, of my own life. I read the dates of each person's birth and death in the reference books. I count the number of years each has lived to ascertain whether the biography is worth writing. It seems more natural to be one of those men than to be myself, because I live in the incredible twentieth century."

Horvath heard some quick footsteps on the stairs. Nervously, he asked Banyay who it was. Banyay lowered his eyes.

A young girl came in. To Horvath she was the incarnation of the love of his childhood nights: the incarnation of the Florentine girl in one of Luca della Robbia's terracottas that his mother had shown him in the worn catalogue from the museum in Florence. That image had been his first love, his first theft, his first treasure. And then, inexplicably, he had forgotten her.

Horvath wondered impatiently, "Shall I wait here until she goes, or shall I leave when she does?"

Banyay introduced the girl as Palma Szentgyörgyi.

"Hasn't anyone arrived yet?" asked Palma. She turned immediately to Horvath, who was confused, apprehensive. "Don't thank Istvan for letting you stay here. I'm the injured party!"

Although she was obviously joking, Horvath thought he could detect an inherent cruelty in her character.

"You see," Palma continued, "it was much easier to visit him here."

Was she referring to clandestine visits? Apparently, or else her words would have been meaningless. That sordid mystery increased his need for fresh air. He heard more footsteps. He had a fervent desire to escape. Ferencz Remenyi walked in.

Ferencz Remenyi might have been called a young man of distinction, or a man about town. He had wavy hair, a luxuriant moustache, and he wore glasses. It was rumored that he was infallible with women, and it was even said that he was responsible for the extravagant reputation of the carnivals of Kelenfold. Horvath envied the easy courage with which he participated in the fight against the Austrians and the Magyars. "He is fighting on the right side," thought Horvath, "but for the wrong reason."

Ignoring the others, Remenyi came straight to Horvath. He opened his eyes wide, thrust out his arms, and exclaimed, "How goes it, old man?" Then, as if Horvath were not there, he turned to the others and said, "Have you heard the latest news? He told the publishers that his books are selling well, and they're all hounding him now!"

Resigned, flattered, Horvath replied, "For Hellebronth I'm doing three mystery novels, and for Orbe a biography of the English poet Chatterton and a complicated adventure novel, to be published under my pseudonym."

"Listen to this," said Remenyi, continuing to address the others. "When he was in Paris he sent Hellebronth a historical novel. Even with influence, he was not able to get it published. You see what a great success he is!"

"I didn't send a historical novel," protested Horvath. "In Paris—"

No one was listening.

"Why don't you follow Anthal's example?" said Remenyi turning to Banyay. "Why do you sacrifice yourself on the *Hungarian Encyclopedia* as if you were starving?"

Four or five others came in. Horvath recognized several of them as perennial students. Someone expressed the hope that Professor Liptay would come.

"I rather wish he wouldn't," said someone else. No one seemed to believe that he meant it. "His life is dedicated to learning," he continued. "We must not let our passions interfere with his work."

A young girl came in quietly. Her hair reached her shoulders, her large eyes were deep blue; she looked like a page—restrained, agile, and dark.

"Why don't you show them the 'museum'?" Remenyi asked Banyay.

"In my opinion, it's depressing," said Horvath.

Banyay liked to show people the "museum." To please Horvath he lied, "I don't have the key. Besides," he added, "you never know what I may find there. When I work on the biographies for the *Encyclopedia*, I imagine that the seventeenth century is in that room."

Palma said with sudden violence, "Istvan never would have considered doing that work for the *Encyclopedia* if it hadn't been for—"

"I suggested it simply as a discipline," said Horvath quickly. "Not as a permanent occupation."

"But you have no stake in all this," she continued. "At least, that was the opinion of Istvan's uncle!"

Horvath perceived the irony in her tone. He reflected that the girl who looked like a page had a kind face. He addressed his defense to her. He mentioned Istvan's weak character and said that an intellect in formation needed sound discipline; smiling, he alluded to the sublime destinies that Professor Liptay predicted for Istvan; he admitted that his friend's interest in the past was almost an obsession; he asked the girl what her name was.

Erzsebet Loczy, Horvath repeated mentally. Somewhat theatrically he resolved that he should not move, or even take a step, that he should stand still, because Erzsebet Loczy was now a part of his destiny. He thought of himself as a cool, majestic, and shadowy chess player at a shadowy, symbolical chessboard.

"If you were true friends," Palma went on, "you would not let Istvan get involved in conspiracies. He's not well—he has a weak heart. The doctors say that a shock could kill him."

Banyay contemplated her with anxious deference, rocking slowly back and forth with his weight first on one foot, then on the other, breathing laboriously.

Anthal looked through the window at the familiar street below. It seemed as if he had never been away from Budapest, as if the city was and would continue to be his "native mountain, where everything, even the past, is our refuge." He looked at the street where, according to the same Hungarian song, "death and disaster are lurking." Opposite was the abandoned vacant lot that was linked in his memory to the first joys of friendship and love.

Others had joined the group now. It was evidently a meeting of the Hungarian Patriots, and those meetings could lead to exile, torture, or the firing squad if intercepted by the police. Horvath knew that everyone in the group was gambling, and that the outcome might be the overthrow of the government, or a bloody defeat.

An unattractive girl urged the group to wait a little longer for Professor Liptay.

"I haven't seen him yet," said Horvath. "I heard he was cataloguing manuscripts at the University library, so I went there the day after I arrived, but was unable to find him. I left him a little souvenir from a French girl, an unknown admirer of his."

Then Horvath tried to talk about literature, and said he wanted to interest Banyay in a biography of Paracelsus. But the others discussed the new leader of the city, the new chief of police who had come from Vienna with a thirst for Hungarian blood.

They explained why that able and unscrupulous man was the cause of all the evils, why he shattered all the patriots' hopes. "The city has changed," they kept repeating. They revealed an amazing ability to relate facts, an irritating inability to reach conclusions.

Horvath did not wish to interfere, but the others had begun to argue. Incredulously, impatiently, he foresaw that they would leave the argument unresolved. With simple logic he concluded, "Someone must kill the chief of police!"

II

The city had not changed: the light, the houses, the shouting, and the people seemed familiar. He walked by the mill and read the name of the proprietor, as he had done many times before during his childhood. He stopped to chat with the old man who sold pencils; he was blind now and as irascible as ever. The café where the coachmen met to drink wine and soda and to play cards reminded him of the long nights during exam week. A few things had changed; but everything was tawdry, familiar, homely. It was incredible that the obese dollseller would be a spy, and that the coffeehouse, of marble like a gigantic lavabo, was the place where a trap would be set. The tailor's wife was standing at the doorway of her house. She looked at Anthal Horvath and her glance was as cold as a blue stone. He whistled "Wenn die Liebe in deinen blauen Augen," and his feelings were what they had always been when, on many previous afternoons, he had passed that same doorway. He also felt some nostalgia, a belated desire to make amends, and resolved to stop squandering his opportunities.

III

At night the impression that nothing had changed was even more vivid. Sitting with Banyay and Remenyi at a marble-topped table on the terrace of the Turf Café, listening to the czardas, drinking beer and waiting, with the rest of the city, for an unlikely cool spell, Horvath felt with displeasure that the years spent in Paris were fading away, as if they had never existed at all, and that the recurrent and shoddy labyrinth of his accustomed life in Budapest was taking their place. For a moment the image of his friends, with their white suits, open coats, and straw hats, seemed repugnant.

"It's good to be together again," said Banyay. His large delicate rose-colored tongue touched his very white teeth; his mouth was slightly open; benevolence and persuasion shone from his beautiful bovine eyes. Then, as he leaned his heavy body forward, he proceeded with difficulty, "I am very interested in the manuscript that was found recently. The life it describes is quite intriguing."

Horvath thought, "Why does he speak of this in front of Remenyi?" and, to change the subject, asked, "How is Professor Liptay?"

"I admire him more every day," said Banyay. "He is a man with one consuming passion: history. But history, as he approaches it, is sometimes like fiction, always like art."

"And now Liptay has another passion," commented Remenyi amiably. "Istvan's future. He wants Istvan to be his disciple, to carry on his work when he is gone."

Horvath was surprised, almost shocked.

"I'm going to buy you another glass of beer, Horvath," said Remenyi, adjusting his glasses and smiling complacently at his friend. "You're thin and you look pale. Is it because you're jealous?"

"Don't listen to him," said Banyay. "The Professor is not satisfied with my method. He says I am not cautious enough."

Remenyi stood up abruptly, showing his irritation. Palma and Erzsebet (the girl who looked like a page) had arrived.

Now Horvath transferred the rancor he had felt toward Remenyi to Banyay. Why had they invited the women? The evening was ruined.

Remenyi admitted that the czardas had degenerated in recent years. "This café," he said, perhaps imprudently, "is the only place where intellectuals can meet. You can still hear some of the old czardas here, and they are played well."

The conversation turned again to Professor Liptay.

"I understand that he is a bit discouraged," said Horvath.

"It's because of the other professors," Banyay explained. "They are constantly involved in politics."

"But Liptay never was," said Horvath.

"I know," said Banyay. "But now he can't avoid it. He dislikes politics, and he will never let the University fall into the hands of politicians."

"Is that his third passion?" asked Remenyi.

"Yes, he's constantly concerned with University politics," said Palma, "but I believe he has acquired a senile passion: the lust for power."

"That's not true!" said Horvath hotly, rising. "Liptay is completely devoted to study. His conduct is exemplary. His life is an irrefutable proof that life should be lived," he added, ignoring the repetitions.

Even Remenyi surveyed him approvingly. Banyay mumbled his gratitude. Horvath drank another glass of beer. It occurred to him that no other music could move him like the czardas, that he liked to be with his friends, and that, after all, he had been born in Budapest. He looked at Erzsebet. "She knows," he thought.

Suddenly there was a disturbance on the terrace. The people got up, forming little groups and talking to each other. Everyone scattered as three gendarmes and a civilian walked between the deserted tables.

The civilian waved at a youth who was trying to escape. The gendarmes overtook him.

"They've captured another student," said Remenyi.

The people watched. Horvath remarked later that the incident had made him feel exceedingly nervous and uncomfortable.

IV

Several days later, on his way to the garden pavilion—Istvan's parents had returned and Anthal had been forced to find other lodgings—Horvath reflected that Budapest had indeed changed, that remaining in the capital would be unpleasant, and that he must try to induce someone to send him to Paris.

He passed the garish coffeehouse; he saw that the front door of the tailor's house was deserted; he entered the pavilion. Banyay and Palma were sitting by the window.

"You look as if you've lost some weight, Istvan," said Horvath.

"Yes, I am feeling much better," replied Banyay in a choked voice.

He had deep circles under his eyes and an expression of astonished fatigue.

They joked about who would be the one to kill the chief of police. They said it would be necessary to hire an assassin; or else one of their own group would have to play the role of a criminal.

"Whoever kills him," cried a voice behind Horvath, "must be someone who has nothing to hope for."

Horvath turned quickly and saw Professor Liptay who, enveloped in a black cloak, was smiling at him with his ironic and serene horse-trainer's face. He was not wearing a hat, and the hair on his temples was graying. His eyes were small and roguish; he had prominent cheekbones and thin lips. He was tall, gaunt, wizened.

"We must find a man who has no hopes, my friend," continued the Professor in his quiet, restrained voice, "a man who knows that his death is imminent, and that nothing can save him."

"Or a man who knows that nothing will save him from a life of misery," said Horvath, and he felt that something indefinable and ominous had slipped into the conversation.

"Better still," Banyay added, "a man with no will, a fool—or else a woman."

"We could ambush him," proposed Horvath. "Take him to that vacant lot." He pointed to the lot they could see from the window, on the opposite side of the street. "Istvan could project a palace there and—"

Horvath proceeded to tell once again the story of how he had discovered Banyay's supernatural powers.

"Istvan and I were studying for an examination. I went up to the pavilion to practice an interminable lesson I had memorized. Istvan was sitting at this desk; there were books strewn all over it. I walked over and absentmindedly arranged some of them; I stacked up some papers and put a stone on top as a paperweight; I aligned the pens and pencils; I closed the bottle of ink. I began to recite the lesson, but very soon I noticed that Istvan was not listening. When I complained about his inattention, he asked me if I had seen a stone on the desk. I looked for it, but it was not there.

"Then he explained that the stone I had seen was simply a projection of his mind. You see, when Istvan concentrates, he can project, or materialize, mental objects. There, now—I suppose he is angry that I have told you. For some absurd reason he doesn't like to talk about it."

When Horvath finished speaking he felt that his last sentence had somehow shattered his listeners's faith in the veracity of his story.

"I've never had much trouble projecting form, color, mass, or temperature," said Banyay unaffectedly. "Weight is more difficult."

"If you projected a house on that vacant lot," asked the Professor, "would people notice it, or simply accept it as if it had always been there?"

Horvath had expected an explicit statement that would confirm his claims before Palma (the only person present who had not known about Banyay's powers).

"Some writers attribute a similar power to Thomas More," he commented. "He projected dragons in the sky."

"At first I projected very simple objects," said Banyay. "A stone or a block of wood."

"Didn't you say that Remenyi was coming?" interrupted Palma with unwonted agitation.

"Yes, he said he would be here at six."

"Well, it's nine now," said Palma.

"That's strange," observed the Professor. "I had arranged to meet him yesterday at the University. He didn't come, or even call to apologize."

They heard someone knocking. Horvath, acting as if he were in his own house, went to open the door. The messenger standing there, seeming to justify Horvath's action, gave him an envelope with his name on it. Anthal took the jagged piece of paper out of the envelope and read: "Please come at once. I am afraid." Horvath recognized Erzsebet's handwriting. He gave the note to Banyay, who thought it was intended for him. Horvath did not correct the error.

"I must go," mumbled Banyay. "I am happy, I am afraid. I am in love with Erzsebet."

V

Horvath did not know where to go that night. He wanted to avoid Erzsebet. His evenings were usually spent with his friends in one of three different places: the Turf Café; a dancehall near the lake, in the Varosliget Forest; or the Gerbaud Coffeehouse. Erzsebet was sure to be in one of those places with Banyay.

He reflected that the rest of the city was completely unknown to him. However, he would not explore it that night. He decided to risk going to the dancehall by the lake.

He was talking to the hat-check girl when he felt an easily recognizable, heavy hand on his shoulder. Banyay suggested that they have a drink.

"I have great news," said Banyay abruptly, seeming to choke with exaltation. "Professor Liptay found a long paragraph about the manuscript in Tavernier. You know, the *Six voyages de J. B. Tavernier, qu'il a fait en Turquie*, et cetera—(Banyay spoke French laboriously, ostentatiously, with a great deal of spitting)—*pendant l'espace de quarante ans et par toutes les routes que l'on peut tenir*. Well, Tavernier says that when he was in Hungary no one spoke of the mysterious corpse that was found at the Tunnel Inn. But when he was in Constantinople in 1637 he met a dealer in precious stones, an agent of his father-in-law, who mentioned the incident in a conversation. Tavernier's interest was aroused, he asked for details, waited patiently and flattered bureaucrats, and finally acquired the manuscript. I've read somewhere that Voltaire and others considered Tavernier an ignoramus."

"Oh, really?" commented Horvath. He was bored.

"But you know Liptay's insistence on method: you must prove everything, suspect everything. I showed him the manuscript innumerable times these past few days, and he always had some new reason to doubt its authenticity. Well, there is a Latin quotation that neither Liptay nor I—"

"What quotation?" asked Horvath.

Banyay stopped talking, perhaps as an implicit reproach to his friend; but there was no malice in his enormous bovine eyes. His huge body shook as he moved to and fro; then he leaned on the counter, drank some gin, and continued to speak impetuously.

"The quotation is from Ovid's *Tristia*. It seems to have been inserted in the text. In a letter the man wrote to a girl in Florence, quoting the lovely verse: 'nulla venit sine te nox mihi, nulla dies.' After the quotation he wrote *Tr.* I, V, 7, enclosed in parentheses. Well, what I am getting at is this: we have examined the paragraph many times, and we believe that the quotation was added later because it is written in a handwriting that appears to be a bad imitation of the writing in the rest of the document. Neither Liptay nor I noticed that the verse did not correspond to the number given. But Tavernier discovered the error, or says he did, and supplies the correct number. I don't recall it at this moment—" Banyay paused, then continued, "But there is something else I want to tell you. Erzsebet would like to see you before she leaves for Nagy-Banya."

Horvath turned pale. He was unable to speak.

Banyay watched him with anxious solicitude and, after a moment's hesitation, filled Horvath's glass.

Horvath took a sip of gin and asked, "What did you say about Erzsebet?"

Then it was Banyay's turn to be speechless. He gazed at his friend with enormous, surprised eyes, with an expression of profound, concerned affection; his breathing was agitated. His fat, trembling hand held Horvath's arm in a steely grip.

"Of all the women in Budapest, why did you have to choose Erzsebet?" he asked sadly.

VI

Horvath had the impression that Liptay had not exaggerated: Budapest was like an immense armed camp. Soldiers and gendarmes were everywhere. He went to the University library; several officials inquired the reason for his visit. The walls were covered with dark portraits of Metternich and (as everyone asserted, as no one believed) of Kollonich, the execrated bishop.

After a series of delays and interrogations, a male secretary in mourning led him to the room that contained manuscripts from the seventeenth and eighteenth centuries. From the corridor he caught a glimpse of an object that was partially draped in black—a large copy camera. Three or four people were hovering around it; one was Banyay. He waved excitedly at Horvath, and indicated an empty chair.

Professor Liptay had asked Horvath to see Banyay, whose condition was, he said, alarming.

"You are the only one who can save him," he told Horvath. "I can't do a thing. He doesn't trust me. You must get him away from his work, his obsession."

Horvath studied Banyay. His friend was agitated, he had lost weight, he looked sickly; perhaps he was happy. Horvath sat for a moment contemplating the incomprehensible figures on the frieze near the ceiling. There was a quotation in gold letters from the eleventh book of St. Augustine's *Confessions*. He stood up and walked over to a bust in one corner of the room. On its base he read: A.M.S. BOETHIVS—CDLXX—DXXV—A.D.—HI OCULI VIDERVNT AETERNITATEM. He surveyed the marble eyes. Two hands pressed heavily on his shoulders, and he turned around.

"They gave me permission to photograph the manuscript page by page," exclaimed Banyay.

Several men were pushing the heavy camera out of the room.

"You can't accuse them of indifference," Horvath remarked. "They want to be despotic, but they still make mistakes."

"Not many," replied Banyay. "I asked for permission to take the document home for just one night. I asked in writing, verbally; I enlisted the help of Liptay, the secretary, the attendant. But it was no use."

"I'm surprised that Liptay couldn't get permission—I thought they respected him!"

Solemnly, Banyay drew himself up to his full height.

"How can you say that?" he asked. "Listen: Liptay is trying to ruin me!"

Horvath reflected that his friend was hopelessly mistaken.

"Absurd, isn't it?" Banyay went on. "Here is an example to show what I mean: except for the few facts I had before, the manuscript is my only source of information about the man who was found at the Tunnel Inn. Can there be any discrepancies between the manuscript and the information I had?"

"I don't understand," said Horvath.

"Well, this is the problem. I learned that the man spent his childhood in Nyiregyhaza; then I saw in the manuscript that he spent it in Tuszer. The word "Tuszer" is above the line and appears to have been written later, because the word below it has been crossed out. But where did I get the wrong idea? From the manuscript, because it was the source of my information. Obviously, then, someone must have made a change in it. But when? At night; during the daytime the readers, guards, attendants are here, and anyone who tampered with it would be observed. Who makes these changes in the manuscript at night? The director of the library, the only official who lives in the building: Liptay."

"I don't believe it," replied Horvath with excessive vehemence. "Why would he want to do that?"

"Palma has found the explanation: he wants me to make a fool of myself so he can draw attention to my mistakes and destroy me. It's a matter of jealousy—he is consumed by senile passions."

"I can't believe it. Why, if you told me that some men from the seventeenth century came here at night and made changes in the manuscript, it would seem more plausible."

Banyay paused and then continued, as if he were thinking out loud, "If only one word had been changed, I might not have noticed. But the manuscript is full of words that have been crossed out, with other words written above them. The lines on many of the pages run through the others at right angles, like the letters some women write. Sometimes it has taken me a whole day to read just one page. Look—"

Horvath looked at the wrinkled opaque parchment without experiencing the slightest feeling of curiosity.

VII

Anthal Horvath was aware of the conflict between several temptations and his lucidity, his will, his prudence.

On the one hand, he feared being doubly disloyal to a friend, disloyal to Erzsebet, cowardly. "But Banyay is not in any danger," he thought. "No one is distrustful of the rich." And then, "Am I in love with Erzsebet?" he wondered. "We must not be deceived by our own lies." It was better not to think of courage; one became confused, and—

On the other hand were peace of soul, self-control, his hope of returning to Paris, his literary career.

Erzsebet wanted to go away with him; she had called several times. He had suggested to Banyay that the girl would be safe at the country place in Nagy-Banya, and now Banyay was getting ready for the trip. They would leave on Friday. Horvath had four days left, four days during which Erzsebet was not to find him.

VIII

A week later Istvan Banyay disappeared. This was Horvath's version of what happened:

Banyay left with Erzsebet for Nagy-Banya on Friday, and returned on Monday. Horvath tried unsuccessfully to see him several times. Professor Liptay told Horvath that Professor Palffy, on his deathbed, had given him 1,300 florins for the Hungarian Patriots.

With a faraway look in his eyes, Liptay had said, "Horvath, my friend, I am in a position to confer a signal honor on you. I am going to give you these florins to turn over to the Patriots. Don't give me a receipt. Don't mention my name. I don't want to be involved in this generous transaction."

Horvath made several efforts to deliver the money, but soon gave up, for he was convinced that the police had the group under surveillance. Then he renewed his efforts to find Banyay—he wanted to dispose of the florins, which, as he said, were burning his hands. When he finally found Banyay, he had the impression that his friend was deliberately trying to avoid him; but then he wondered whether he only imagined that. Banyay agreed to turn the money over to the Patriots. The two old friends drank a glass of beer together at the Turf Café.

When they were about to say good-bye, Banyay stammered, "At Nagy-Banya I learned that Erzsebet loves you."

He spoke with bitterness, but without reproach.

That was the last time Horvath ever saw him.

IX

Banyay's parents discarded their objections to Horvath and received him like a son. They told him, with frequent repetitions, everything they knew about Istvan's disappearance: details about his actions during the morning of the day he disappeared, or during the days preceding it—an incomplete, perhaps futile, account of his past. But it was their treasure, and they wanted to share it with him.

Janos, the last person who had seen Banyay, was brought up from the remote cellar, where he drank and made speeches to himself, to give his version of the events. Horvath heard the prolix story from his damp, quivering lips. On Friday, Janos had driven Miss Erzsebet and Mr. Istvan to Gödölö, where they took the train to Nagy-Banya. The young lady scarcely spoke during the ride; Mr. Istvan seemed happy, and lavished his attentions on her. On Monday, Janos drove to Aszod to meet Mr. Istvan, who was alone and seemed depressed.

"At nine o'clock this morning," the coachman continued, "he ordered me to get the carriage ready."

The last time the coachman saw Banyay, who was sitting at his desk by the window, was when he went out to prepare the carriage.

Banyay's parents asked Horvath whether they should notify the police. At first Horvath said no; then they decided to ask Professor Liptay for his opinion on the matter. Palma went to see him, and the Professor hinted that it might not be wise to dispense with the help of the police.

Horvath accompanied Mr. Banyay when he went to see Commissioner Hegedüs. Old Hellebronth had told Horvath that Hegedüs was very fond of reading. "He is well acquainted with all the books confiscated by the police." Without understanding the man's equanimity, Horvath admired it.

The Commissioner, who appeared to be alarmed by Banyay's disappearance, confirmed the fact that the police had not been notified of the matter; then he promised his active cooperation.

Mr. Banyay left the office feeling hopeful. He invited Horvath to dinner. Palma was with Mrs. Banyay, waiting for them.

The girl stayed until quite late. Horvath escorted her to the door. When they were alone, he said, "I think it was wrong to go to the police. I don't know why Liptay advised that."

"The explanation is obvious," said Palma. "Liptay is a traitor."

He watched the girl as she went away.

"She's obsessed," he thought. "Weakness may bring people closer together, but madness does not."

He went back to talk to Mr. Banyay. They conversed until dawn.

"You can't leave at this hour," the older man said. "With the state of siege, it would be dangerous. You can sleep in Istvan's room."

Horvath obeyed.

X

The next morning he decided to start his own investigation. He did not make much progress with the blind pencilseller, whose temper was as caustic as ever. The tailor's wife received him with obvious pleasure, but when he tried to talk about Banyay she said, "a girl likes a man to talk about her, not about some other man." Horvath humored her and felt he was being disloyal to his friend.

But the obese dollseller was to supply the revelation. The previous morning the woman had seen a group of men arrive. One, a thin man in a gray suit, with a very white, very large bony face, with eyes like two small black dots, waited opposite Banyay's pavilion, while the others went into the coffeehouse.

"And what did you do?"

"Why, nothing," said the woman. "I was on my way to the pharmacy and I didn't stop. As I passed the pavilion, I saw Mr. Istvan in his room, sitting by the window. Suddenly I felt so frightened it seemed my ears were ringing. I said to myself, 'Keep calm,' and I stood still for a moment. Then Janos, the coachman, came out of the pavilion. The man who was standing across the street took out his handkerchief and the men came out of the coffeehouse and all three went into the pavilion."

"And then?"

"My husband came along, and I had to go with him," said the woman with a show of irritation.

"Who were those men?"

"Don't tell me you don't know. Investigators!"

Horvath did not mention the incident to Banyay's parents.

Now the search for Banyay would be more difficult. Before continuing it, Horvath wanted to do a favor for his friend. He went to the editorial offices of the *Hungarian Encyclopedia*, said that Banyay was ill, and offered to replace him until he was better. They accepted his services.

"I did this," he told Palma, "as a kind of pledge, as if I were giving something as security."

Possibly he did it to convince himself that Banyay would return, or to atone for something.

He went to three or four meetings of the Hungarian Patriots. They discussed plans to kill the chief of police. They spoke of Liptay. He realized, without undue surprise, that now they considered Liptay a **traitor.**

Banyay's parents urged him to stay and live with them. Mrs. Banyay had hinted at the possibility before; her husband had reasoned, "Horvath is Istvan's closest friend; with Istvan gone, he represents him, in a sense."

With what seemed like excessive emotion Horvath told Palma one afternoon, "I could be happy now. I no longer have any financial worries. I always dreamed of living in a place like this pavilion. Your hand in mine comforts me. But I shall not replace Istvan only in pleasant situations. I shall continue to work on the *Encyclopedia*. I shall work on the biography of the man who was found dead at the Tunnel Inn."

His words, perhaps selfish, perhaps ignoble, and the tone of voice in which he uttered them, seemed unrelated.

"I've read the document," said Palma. "I don't know how Istvan could have thought it was authentic. It's obviously a fraud, a paraphrase of Istvan's own life—crude, badly written, showing no talent whatever. I'm sure it was written by Liptay or by one of his henchmen as a joke on Istvan."

He felt the desire to break with Palma. He stopped seeing her when Erzsebet came back.

At the University there was a ceremony to honor a new official. Liptay, who was the only Hungarian present, read a speech flanked by Austrian soldiers and guards.

The Patriots met again. One girl said that Professor Liptay had committed the indignity of appearing at the ceremony to avoid being discharged at the end of his long career. She said that she too had lost faith in him: his expulsion from the Hungarian Patriots was voted unanimously except for one abstention (Horvath's).

Then a quiet man stood up and asked that he be permitted to kill the chief of police. They agreed, and set the date: 17 March. Someone said that traitors should be punished, and therefore they would have to kill Professor Liptay. Horvath scarcely heard, for he was thinking of Banyay and of the Professor, with whom, under the austere gaze of a bust of Leibnitz in a small smoke-filled room, he had spent moments of exalted and generous happiness, of unconditional faith in intelligence, of utter devotion to study and to collaboration in study. He felt ill, he thought he was going to faint. He stood up. He offered to assassinate Liptay. They accepted his offer and set the date: 17 March.

Then neither the methodical prolixities of life, nor physical pains, nor cold nor heat, could awaken him from a throbbing sensation of unreality. He would have preferred to confess everything to Erzsebet; but if he had she would no longer have been that inviolate refuge. Somehow he did not believe that the time when he was to kill Liptay would ever really come.

Erzsebet's company consoled him. They walked together through the tree-lined streets on the west side of Buda, not far from the train tracks. Horvath would speak of a book he planned to write, and ask for permission to dedicate it to her. And he would wonder, when he looked at the deep clear tremulous green of the leaves dappled by afternoon sunlight as if he were seeing it for the first time, whether the secret exaltation that glowed within him was because of the green or because of Erzsebet.

PART TWO

"Straight was I carried . . ."

Thomas Chatterton, *The Storie of William Canynge.*

Anthal Horvath was writing his "Communication to My Friends":

" 'Before me, my desk; beyond, the window.' I don't know why these words come to me now: they are the first words of the first novel I ever wrote; they could also serve to introduce these pages, the last I shall ever write: my confession. Everything has changed. That is why I am in this situation. And that is why I must justify an act that might have seemed absurd before I went to France; now it will be thought of as infamous. It will be difficult to convince my friends (I know how anxious they are to be convinced). They never left Budapest as I did; they participated in that gradual process of transformation. They will never know how quickly time passed in Hungary, how many changes it brought. When I came back from Paris, I did not perceive at once that this familiar world was actually a different one. I did not even perceive it when Istvan disappeared. Slowly, without pathetic revelations or startling disclosures, I became a part of that nightmare. This morning of 17 March came after my melodramatic, unreal meeting with Remenyi, a symbol of the true nature of things."

He continued to write; he had awaited the arrival of 16 March with terror.

"As I think of it now, that tremendous day seems to have been a very long one, and I see myself lost in its immensity and in the dreams I had at night: dreams that seemed to prolong it even more."

In the morning he sent a message to Erzsebet to remind her that she had promised to go out with him. Then, for a long time, he cleaned his revolver. He had an incipient impulse to talk to the revolver, as Hamlet talked to Yorick's skull, and he imagined himself in the role of a spectator listening to those fantastic future dialogues.

Erzsebet came at one that afternoon. Horvath had told her nothing; neither had Palma (the two saw little of each other now). Horvath wrote:

"I felt Erzsebet's absence of worry like a harsh reproach and I would have given my happiness, perhaps our happiness, in order to keep from being disloyal to her."

But if he told her about his pact with the Patriots everything would be ruined.

He was able to guard the secret that he would kill Professor Liptay on the following day, but he was not able to keep his manner from suggesting that he was hiding something from her. He made too many jokes, and his gaiety was exaggerated. Although he had not drunk a drop of alcohol, afterward he had a vague memory of having experienced intoxication. He realized that his conduct was alienating him from Erzsebet, and yet he persisted in his perfidious, lonely, and foolish games. He weighed himself in a pharmacy, and with unjustified, secret elation he gave her the piece of paper that recorded his weight, and asked her to keep it. It amused him to know, when she did not, that she would read the paper in a completely altered future where it—those numbers and the uncertain memory of the scene—would have a sentimental value.

Then they walked through the zoo. At dusk they heard the screeching of the peacocks (that night, his dream was like a deep mirror, and he saw the peacocks again, perched at different heights in a dark circle of trees all around him, and when they screeched he awoke in anguish because he knew he would never see Erzsebet again). They parted at ten o'clock that night, and he could not bear to see her go.

"But as this happens every night," he wrote, "Erzsebet was not alarmed."

He went home, thinking of Erzsebet; but when he arrived, when he ascended the first few steps of the stairway, he could no longer remember her. Upstairs, within the four walls of his room, was the lonely interval of waiting, the night of unending horrors, the dawn of the unbelievable day when he was to kill Liptay. "It would be horrible," he said in order to change his thoughts (and "horrible" was the first word that occurred to him) "if the Professor happened to be upstairs."

He heard a boy selling newspapers in the street. He went down and bought a paper. He hoped to find some news that would save him from the nightmare. The news he found made him lose all hope. "Today at four o'clock," he read, "a group of young people entered the office of the rector of the University and tore the portraits of Metternich and Bishop Kollonich off the walls."

He went back up to his room. Why had he promised to kill the Professor? Horvath's wretched joke had ruined Banyay: suicide was not good enough for him. His soul needed an atrocious awakening from that unreality. He wanted to feel the punishment in every fiber of his being.

Very late that night, Palma appeared in his room. She had the hard, strange expression of a fanatic and a determination that he found inscrutable. It had been a long time since he had seen her.

"How much money do you have?" she asked.

Horvath took out his wallet and counted the money.

"Eighty-four florins."

"That's not very much."

He did not know what to say. Perhaps it was not much. Palma had not explained why she had asked him. He had not often had that much money.

"Get ready," the girl ordered. "You are coming with me."

Horvath looked at her.

"I was certain that something serious was happening," he wrote. "I felt overwhelmed by a secret and unbridled joy. I was saved." He longed for any adventure, any calamity; he thought out loud: "Even my own death!" When he said that last word, he felt a sudden eagerness, then confusion, then fear. He wondered, Is she secretly working with the police? No, that was absurd. Palma was "decent to the point of incompatibility," as Liptay had said. Or was she sent by the Patriots? Had he done something wrong? Then he felt a kind of awakening: no longer any joy or eagerness, or confusion or fear. He had done something wrong, but not to the Patriots. He would not refuse to go with Palma.

"I didn't care about myself and it was useless to think about Erzsebet until I had atoned for that wrong," he wrote.

Meanwhile Palma, with silent determination, busied herself with strange preparations. She had taken a box of tea, a bottle of gin, two loaves of bread, and some fruit from the little room where Janos prepared breakfast. She wrapped the things in a blanket that she found in the closet. She examined the clothes hanging there and finally chose a blue cloak. When Palma was not looking, Horvath took the revolver from the night table and put it in his pocket.

"Please bring these," said Palma, giving him the cloak and the blanket.

They left without speaking. On Krisztina Street, in front of the Summer Theatre, they boarded a rickety streetcar. It was almost empty: at one end there was a sleeping girl (she was young, pale, ragged, and she held a child in her arms); at the other, two men were shouting at each other, commenting on a conversation they had had earlier. They were coming from a wake. Horvath wanted to ask Palma where she was taking him. He postponed the question; in order to be heard, he would have had to shout. The men got off at Atlos Street. Palma and Horvath got off at Etele Street, and walked west. Horvath wrote later that an unaccustomed timidity prevented him from speaking. They came to the spring of Aesculapius, and approached a cluster of trees, vast and obscure in the night. To the right, a street lamp projected a circle of light. Just beyond the circle, on the ground against the tree, there was a mound. Palma stopped beside it.

"How goes it?" said the mound.

For an instant Horvath thought he could identify that unknown voice. Then he wondered if the man was disguising it on purpose. Why was he crouching like that? Why did he not stand up?

"Did you bring anything, Palma?"

Palma, kneeling, speaking persuasively, enumerated what they had brought as if she were addressing a child or a sick person.

"All right," replied the voice from the darkness. "They are giving me forty-eight hours. If I have not crossed the border by then, it will be too late. 'Let's play fair,' they tell me as if they meant it."

Horvath recognized the invisible speaker.

"It's their idea of a joke," he continued. "They are just doing it to arouse my hopes, to postpone my death for a little while. They think I cannot go very far. But they will not find me. I am sure I can get across the border before the deadline. If not—"

Remenyi stopped, as if his emotion choked him. Horvath was impressed; he had never observed in Remenyi anything but sufficiency, vanity, disdain.

"Palma, dear Palma," continued Remenyi in a whisper, "don't tell me that you forgot the revolver—"

There was a silence; then Palma began, "I wasn't able—"

"I brought you my revolver," said Horvath impulsively. Moving to the right, he entered the orbit of light; he pulled out his revolver and held it out rigidly. "Take it," he said.

The weapon shone in his hand. To reach it, Remenyi would have to enter the illuminated zone. Horvath saw him tremble, move, like an animal in agony. Palma took the weapon and gave it to Remenyi.

"Thanks, my friend," he said with painful slowness. "I'll pay you back with some advice: get away from here as soon as you can. If you stay, they'll get you. I saw Erzsebet today. You must save her. She loves you."

At that moment they heard the clatter of horses' hoofs on the pavement. Almost immediately, two foaming black horses could be seen through the leaves.

"The coach is here," said Palma. She turned to Horvath. "I asked you to come because I thought we might need you. Thanks. Go back now. I am going with Ferencz."

"Do you know anything about Istvan?" asked Horvath.

"I can assure you of one thing," replied Remenyi. "The police do not know what happened to him. They haven't found him. He simply disappeared."

Palma helped Remenyi up.

Dawn was breaking. Horvath went away. His footsteps echoed martially in the empty streets. He felt his own futility and knew that he should cling to that feeling: he was like a door standing ajar— He thought out loud, "Tomorrow I shall need a revolver." He passed the pharmacy he and Erzsebet had visited the previous afternoon. It was open. He went in.

"What can I do for you, Mr. Horvath?" asked the pharmacist.

"I want a strong poison," he said. "My house is full of rats."

"Arsenic," said the man.

There was no difficulty, there was no delay.

And then he was out in the street again, uneasy with the package, with nothing to do, in front of his house with no pretext for postponing the moment when he must enter his room and wait.

He mounted the stairs, went into his room, closed the door, looked around, looked at the bed where he would have to lie down. Then his heart began to beat faster and it felt heavy, enormous. He put his hand on his chest and, trembling, fell into the chair by his desk.

After a brief hesitation he decided to write this "Communication to My Friends," but first he opened the package of arsenic and took the bottle to the room next to his own, the room known as the "museum." No one went there; no one would be poisoned by mistake. He wrote:

"Perhaps I could justify myself. But unfortunately there is no possible justification for my conduct. At least, not today; but yesterday— Time is the key to all this; if time is successive, if the past is extinguished, then there is no use for me to try to find an excuse. Everything has changed so much. Incredulously, I repeat that I was never conscious of committing a real offense. But that is probably the doctrine of criminals: they can justify all their actions, all their moments. To outsiders, those actions and those moments depict the crime. Of course, mine was not a crime—only a joke, a miserable, stupid joke.

"I have to write this down. As I try to vindicate my conduct, which will doubtless deserve and achieve oblivion, I shall find the way to describe a magical thing, to communicate my frightful destiny to posterity, the interplay of magic, atonements, pledges, and death, in which my soul was entangled. Writing will mitigate the pain of my long wait (which now, unexpectedly, is drawing to a close).

"Janos, the coachman, has just brought my breakfast. Now he is arranging the room. This interruption keeps me from writing. But I must write, before he goes away.

"To go back to the beginning of this confession, I believe that the time has come to complete it with a sentence like: 'Through the window I see the street, and in the street there is a thin man.'

>We must die, said the valiant Charles.
>I am not afraid of that.

"But now I am waxing heroic. It displeases me to feel that I am not in control; I feel I am either drunk or delirious. To be natural and sincere I should have to have more time at my disposal, more tranquillity.

"I forged the story of the man who was found dead in the Tunnel Inn, the manuscript that Professor Liptay found—Istvan's obsession.

"If I consider my close friendship with Istvan and the consequences of this innocent, abject joke, then no explanations are possible. I should keep silent and die; but mere death is not, perhaps, sufficient punishment. Since even the most vicious criminals are given the right of defense—not as a consideration for them, but for the morality they have transgressed and which, by defending themselves, they acknowledge—I shall try to defend myself. I shall try to give a chronological narration of the events, in the hope that I shall appear, in the light of that account, as an imbecile, perhaps, but not as a fiend."

While he was still in Paris, Horvath received a letter from Hellebronth, the publisher, asking him to write a novel for *Clio*, his unscrupulous collection of historical novels. Horvath began the work eagerly, impetuously; when he reached the middle of Chapter XV, he realized that the book was uncomfortably similar to his vivid memories of *The Two Dianas*. He tore up the pages he had written and tried not to think about it again. A few days later he spoke of Istvan to a French girl, and in a flash of memory he recalled the man who had been found in the Tunnel Inn and how Istvan had urged him to write a story about the incident. He worked hard, but that second historical novel was a failure too.

One night he went with some friends to see *Chatterton*, by Alfred de Vigny. He recalled the event:

"Even now, in this unfortunate, extreme situation, I seem to feel the echo of an exaltation when I remember the glorious exaltation of that night as I went home on the Boulevard Saint Germain and the Rue du Bac. Then I read everything I could find about the poet who invented manuscripts and poets."

Helene Richter's study and Wilson's biography convinced him of the urgent need for a new biography. He spoke about it to Madeleine (in an outburst of false fanaticism, he added: "Erzsebet, I should like to offer you a pure soul, an empty past; I have given you what I have.") and it occurred to her that they could play a joke on Istvan: forge the lost manuscript, the manuscript that was found in the pocket of the mysterious man who died in the Tunnel Inn. Horvath pretended to be enthusiastic, and told her everything he remembered about the case, but he was certain that the plan would soon be forgotten. Madeleine, however, could not sleep that night and she devoted her implacable ardor to the plans for the manuscript. Horvath would write the story in rough draft and she would copy it, for if he had written directly on the parchment—even if he had tried to change his handwriting—Istvan might have recognized it. Horvath offered a feeble objection: he said he did not know how to invent the man's life story. Madeleine was sure he could do it; after all, he had written many novels. He reminded her that all his attempts to write historical novels had failed. She said that he could simply relate the life of Istvan, with a few variations; that would be easy and would make the joke more ingenious.

Then Istvan's uncle (who had never shown an interest in Horvath's literary works) heard that Horvath was writing a historical novel. The project became the subject of most of their conversations, and soon the affection he had felt for Horvath evolved into genuine devotion. One afternoon he came up to the garret and found Horvath reading the manuscript. He asked about it.

"I should have said that it was one of the sources of my historical novel," Horvath wrote. "Instead I said, 'My historical novel.' The Count did not seem to be surprised. He showed an alarming impatience for the work to be finished, to be read. I told him that it was almost finished, but that it might not be published for some time because Hellebronth had lost interest in my historical novels. The Count smiled with purposeful cunning; I did not ask what he planned to do; he went away looking preoccupied."

A few days later Horvath learned that the Count had written to Hellebronth and Professor Liptay, asking Hellebronth to let him subsidize the publication of the book and urging the Professor to persuade Hellebronth to let him subsidize it and to publish the book at once.

"That correspondence," Horvath wrote, "must have been the source of the rumors (heard by Remenyi) that I had sent a novel to

Hellebronth from Paris, had used some influence, and still had not been able to get it published."

Horvath confessed that he enjoyed writing the "life" of Istvan. Istvan wrote about Palma and Erzsebet in his letters to Horvath, who had not yet met them.

"In my story the hero believes he is in love with Palma, and then falls desperately in love with Erzsebet. And here I must point out something magic in that forged manuscript, a presage that somehow redeems it from being merely a fraud: the description of the love inspired by Erzsebet is a pallid but faithful description of the love, the adoration I feel for her now."

Madeleine's task was arduous. A person with less determination—a normal person—would have abandoned it. In the first place, she did not know Hungarian: she did not know the meaning of the words she had to write.

"And therefore," continued Horvath, "it was not surprising that she omitted some z's, some diaereses. I overlooked those omissions, or else I stressed their value as a proof of the antiquity of the manuscript."

Further, Madeleine realized that she should not use the handwriting of a woman of the twentieth century: she copied the crabbed writing of the first (possibly apocryphal) manuscript of the *Chronicle of the World* by Szekely, which a compatriot had sold to Count Banyay.

After much care and much labor, Madeleine and Horvath finished the "document."

"But I did not really plan to use it as Madeleine intended."

And still he played the game he did not believe in, pretending to believe in it. He suggested changes. To say that the hero had spent the summers of his childhood in Nyiregyhaza, he observed, lacked subtlety. Horvath and Istvan had spent many of their vacations in Nyiregyhaza at the country estate of Istvan's family. If there were no differences between Istvan's life and the hero's, the parallelism would be too obvious. And so Horvath suggested crossing out Nyiregyhaza and writing above it "Tuszer." At first Madeleine refused to spoil her painstaking work; but then she agreed and even insisted on making other corrections, because she discovered that they made the document look more genuine. They wrote that the hero (like Istvan) hoped one day to explore the jungles of India; then they crossed out "jungles of India" and wrote above the line "deserts of the Indies." And so with inversions, coincidences, anachronisms, variations, and metaphors, they completed Istvan's biography.

"My return to my own country was rather sudden, and it brought an end to the custom, which I had come to enjoy, of seeing Madeleine."

A farewell that was pathetic because of his haste; the possibility that their parting was a definitive one; the distance that separated them; nostalgia for France, which included all the persons and all the things he had left behind convinced him that he was in love with Madeleine. Before leaving he had promised her, halfheartedly, that he would play their joke on Istvan. And when he reached Hungary he knew that he could not be disloyal to Madeleine: that would have been like repudiating France.

"Besides, I found Istvan obsessed by the Tunnel Inn incident (I might almost say: in urgent need of a lesson). The very night I arrived he gave me the note telling what he had found out about it. I was relieved to see that, since I had made some mistakes when I forged the manuscript, Istvan would not be deceived by it."

Horvath had forgotten that the manuscript was written in a dialect, "in an unidentified Hungarian dialect"; he wrote it in modern Hungarian, with a smattering of archaisms (he did not worry whether they were all from the same period). He had forgotten that the pages had writing on only one side and that the paper was smooth and shiny (his wrinkled parchment seemed so genuinely old!). As for the ink that was imperceptible to the touch, perhaps he remembered it; it must have seemed like a rather unimportant detail, one that could be ignored.

"There was no need to worry, I thought: the hoax was inoffensive and Istvan would see through it immediately. Then I thought of how sad my little Madeleine would be if she knew about all the flaws in our work, and I felt that I was to blame. Since Madeleine's plan had failed, I would do all I could to keep my part of the bargain. I was afraid of the future: afraid that I would awaken from this dream of deception and would reveal to Istvan our plan to trick him. But I was guilty of another infidelity to Madeleine: I took a precaution to assure that the apocryphal nature of the document would not pass unnoticed."

The manuscript would not be found by the ingenuous Istvan, but by Professor Liptay. Horvath remembered that the Professor was cataloguing manuscripts in the University library; he remembered "The Purloined Letter" by Poe, and knew the safest place to hide the manuscript (so Liptay would be sure to find it). When, that same night, he went to the library, Liptay was not there. In his office there were three large baskets filled with manuscripts—no one would notice that one more had been added to the pile.

"Liptay found the document four days later. I don't know whether he examined it carefully; at any rate, he gave it to Istvan, who was deceived by the manuscript. Istvan studied it several times with Liptay, who also was deceived. (When Liptay tried to dissuade Istvan from the work, I don't believe that he suspected the manuscript was a fraud, or that he was envious; he simply wanted to cure Istvan of a monstrous obsession.) The manuscript deceived us all: in a sense, it deceived me too (but then it would be necessary to admit that it did not deceive Istvan or Liptay).

"That is the atrocious revelation. I was deceived about the implications of my work. I do not claim that the manuscript found in the dead man's pocket at the Tunnel Inn in 1607 was the document Madeleine and I prepared in Paris in 1904. It was instead a photographic copy of our manuscript, Istvan's photographic copy, the one he made that afternoon at the University library when the authorities refused to let him take the manuscript home to study at night. That was why the manuscript found in the Tunnel Inn, although it had the same number of pages as mine, had writing on only one side of the page; that was why the paper was smooth and glossy; that was why the ink blended into the paper. The Turks and the traitors who assisted them believed that the document was written in an unknown Hungarian dialect: it was simply modern Hungarian (which they could not foresee).

"But there are other ways to identify the document that was found in the seventeenth century. One is that the lines crossed each other at right angles. Another is that the source of the passage from Ovid was given incorrectly. I added it at the last moment (with extraordinary brilliance, Liptay and Istvan discovered that it had been interpolated) as a last countersign and a greeting. The countersign was concealed in the error of the quotation, which Tavernier explained; the greeting was an affectionate tribute to the absent girl: Madeleine or Erzsebet (now I am so nervous, so confused, I do not remember which one). Istvan saw through the symbols and the deformations and discovered that the life described in the manuscript was his own. He never admitted the discovery to himself; he was never conscious of it; but his reactions were unmistakable. Istvan said that his information on the man's life was gleaned exclusively from the document. He said also that the discrepancies between his information and the contents of the document could only be explained by the Professor's malevolent changes. But those changes were made by me before he ever saw the document. I was foolish to have written that the man had summered in Tuszer during his childhood; Istvan knew that he had summered in Nyiregyhaza. The night by the lake when Istvan told me that Tavernier, in the seventeenth century, had discovered the error in the quotation, I knew that I had entered a magic world.

"As for Istvan, he only entered the past. It was he who carried the photographic copy of the manuscript to the seventeenth century in the pocket of his cape.

"I can evoke the scene of his departure. He was—as the dollseller said—in the pavilion, at this desk, by this window. On his left he had, as I have now, the door to the 'museum.' He was wearing his blue cape and he was working on his copy of the manuscript I forged. Janos, the coachman, put the room in order and left. Then Istvan saw some men who came from the direction of the coffeehouse approach a thin man in a gray suit who had been standing across the street. They walked toward the pavilion. Istvan knew that it was the secret police; he thought with desperate intensity of the room beyond the door on his left, the 'museum.' He had always imagined that the seventeenth century was in that room. Now, obsessively, he concentrated his imagination of that century on a room in the Tunnel Inn, the inn that had stood on the spot where his grandparents built the pavilion. He put the manuscript in the pocket of his cape, opened the door, and entered the room. He had time to fasten the bolt. He was very excited. His heart, which had always been weak, failed. But Istvan did not die in the 'museum'; he dropped dead in a room of the Tunnel Inn, in the seventeenth century.

"Now I shall pass through the same door. Janos has gone. Several men who came from the direction of the coffeehouse have joined a thin man in gray who was standing across the street. Now they are all coming this way. They will not find me. I am going to the 'museum,' with the glass of water that Janos brought me with breakfast. Although Istvan's journey to the past proves that successive time is a mere illusion of men and that we live in an eternity where everything is simultaneous, I lack the imaginative powers of Istvan, who was able to recreate objects and centuries. I do not have the seventeenth century in the next room as a refuge. I have only a glass of water, a little arsenic, and the example of Chatterton."

The Perjury of the Snow

> "Among the works of Gustav Meyrink we shall remember the fragment entitled *The Secret King of the World*."
>
> Ulrich Spiegelhalter, *Oesterreich und die phantastische Dichtung* (Vienna, 1919).

Reality (like large cities) has spread out and attained new ramifications in recent years. That has influenced Time: the past recedes with inexorable swiftness. The Second World War is confused with the First, and faces that were once ugly assume, with time, a certain dignity. Widespread enthusiasms, popular pastimes, notorious crimes, names that were familiar to everyone have been forgotten. It should not surprise us, therefore, that for some readers the name Juan Luis Villafañe evokes no memories. Nor will it surprise us to learn that the following story, which shocked the country fifteen years ago, is viewed today as the tortuous invention of a discredited fantasy.

Villafañe was a man of vast but undisciplined scholarship, of insatiable intellectual curiosity; further, he possessed that modest and useful substitute for a knowledge of Greek and Latin: a knowledge of French and English. He wrote for *Nosotros, Argentine Culture*, and other magazines; he published his best articles anonymously in newspapers; and he was the author of more than one senator's best speeches. I enjoyed his company. I know that his life was licentious, and I am not sure how honest he was. He drank heavily; when he was drunk he talked about his adventures with methodical crudity. That was surprising, because Villafañe was usually "clean spoken" (as one of his best friends, a composer from Palermo, used to say). He treated love and women with a dispassionate scorn that was not devoid of courtesy. However, he believed that it was a national duty, *his* national duty, to possess all women. As for his appearance, I can recall his resemblance to Voltaire, the high forehead, the noble eyes, the imperious nose, and the slight stature.

When I published a collection of his articles someone tried to find similarities between the style of Villafañe and that of Thomas De Quincey. With more respect for the truth than for his feelings, an anonymous commentator wrote in *Azul*:

"I admit that Villafañe's hat is large; but I do not admit that this disproportionate attribute, or the epithet 'high-hatted dwarf' are enough to proclaim an identity, even an exclusively literary one, with De Quincey; but I agree that our author (considered as a person) is a dangerous rival of Jean-Paul (Richter)."

I shall transcribe below his account of the terrible adventure in which he was more than an observer; an adventure that is more complex than it appears at first glance. All of the characters who were involved in it died more than nine years ago; the events occurred at least five years before that; perhaps someone will protest, and say that the document resurrects from well-deserved oblivion things that were better left forgotten, that never should have happened. While I do not dispute that opinion, I shall merely keep the promise I made to my friend Juan Luis Villafañe on the night of his death, that I would publish the story this year. However, in view of possible objections, I have at times permitted myself certain ingenuous anachronisms, and I have introduced changes in the attributes and the names of persons and places; there are other purely formal changes, which I scarcely need mention. It will be enough to say that Villafañe was never concerned with style and that, accordingly, he observed very strict rules: he meticulously eliminated the "thats" required by his text, and eschewed the repetition of words at all costs, even when the result was obscurity. But my corrections would not have offended him. He believed that Shakespeare and Cervantes were perfect, and he was not unaware of the fact that his own writings were merely rough drafts. The changes I mentioned are important only to me. I am telling today, for the first time, the story that fully reveals and enables us to understand a tragedy whose causes or explanations were never known, although its horrors were.

Finally, I shall add that some of Villafañe's opinions about the lamented, the immortal Carlos Oribe (each day my pride in having been his friend increases) were simply due to his virile but indiscriminate aversion to all of us who were members of the younger generation.

A. B. C.

AN ACCOUNT OF THE TERRIBLE, MYSTERIOUS EVENTS THAT OCCURRED IN GENERAL PAZ (CHUBUT)

It was in the blatant desolation of the town of General Paz that I met the poet Carlos Oribe. My newspaper had sent me on tour to report on government inefficiency and to prove that Patagonia was being neglected. I could have done both of those things without leaving my desk; but, as the candor of businessmen is unappealable, I went, I spent, I grew weary. One obstinate midday I arrived by bus, especially fatigued and dusty, at the Hotel America in General Paz. The town consists of that unfinished and perhaps extensive building, a gasoline pump displaying the national colors, the Municipal Delegation, and, surely, a few more houses than those I remember. My memory of the town is almost gone, but it is associated with a terrible experience: what I did, what I shall do, no longer matters: in life, in dreams, in my hours of sleeplessness, I am only the persistent memory of those events. Everything, even my first impressions of the day—the smell of wood, straw, and sawdust from the store (which was a part of the hotel), the streets white with dust, illuminated by a vertical sun, and, in the distance, seen from the window, the forest of pine trees—everything was contaminated by a sinister and more or less precise symbolical meaning. Can I recall the sensation I had the first time I saw the forest? Can I imagine it as a simple grove of trees, somewhat incongruous in that rocky wilderness, but still untouched by the horrors it now evokes for all time?

When I arrived the proprietor took me to a room that contained the luggage and clothing of another traveler, and begged me not to delay, because lunch was ready. At first I ignored his request but then, aware that the others were waiting, I hurried down to the dining room where I would hear the beginning of the story that was to change, with secret violence, the lives of so many persons.

The proprietor of the hotel moved his chair back slightly and, without rising, introduced me to each of the persons seated at the long table: the Municipal Delegate, a traveling salesman, another traveling salesman— The hope that I would not see any of those faces after the following day and, above all, the triumphant din of the radio, kept me from hearing their names. But I heard one name clearly—Carlos Oribe—and with a smile that was indifferent to my surprise, my incredulity, I extended my hand to a young man whose voice was so shrill and unpleasant that it seemed like an affectation. He must have been about seventeen; he was tall and stooped; his head was small, but a disorderly shock of hair gave it an extraordinary magnitude; he appeared to be very nearsighted.

"Oh, so you are Oribe? The writer?" I asked.

"The poet," he replied with a vague smile.

"I did not imagine you were so young," I said sincerely. "Did you catch my name?"

"No, sir. I never listen to introductions."

"I am Juan Luis Villafañe," I said, convinced that this would serve to identify me adequately.

Perhaps I should explain that only a few months earlier I had published an article entitled "An Argentine Promise" in *Nosotros* in which I spoke favorably of Oribe's book. It is true that in *Songs and Ballads* I had found a conspicuous ignorance of our national themes and traditions (never-failing among young writers of some talent); a scrupulous study, I would almost say a fervent imitation, of foreign models; and—this discouraged me—much vanity, a few effeminate quirks, and a marked lack of concern with syntax and logic. But it is also certain that an authentic poetic instinct and a passion for literature, perhaps less discreet than oppressive, but always beautiful, were evident throughout the whole book. There is no shortage of geniuses—or, at least, of persons who act as if they were geniuses; I readily admit that Oribe might easily be confused with the latter. But I should like to point out this distinction: such persons are basically indifferent to art. And because of that distinction, which may not be interesting, which may not apply to books, I rejoiced at Oribe's entrance into our literature.

"Well, if we've met before," Oribe snapped in his most strident tone of voice, "the radio has deafened my memory, too."

Before I said something irreparable, I hastened to explain, "I thought you would recall my name because I wrote about your book in *Nosotros*."

His candid face lighted up with genuine interest. "Oh, that's too bad!" he exclaimed, suddenly repentant. "I didn't read it. I never read newspapers or magazines. I only read *La Nación* when it publishes my poems."

I told him about my article in praise of *Songs and Ballads* (I did not feel then, nor do I feel now, any need to justify it), and I mentioned several verses that I had considered especially felicitous. Suddenly I found myself being patted on the back effusively, and congratulated.

"Excellent, excellent!" Oribe repeated over and over, in a tone that revealed a generous desire to encourage me.

No one, however, should believe that this dialogue caused a breach between us. Two days later we made the trip to Bariloche together. In that interval the terrible misfortune had occurred.

The only passengers on the bus to Bariloche were a lady in mourning, Oribe, and I. We were depressed and in no mood to talk. It became obvious, however, that the poor old woman wanted to start a conversation. The bus stopped for gasoline, and we went outside to walk around.

"I don't feel like giving her the pleasure," said Oribe with unsuspected harshness.

He was referring, naturally, to the woman in mourning.

I was of the opinion that a conversation with her would probably be dull, but not too horrible, and that, in any event, we could scarcely avoid it.

A few minutes later the woman leaned over to ask me if the next town was Moreno. I was about to answer her when, suddenly, Oribe sat down in the aisle, crossed his legs, threw up his hands and shouted raucously:

> Seated on the floor, which is, after all, the truth;
> Let us talk with sadness of the deaths of kings
> And speak of epitaphs, tombs, and worms.

Oribe's action was probably childish, exaggerated, out of place. But, along with his confused motives, there was perhaps a benevolent intention: he wanted to dispel our melancholy. The woman laughed heartily and the three of us began a conversation—precisely what Oribe wanted to avoid. But, of course, he was sensitive to any tribute, and the woman, like so many other people who met him, was obviously impressed. I concealed my opinion: I thought that those verses were an improvised translation from Shakespeare, and that the gestures were a reproduction of Shelley's.

But I do not wish to suggest that plagiarism dominated all of Oribe's actions. Some anecdotes can give an accurate portrait of a person.

For example, that first afternoon at the hotel, as I was trying to take a nap, I heard Oribe's voice, which seemed to come from the garden, reciting, indomitable as the phoenix, the *Death of Tristan*. Finally I decided to ask him to join me for a cup of coffee. When I went out to the garden, Oribe was nowhere to be seen. The hotelkeeper appeared at the door; I asked him if he knew where Oribe was, if he had seen him.

"No," shouted Oribe from above. "No one has seen me," and he went on impudently, "Here I am, up in the tree. I always climb a tree when I want to think."

That same day, at dusk, we were talking to the Delegate and some of the travelers. Oribe seemed to be interested in the conversation. Suddenly he began to show signs of increasing impatience and finally he ran into the house. The man who was speaking forgot what he was talking about and the rest of us tried to conceal our surprise. Oribe came back, with an expression of beatific relief on his face. I asked him what was the matter.

"Nothing," he replied, with ingenuous composure. "I went to look at a chair. I had forgotten what chairs looked like."

I am afraid I have not conveyed my thoughts about Oribe accurately. Nothing is more difficult than to find the right word, without being deficient or excessive. I have reread these pages and I am afraid that the malicious, or unconscious, or apparently unjustified conclusion may be that these two rather grotesque anecdotes express the only originality I attribute to Oribe. But we must not forget his *Songs and Ballads*. For if the reader likes his verses, or not, they are the indisputable heritage of all men, who will never weary of singing their praises. And, above all, we must not forget his impassioned poetic temperament. Carlos Oribe was intensely literary, and he wanted his life to be a work of literature. He emulated his favorite models—Shelley, Keats—and the life or work that resulted is no more original than a combination of memories. But what else can be achieved by the most audacious intelligence or the most laborious fantasy? We who observe him with sympathy tempered by a routine critical sense believe that his passage through the very brief history of our literature will be, forever, like a symbol: the symbol of the poet.

But to return to that day when we were lunching at General Paz: as I said, the table was in front of a window; from the window we could see the forest of pine trees in the distance.

"Is that a ranch?" someone asked (I forget whether it was Oribe, or one of the travelers, or I myself).

"Yes, it's called 'La Adela'," replied the Delegate. "It belongs to a Dane, Mr. Vermehren."

"He is a very proper man, Señores," said the hotelkeeper. "A very strict disciplinarian."

"That's not all, Don Américo," said the Delegate. "Here they are in 1933, in the middle of civilization; and yet they live as if it were twenty years ago—as if they were completely isolated from the rest of the world."

Oribe stood up. "I propose a toast to civilization," he bellowed stridently. "I propose a toast to the radio!"

The thought crossed my mind that civilization had come to all parts of the country except to our tiresome *farceur*. The others surveyed him impassively. Oribe sat down.

"The case of 'La Adela' is incredible and mysterious," said the Delegate absently.

Incredible and mysterious because life on the ranch was a little outmoded? I wanted to ask him to explain, but I was afraid that Oribe would discover my curiosity and I would have his derision to cope with. Looking taciturn the hotelkeeper left the room. But, as it turned out, I did not need to ask for an explanation after all.

"Do you see that large wooden gate?" asked the Delegate.

We stood up to look. In the forest of pine trees we could see a white gate under a small canopy.

"No one has gone in or out through that gate for a year and a half," the Delegate continued. "Every day at the same time, Vermehren comes to the gate in a small carriage drawn by a white mare. He meets the delivery men and then returns to the ranch. He scarcely speaks to them. 'Good afternoon,' 'Good-bye.' Always the same words."

"Can we see him?" asked Oribe.

"He always comes at five o'clock. But I wouldn't get within shooting distance, if I were you. And, speaking of shooting, Vermehren has said that his Browning would take care of anyone who tried to come to see him. I heard that from the hired man who managed to escape."

"Managed to escape?"

"That's right. He is holding the people on his ranch captive; they are practically recluses. But I'm sorry for the girls."

I asked who lived at "La Adela."

"Vermehren, his four daughters, a few servant women, and a farm laborer," replied the Delegate.

"What are the names of his daughters?" asked Oribe, wide-eyed.

For a moment the Delegate seemed to be debating whether to answer the poet's question or to insult him. Then he said, "Adelaide, Ruth, Margaret, and Lucy."

Immediately afterward he embarked on a lengthy and totally irrelevant description of the forest and gardens of "La Adela."

I had heard the story of Louis Vermehren in Buenos Aires. He was the youngest son of Niels Matthias Vermehren, who had attained distinction as the only member of the Danish Academy to vote for the awarding of a prize to a book written by Schopenhauer. Louis Vermehren was born around 1870. He had two brothers. Einar, like him, became a clergyman. The oldest boy, Matthias Mathildus Vermehren, became a sea captain and was famous for the way he disciplined his crews, for his unkempt appearance, for his terrible piety, and for taking his own life in the land of King Charles "after abandoning his ship like a rat one night during a shipwreck" (H. J. Molbech, *Annals of the Royal Danish Navy*, Copenhagen, 1906). Einar and Louis Vermehren gained a degree of notoriety because of their fight against High Calvinism. When that fight overstepped the boundaries of rhetoric and the peaceful skies of Denmark were illuminated by burning churches, the government intervened. (Einar commented later: "In a liberal country Louis revived passions that had been dormant for three hundred years; if he had been living in the sixteenth century, he would have burned Calvin himself at the stake.") Representatives of the Crown asked the Arminian pastors to sign a compromise. Einar was among the last to sign and then, like the surprise ending of a story, it was learned that the leader of the religious agitation was not he, as people had believed, but Louis. The latter, in fact, made no concessions. Although his wife was not well (their daughter Lucy had just been born), he made up his mind to leave Denmark. Soon afterward, one November afternoon in 1908, they sailed from Rotterdam for Argentina. His wife died during the crossing. Her death shocked Vermehren, who had thought only of his religious battles and his brother's duplicity. Her death seemed like an irremissible punishment and an atrocious omen, and Vermehren decided to find sanctuary with his daughters in some lonely place. He chose Patagonia, at the very bottom of Argentina, at the bottom of "that lonely and never-ending country." He bought land in Chubut and began to work very hard in order to busy himself with something. It was not long before he developed a passion for work. He was able to borrow large sums of money and, with almost inhuman discipline and will power, he created an admirable establishment; he planted gardens and built shelters in the wilderness; and in less than eight years he had paid his enormous debt in full.

But now I shall return to that first afternoon in the Hotel America.

It was time for tea. We had *yerba mate* in large earthenware cups, and crackers. I remembered our plan to catch a glimpse of Vermehren when he appeared at the gate.

"It's almost five," I said. "If we don't go outside this minute, we'll miss seeing Vermehren. We're quite far away, you know!"

"In our room we shall be close!" shouted Oribe.

I followed him with resignation. When we were in the room (I believe I already mentioned the fact that we were sharing a room), he flippantly opened a suitcase plastered with hotel labels and, acquiring the look and smile of a sleight-of-hand artist, took out a very fine pair of binoculars. He motioned me to the window, raised the glasses, and began to focus them. I waited for him to offer them to me.

In the distant forest my eyes perceived the covered gate and, beyond it, a narrow road that disappeared darkly among the trees. Suddenly a white spot appeared; then I saw that it was a horse drawing a little carriage. I looked at my companion; he appeared to have no intention of letting me borrow the glasses. I reached over and grabbed them, found the right focus, and then, very clearly, I saw a white horse drawing a yellow carriage with a man in black sitting there stiffly. The man got out of the carriage, and when I saw him walk to the gate, very small and brisk, I had the strange impression that in this one movement I could see a superimposition of past and future repeated actions and that the image magnified by the glasses existed in eternity.

I congratulated Oribe on his excellent glasses and we went to have a drink.

"Gentlemen," shouted Oribe shrilly, "Listen. After what I have seen this afternoon, I shall not leave General Paz without paying a visit to 'La Adela'."

The hotelkeeper took him seriously.

"I wouldn't, if I were you," he said coldly. "The Danish fellow's head may be sick, but his hand isn't. And do you know what his dogs are like? If they get hold of you, they will tear you to pieces, my friend!"

To change the subject, I asked Oribe about his friends in Buenos Aires.

"I have no friends," he replied. "I don't believe it would be too presumptuous to give that title to Mr. Alfonso Berger Cárdenas, however."

I did not question him further. I felt that Oribe was a monster or that, anyway, we were two monsters of different sorts. I had glanced at a book by A. B. C.; I had written about the man who was the precocious author of *Embolism* and of almost all the mistakes a contemporary writer can make without even trying (almost all: he still had some stories and essays in preparation). There is not much point in saying that my opinion of him has changed now. Berger is my only friend; if I dared, I would say that he is the only disciple I leave behind.

But then I thanked Oribe for the information and added, "I'm going to the room to write. I'll see you later."

Perhaps I was impatient with him. Perhaps he deserved it. As I remember him, though, he was a pathetic figure. I can see him as he looked that night in Patagonia: gay, offensive, energetic, standing on the very threshold of an unsuspected maze of persecution.

He left the hotel around ten-fifteen that night. He said he was going to take a walk, to think about a poem he was writing. It was so cold that this was an outrageous thing to do, even for Oribe. I didn't believe him, nor did I answer; I watched him as he went out gloomily, like someone going to keep a horrible rendezvous. Then I went out. It was a dark night. Although I walked for a long time, I did not encounter Oribe. I entered the forest of pine trees. I am not afraid of dogs; at home, when I was a child we always had a dog, so I know how to handle them. Then the moon came out and it began to snow. I was about fifty yards from the hotel, but the snow was so heavy that my boots were covered with it when I reached the door. Oribe was waiting for me inside, stupefied by the cold. He spoke about his poem, and again I did not believe him. We had a few drinks. He needed them; probably I did, too. I told him about my expedition. I must have been slightly drunk. It seemed to me then that Oribe was a great friend, worthy of confidences, and I forced him to stay up until dawn while I chattered and drank.

The next day I awoke very late. Oribe was standing by the window; I saw him throw up his hands in amazement.

"The end of another myth!" he exclaimed.

I did not ask what he meant; I did not want to know; I wanted to sleep. But he kept on talking.

"At this very instant a car is driving into 'La Adela.' I demand an explanation!"

He went out of the room. I began to dress. Presently he came back. His depression was very noticeable, it was almost theatrical.

"What happened?" I asked.

"The ban on entering the ranch has been lifted. One of the girls is dead."

We walked slowly out of the hotel together. The proprietor greeted us from an old automobile.

"Where are you going?" Oribe inquired with his natural impertinence.

"To Moreno, to get a doctor. The one in this town is impossible. I went to see him this morning, and asked him to go to the ranch to issue the death certificate; now they tell me that he never came. I sent a boy to his house and they said that the doctor had left for Neuquén!"

One of the travelers from the hotel asked us if we were going to the wake.

"Of course not!" said Oribe.

"But you can go if you want to," said the hotelkeeper. "The whole town will be there."

Oribe's mind was made up. Perhaps he was right; perhaps the wake would be unpleasant; but I was irritated that he was making decisions for me and interfering in my affairs.

We did not know what to do that afternoon. We could not leave town because there was no bus until the following day. Everyone in General Paz was at the wake. We did not feel like talking. I thought about the dead girl. Oribe must have been thinking about her too. I did not dare to ask whether he knew the girl's name (in general I treated him with a superior air; but on some occasions I was shamefully cautious, as if his opinion of me really mattered).

"Do you want to go to the wake?" he asked finally.

I agreed to go. We walked, because there were no vehicles of any kind left in General Paz. It was almost nightfall when we made our silent entrance into the grounds of "La Adela" with a shared solemnity that might be construed as a touch of madness or an omen.

"I see they have tied up the dogs," whispered Oribe.

"Naturally," I replied, "since people have been invited."

"I don't trust country people," he said, looking nervously over his shoulder.

It took us ten minutes to walk down the long road between the trees. Then we came to a clearing (it was surrounded, in the distance, by groves of trees). The house was at the rear. Perhaps I had seen homes like Vermehren's in photographs of Denmark; in Patagonia it looked rather startling. It was a very wide, white house several stories high with a thatched roof and boarded-up windows.

We knocked; someone came to let us in. We entered a vast, brightly lighted hall (extraordinary for a country house). The doors and windows were painted a dark blue, and there were shelves filled with objects of porcelain or wood, and bright-colored rugs on the floor. Oribe said that when he entered the house he had the impression of entering an isolated world, more isolated than an island or a ship. It was true that the objects, the curtains, and the rugs, the red, green, or blue of the walls and the picture frames gave the interior an almost palpable atmosphere. Oribe took my arm and whispered, "This house seems to have been built in the center of the earth. No birds will sing their morning songs here!"

That was simply an affected, unpleasant exaggeration; but I have transcribed it because it expresses quite faithfully what we felt when we entered the house.

Then we came to an enormous room with two large fireplaces where pine branches were crackling and sputtering in two huge fires. In the shadow of a remote corner I saw a group of people. Someone stood up and walked over to greet us. We recognized the Delegate.

"Mr. Vermehren is grief-stricken," he informed us. "Grief-stricken. Come and say a few words to him."

We followed him. Vermehren was sitting in a large chair, surrounded by silent men. He was wearing a black suit; his head (his face looked very white and flabby) was slumped down on his chest. The Delegate introduced us. No movement, no reply showed that the introduction had been heard, or that Vermehren was alive. The little group around him maintained silence.

Soon the Delegate asked, "Would you like to see her?" He motioned with his hand. "She is in that room. The girls are in there with her."

"No," I said quickly. "Later."

I looked around. The room was very high, and at one end there was a kind of loft or balcony that extended along the whole width of the wall. The loft had a red railing; behind it there were two red doors. A heavy green drapery, like the curtain in a theatre, hung from the balcony and covered that end of the room.

Oribe leaned fearlessly against a floor lamp decorated with eagles, which was next to Vermehren's chair. He asked me somewhat timidly, "What are you thinking about?"

Immediately I lied, "I am thinking that it has been a long time since I have written anything for my newspaper. But I can't find anything to write about."

"What about this?" asked Oribe.

"Why, of course!" said the Delegate.

"No. I don't dare," I replied.

"It would be an honor for Mr. Vermehren," insisted the Delegate.

"Well," I said, "if I had a photograph of the girl—"

I felt like a scoundrel. The Delegate and Oribe were both enthusiastic.

"Mr. Vermehren," said the Delegate in a very loud voice that revealed a touch of indecision. "The gentleman, here, is from the newspapers. He would like to write a little article for the obituary column."

"Thanks," murmured Vermehren. He made no gesture whatsoever. His head was still slumped down on his chest. I shuddered, as if a dead man had spoken. "Thanks. The less we talk, the better."

"All the gentleman wants," insisted the Delegate with a nod in my direction, "is a photograph. It is necessary for the article."

"Your daughter deserves that tribute," added Oribe, candid and heartless.

"All right," murmured Vermehren.

"Are you going to give us the photograph?" asked Oribe.

Vermehren nodded. He had no strength to fight against such persistence. As for me, I was almost tempted by compassion, I almost wanted to help him— But I let them make the arrangements.

"When can we have it?" asked Oribe.

"When one of the girls comes, I'll ask her to get it. I would get it myself, but I am tired."

"I would never allow that!" said Oribe with dignity. And then he asked, "Where is it?"

"In my bedroom," mumbled Vermehren.

Oribe stood stiffly for a moment, with his head raised and his eyes closed. Then with a sudden movement, like a sudden inspiration, he darted behind the green curtain. He appeared at the top of the loft; he looked with indecision at the two doors. He opened the door on the left and disappeared from view.

The Delegate, who had been looking up calmly in the direction of the loft, opened his eyes wide in amazement.

"What in the world!" he said.

I had to invent some explanation to avert an imminent catastrophe.

"He is a poet, just a poet," I repeated fatuously.

Oribe appeared again, was lost from view, and then emerged from behind the curtain. He had a photograph in his hand. I wanted to see it; he held it out to Vermehren. I remember that I trembled as I heard him ask, "Is this the one?"

For an interval that seemed long, but was perhaps only the fraction of a second, Vermehren sat still with his head slumped down on his chest, as if he were sleeping and in pain. Then, as if the proximity of the photograph had reawakened him, he stood up. He lighted the lamp. He was tall and thin, and the thin lips and the large blue eyes in his flabby, white, and effeminate face seemed to express coldness and cruelty.

At that moment one of the girls came into the room. She put a hand on Vermehren's shoulder and said, "Now, father. You mustn't get upset, you know." She turned out the light and went away.

Oribe said that the Delegate commented later on the insistent way in which I had looked at the girl.

I went to sit down on a sofa near a hallway that led to the dead girl's room. The people who went to see her had to pass me. I remained there for a long time; perhaps for hours. I saw one of the Vermehren girls go by. I saw Oribe go by; I saw him come out of the room; he refused to look at me; he had tears in his eyes. I saw another Vermehren girl go by.

Finally I got up and told Oribe it was time to go. I have never liked to look at the dead: because then I cannot remember how they looked when they were living. I asked him if he had the photograph; he said that he did, and his voice was trembling. When we were outside I asked him for it. There was so little light that we could scarcely find the road.

At the hotel Oribe asked for a glass of anise. I did not feel like drinking. I was not able to fall asleep until almost eight o'clock in the morning. The night seemed very short, although we were sad, silent, and awake. I don't believe Oribe was able to sleep either.

When I finally awoke I felt depressed, and I stayed in bed until noon.

Oribe went to the funeral. Then we took the bus back to Buenos Aires, through Bariloche, Carmen de Patagones, and Bahía Blanca. That first afternoon Oribe was very dejected; but, even so, he behaved more foolishly than ever.

Before we parted he asked me to show him, for the last time, the photograph of Lucy Vermehren. He took it anxiously, looked at it very closely for a few seconds, and suddenly closed his eyes and returned it to me.

"That girl," he whispered as if he were groping for the right words, "that girl has been living in hell."

I confess that I did not question whether what he said was true. "Yes, but those are not your own words," I told him.

"That doesn't have the slightest importance," he said with aplomb, and it occurred to me that I had revealed to him the stubborn poverty of my spirit. "Poets lack identity, we occupy vacant bodies, we animate them."

I don't know whether he was right. I have justified some of his actions by attributing them to a perhaps immoderate desire to improvise a personality; it might have been more equitable to have ascribed them to literary motives, to think that he treated the episodes of his life as if they were the episodes of a book. But what I cannot overlook is that, although the words he used in speaking about the photograph of Lucy Vermehren were not his own, they gave him the power of divination that antiquity attributed to poets.

I saw very little of him in Buenos Aires. I know, because the maids at my boardinghouse told me, that he telephoned a few times when I was out. The last memory he left me, and the most vehement one of all, was the night when he came into my office at the newspaper with his hair dishevelled and his eyes bulging out of their sockets.

"I want to talk to you," he shouted.

"Well, I'm listening."

"Not here," he said, looking around. "Alone."

"I'm sorry," I said. "I still have part of my column to write."

"I'll wait," he said.

He just stood there staring at me. He may not have done it to unnerve me; but the fact is that I began to feel downright shaky. "You won't win this round," I thought, and with complete calm, I should almost say, with deliberate slowness, I continued to work on my article.

When we went out, it was raining and the weather had turned cold. Oribe tried to walk under the shelter of the buildings; I forced him to walk near the street. I watched him get soaking wet and start to cough. I postponed the moment when I would speak to him.

"Well, what do you want?" I asked finally.

"To invite you to go on a trip with me. To Córdoba. As my guest."

He not only had money; he had the effrontery that goes with it. I was angry, too, that he considered himself such a good friend of mine. Why would I want to take a trip with him? Our experience together in Patagonia had been purely accidental.

"Impossible," I said. But today it is a satisfaction to know that I was polite, that I added, "I have too much work right now."

He kept urging me to come in a plaintive voice but succeeded only in increasing my irritation. When he was convinced that I would not go with him, he said, "Well, I must ask you a favor."

It seemed to me that he had asked enough already.

"I don't want anyone to know that I am going to Córdoba," he continued. "Please don't tell anyone."

After that I never asked the maids if he had called. I forget whether I kept the secret about his trip. I thought then, and at times I still think, that Oribe never really wanted anyone to keep a secret for him. But my conscience is clear: nothing, neither my words nor my silence, could have made a difference in the way things turned out.

Two months after the night when my hostile eyes saw him disappear, impassioned and futile, into the bright lights of Buenos Aires, two months after the night when he entered a circumscribed sphere of anguish and persecution, a soldier found his body in a garden in Antofagasta, Chile. Louis Vermehren was arrested a few days later, and confessed to the murder; but neither the local crime experts nor those who were sent from Santiago were able to explain his motive. All they could learn was that Oribe had passed through Córdoba, Salta, and La Paz before arriving in Antofagasta, and that Vermehren had passed through Córdoba, Salta, and La Paz before arriving in Antofagasta.

I took it all quite calmly. I thought I would write a series of articles describing Vermehren's persecution of Oribe, and allude at the same time to the persecution of enlightenment by the Church. But I rejected that idea because I felt I should do something more worthwhile than that; and so, after much difficulty, I finally convinced the same director who had sent me so unnecessarily to Patagonia that he should allow me to go, at the newspaper's expense, anywhere I wished, inside the country or out of it, to investigate the murder of Oribe.

It was a Thursday. Some friends arranged for me to have a seat on the Air Force plane to Bariloche the following Sunday; then I bought a ticket for the commercial flight to Chile on Wednesday.

Without the hope of learning anything, I visited a Danish woman named Bella. She lived in Buenos Aires and was married to an engineer who worked in Tres Arroyos. Of course I had no guarantee that a person born in Denmark would know about Vermehren; but it seemed conceivable, because few Danes lived in Argentina and they all had some news of each other or knew who had. Bella introduced me to a Mr. Grungtvig of Tres Arroyos, who was passing through Buenos Aires. That night at the Germinal, while we listened to tangos, Grungtvig told me almost everything I know about Vermehren. We met again the following night. He gave me more information about Vermehren and at dawn we were still there, melancholy and fraternal, talking about the sterile, proper aversion we all feel for the authorities, convinced of the desperate future of political life on this earth and, especially, in this country; but we did not feel depressed by our predictions and our resignation; the tangos filled us, the Dane and me, with a secretly shared patriotic fervor and gave us an indiscriminate will to act, an aggressive joy.

I arrived in Bariloche on Sunday afternoon. I arranged for the chauffeur who brought me from the airport to the hotel to drive me to General Paz the next morning.

We left early and drove all day. I asked the chauffeur if Dr. Battis still practiced medicine in General Paz. He said he knew nothing about General Paz.

At last we arrived at our destination. Covered with dirt and sick with fatigue, I got out in front of the doctor's house. Dr. Battis opened the door; he introduced himself and held out a hand that was extraordinarily pale, damp, and cold. He was not tall; his hair and moustache were parted exactly in the center with parallel waves on each side. He served me a horrible drink—it turned out to be a wine that he himself had made—and he praised his radio (which made it possible for him "to hear the Colón Theatre and the speeches of a number of men in public office") and then invited me to sit down. When he learned that I was a reporter and that I was not going to do a story about him, his amiability gradually diminished.

"I came to ask why you did not want to go to 'La Adela' to issue a certificate of death for Lucy Vermehren."

He opened his eyes wide and I thought for a moment he might hurl the radio at me and make me cough up his absurd drink (which would not have been difficult). Undoubtedly he wanted to appear to be a man of importance and to talk, but not about the Vermehren case. His attitude was understandable: he did not know where our conversation might lead, and no decent person wishes to be involved with the police. Before he had a chance to answer I explained: "Make up your mind whether you want to talk to me or to the authorities. If you talk to me, I assure you that you won't regret it. I am making this investigation on my own initiative and I don't plan to tell anyone about the results. Make up your mind."

The man swallowed a glass of his own wine and it seemed to revive him.

"Well," he exclaimed triumphantly, "if you will promise to be discreet, I'll talk. I examined Miss Vermehren a year and a half before the date on which they say she died. At the time I saw her, she could not have lived for more than three months."

"And, if you had issued the certificate, you would have been admitting that you made a professional error," I interpreted without enthusiasm.

"If you want to look at it that way," he commented, rubbing his hands together, "I have no objection. But this much is certain: Miss Vermehren could not have lived for more than three months after the date on which I examined her. At the most: four months, five. But no longer than that."

I returned to Bariloche that same night. The next morning I took the plane to Buenos Aires. During the flight I had dreams; my emotions and perhaps the tenacity of the movement and my fatigue must have been the cause of those horrible fantasies. I was a corpse and, in the dream, my desire that the trip would end was the desire that they would bury me. I dreamed that all my friends were ghosts of persons who had died; soon they would die as ghosts, too. An unspecified fear kept me from seeing the photograph of Lucy Vermehren; what I looked at, what I adored, what I touched was no longer a photograph. Then there was an atrocious change; when I looked at it again, although I had never stopped looking at it, I was punished for this retrospective interruption: the image had been erased, the paper was blank, and I knew conclusively that Lucy Vermehren was dead.

We reached Buenos Aires at dusk. I was tired, but, since that would be my last night in the city, I wanted to see Berger Cárdenas before I left for Chile. I telephoned his home; he answered the phone himself and said that he was not in; I told him I would be over that evening.

Years have passed since that visit, but as I remember it today I feel again the same repentance and the same disgust. Berger must remain a symbol, the mere memory of him incessantly conjures up those horrors; but the evolution of our feelings is so inscrutable that he became the most conspicuous of my friends and, I might even add, the best nurse and servant I had during the unending miseries of my long illness.

Walking between enormous dogs that silently appeared and disappeared again in the darkness, I followed an evasive doorman through a series of irregular courtyards and then through a garden where there was a pavilion with an exterior staircase, and a single tree, which at night looked infinite. We ascended the stairs, opened the door, and I entered a brightly illuminated room; the walls were covered with books. Flushed and benevolent, Berger got up from an ugly chair with metallic arms and walked over to greet me.

I did not waste any time on courtesies. I asked him if Oribe had written anything about his trip to Patagonia.

"Yes," he replied. "A poem. I still have it."

He opened a drawer that was stuffed with dirty crumpled papers; he groped about and pulled out a notebook with a red cover. He prepared to read.

"I copied it," he said. "In my own handwriting."

"That doesn't matter," I said, taking the notebook. "I can decipher even the worst scrawl."

The title made me shudder: "Lucy Vermehren: A Memory." I read the poem and it seemed like the weak and periphrastic fixation of intense feelings; but this is a subsequent opinion and I confess that at that moment I felt only a confused, although violent, emotion. A work should not be judged by the emotion it evokes. But, because the poem caused me to experience that sort of reaction, it stands out among all the others Oribe wrote (in spite of his fervid attempts to imitate Shelley, our poet usually displayed more verbal felicity than sincerity). The lines I read had some formal defects and they were not always euphonious, but they were sincere. As I do not have a copy of the scandalous posthumous collection in which the poem is included, I must quote it from memory and—unfortunately—all I remember is one of the weakest stanzas. The first line is poor; the words "wood," "heath," and "myth" are analogous poetic values and do not provide mutual support. The second line, which competes with the most shoddy triumphs of the Spanish poet Campoamor, is unworthy of Oribe. In the last line the caesura does not fall naturally; and I do not like the word "desperation." The whole miserable stanza may not reveal any influences; there are, however (at least in my opinion), vestiges of Shelley; but my forgetful ear is not able to identify them precisely.

> I found a myth, a pine wood in a heath,
> And Sweet Lucia. Now she lies in death.
> Rise, Memory, and write her praise!
> Though desperation fills Oribe's days.

I asked Berger whether Oribe had told him anything about his journey.

"Yes," he said. "He told me about a most unusual adventure."

Berger began with the "mystery" of the pine forest and continued:

"You will remember that Oribe left the hotel one night around ten o'clock on the pretext of meditating on a poem he was writing. The night was very dark (so dark, he told me, that he did not realize he had been walking in snow until he looked at his boots, back at the hotel). He found his way, gropingly, to the pine forest. The dogs did not come out; he was glad of that, because he was afraid of dogs, although he said he knew how to handle them."

"He had dogs when he was a boy, didn't he?" I asked.

"Yes, I think he said something about that— Suddenly he realized that he was in front of the main building of 'La Adela.' He said he circled it, opened a side door, and plunged haphazardly into that strange house; he went through rooms and corridors; finally he came to a spiral staircase behind a green curtain; he went up the stairs and from a balcony he saw an immense living room where a man in black was conversing with three girls (they were the first persons he had seen in the house). He said they did not see him. He paused briefly before the two doors on the balcony, then opened the door on the right. Lucy Vermehren was there."

I felt nauseated and whispered, "What happened then?"

"Oribe emphasized two points," Berger explained methodically. "First, that the girl did not seem surprised when she saw him. He told me it was as if she had been expecting him, in a sense. I asked him to explain what he meant, but you know how obstinate and rude he could be. The second point was the virginal docility with which the girl surrendered to him."

His face was florid and his eyes expressionless as Berger gave details. I was disgusted: with myself, with Oribe, with Berger and the world. I should have preferred to abandon the case; but I felt as if I were in the middle of a dream, and perhaps I knew that I should not make any decisions just then because my sense of responsibility at that moment was no greater than that of a person in a dream. Besides, I began to perceive (very belatedly, to be sure) an explanation for what had happened, and I made the mistake of wanting to confirm it or reject it, to end my uncertainty. The next morning I left for Santiago.

I told myself that I should not hate Oribe. With an insecure attempt at objectivity, I asked myself if what made me so angry about Oribe's story was the fact that the girl was dead. And that, precisely, was why Oribe had told it: because the girl was dead and because the story of her life and the episode of her death were romantic. He treated reality like a literary composition, and he must have imagined that the antithetical value of that anecdote was irresistible. His conduct was ingenuous, actually coarse, and I reflected that I should not judge Oribe too harshly since he was guilty, not of iniquity as a man, but of incompetence as a writer. But it was no use. Those thoughts did not mitigate the vehemence of my rancor.

As soon as I arrived in Antofagasta, I called on the chief of police. He was not impressed by my letter of introduction, although it was signed by our director; he listened to me stolidly and gave me a permit to visit Vermehren whenever I wished.

I went to see him that very afternoon. When I looked into his stonelike eyes I could not tell whether he recognized me. I asked him several questions. He began to insult me, slowly; his words were barely audible but his voice seemed to release a torrent of hatred.

I let him talk. Then I said, "All right. I was making a private investigation, not intending to publish the results. But you've caused me to change my mind: I shall publish the information Dr. Battis gave me, and I won't bother anyone else."

I left at once and did not go to the jail the next day.

When I returned he was almost polite. He scarcely alluded to the previous interview.

"I cannot explain this matter without referring to my poor daughter," he said. "That is why I was reticent to talk about it."

He confirmed the doctor's story; he added that one night, after Lucy had gone upstairs to bed, one of the girls said that it seemed incredible that a change—the definitive change of death—could be introduced into a life like theirs, where each day was the same as the one that preceded it. He remembered her phrase, and during a night of insomnia, when credulities and plans are most urgent, he decided to impose on his household a life of scrupulous repetition so that time would stand still for them.

He had to take some precautions. He forbade the persons in his house to leave it; he forbade those from the outside to enter. He went out, always at the same time, to receive supplies and give the orders to the men. The life of those who worked outside was exactly as it had been before. It is true that a farmhand ran away; probably not because he wanted to save himself from a terrible discipline, but because he must have discovered that something strange was happening, something that he could not understand and that, therefore, intimidated him. Inside the house there had always been strict order and the system of repetitions occurred naturally. No one ran away, or even looked out of a window. All the days were the same. It was as if time stopped each night: as if they were living a tragedy that was always interrupted at the end of the first act. A year and a half went by. He thought he was in eternity. And then Lucy died suddenly. The date predicted by the doctor had been postponed by fifteen months.

But on the day of the wake a revelation occurred: a person who supposedly had never been in the house before was able to go to a definite room, without receiving directions from anyone. That became apparent to Vermehren when Oribe gave him the photograph of Lucy; and then Vermehren turned on the lamp to see the face of the man he had already decided to kill.

A few days later I was back in Buenos Aires and Vermehren had died in his cell. It was said (I do not wish to identify the source of the infamy here) that I had some connection with his death, that I took advantage of not being searched to bring him the cyanide he requested in return for a confession. But the outcome predicted by the same source did not materialize: I revealed nothing and the Chilean police did not detain me.

Now I am afraid that I may have revived the calumny; some will allege that the information I obtained from the doctor, and the mere threat of publishing it, would not have been sufficient to induce Vermehren to confess; they will overlook the difficulty I would have had to obtain a poison in Antofagasta; they will consider the publication of this story as the missing proof. But I hope that the reader will find evidence (on one of these pages) that I could not have been involved in Vermehren's suicide. To establish the evidence, to indicate the preponderant part that fate played in the events at General Paz, and to temper, as much as possible, the guilt that tarnishes the memory of Oribe were the motives that enabled me to write this account of events and passions in a world that no longer exists for me, in my present state of illness and at the very brink of my own disintegration.

Juan Luis Villafañe's manuscript breaks off here.

When I wrote "Juan Luis Villafañe's manuscript breaks off here," I meant to show that in my opinion the account is unfinished. I would add: deliberately unfinished. It is true that the last sentence tries to achieve the pomp, the patheticism, and the bad taste of an ending. Of, above all, a false ending. It is as if Villafañe had been trying to confuse his readers so that they, recognizing the ending, would accept it without remembering that certain explanations were still lacking, as well as a considerable part of the story.

Now I shall try to fill in the gaps. What I am adding is merely my own interpretation of the facts; but I am confident of its validity, since all the premises on which it is based can be found in this document or in the character traits that the document attributes to Oribe and Villafañe. I have not withheld my conclusion with the literary or childish aim of reserving a surprise for the final pages; I have wanted the reader to follow Villafañe, free from any suggestion from me; if the outcome seems too clearly predictable, if, independently, we have reached the same conclusion, I shall take the liberty of considering our concurrence as an indication that my interpretation is not unjustified.

First, let us look at the two people who complement each other like the figures in an engraving: Carlos Oribe and Juan Luis Villafañe, of symmetrical destinies. But then the plot will seem too simple, the symmetry too perfect (not for a theorem or for mere reality; for art).

To describe Villafañe by speaking of gray eminences, although that is not essentially a distortion of the facts, is an error, because it is an apparent distortion. I have already said that Villafañe usually worked anonymously, indirectly, that his best articles were unsigned, and that more than one brilliant and stormy discussion in the Senate was an imaginary dialogue, an intrinsic monologue in which Villafañe, impersonated by various senators, made proposals and offered refutations.

As for Carlos Oribe, there is one question that many people prefer to ignore. I feel they are wrong in doing that, for if no one discusses the matter, it will be exaggerated or forgotten, and the story will suffer accordingly. I shall let others be ashamed of their idols, strip them of their human qualities, and convert them into symbolical personages on a street, at a student party, and in never-ending assignments for scholars. I knew Carlos Oribe; I admired him—as he was. But I must confess, without embarrassment, that Oribe has frequently been guilty of plagiarism. In speaking of this delicate subject, it may be appropriate to recall Oribe's words regarding the plagiarism of Coleridge: "Did Coleridge have to copy Schelling? Did he do it *in forma pauperis?* Not at all. That is the enigma."

The enigma does not exist for Carlos Oribe; he imitated others because his mind was the master of the imitative arts. To disapprove of imitation in him is like disapproving of it in a dramatic actor.

But let us summarize the story: from the hotel window in General Paz, Oribe and Villafañe see a pine forest in the distance; it is "La Adela," a cattle ranch that no one has entered or left for a whole year. One afternoon Oribe says that he will not leave town without visiting the ranch. That night, on an incredible pretext, he goes out of the hotel. Villafañe goes out, too. The next morning Lucy Vermehren dies and the ban on entering "La Adela" is lifted. Oribe does not want to go to the wake; but he goes and moves about the house as if he has been there before. Then Vermehren kills Oribe.

My conclusion is not unpredictable: Vermehren was mistaken. Oribe did not enter his house before the wake. The person who entered the house was Villafañe.

As the reader will observe, all the facts that lead to this conclusion are contained in Villafañe's version of the story. The part played by (a) Oribe and (b) Villafañe would then be clarified as follows:

a) To make it appear that he is going to enter Vermehren's house, Oribe defies the inclemency of that Patagonian night. But he does not even enter the forest. He is afraid of dogs; he is afraid of them even when he is with Villafañe.

On the day of the wake he was able to go to Vermehren's room because Villafañe had given him a detailed account of his visit to "La Adela" the night before. That is borne out by the facts. Villafañe had drunk heavily that night; as he himself said: "It seemed to me then that Oribe was a great friend, worthy of confidences." We know what Villafañe's alcoholic confidences were like: he told them with "methodical crudity." Those two words clarify everything: the confidences were methodical—and Oribe was able to find Vermehren's room on the night of the wake (Villafañe had been in Lucy's room; that explains Oribe's indecision between the two doors on the balcony); the confidences were crude—Villafañe experienced disgust and horror when he heard Oribe's apocryphal story. What he heard was really the story of Villafañe and Lucy Vermehren; what he heard, after Lucy Vermehren's death, was the same story he had told, the same wretched act he had committed, made obscene by alcohol and perhaps by the tradition of conversations among men, made fatuous by his victory.

Oribe appears to be distressed by Lucy's death. But the narrator comments: "His depression was very noticeable, it was almost theatrical." Oribe was actually like a good actor, he imagined his part clearly, he found it easy to identify himself with the character he was playing.

Finally: he twists the facts around and appropriates the experiences of others. For example:

From a window the two watch Vermehren as he arrives at the gate; they are both looking in that direction, but the one who sees is Villafañe, because he has the glasses and Oribe is nearsighted. In the presence of the hotelkeeper Oribe says, "After what I have seen this afternoon, I shall not leave General Paz without paying a visit to 'La Adela'."

Oribe says that he did not see the snow falling because the night was so dark, that he did not notice the fallen snow until he was back in the hotel where he saw his snow-covered boots. But I maintain that no snow fell while he was outside; otherwise he would have seen it. As Villafañe said, "Then the moon came out and it began to snow." Another falsification: Oribe did not see snow on his own boots; he saw it on Villafañe's.

It was not hatred alone that caused Villafañe to present those facets of Oribe's character; it was also a scrupulous desire not to keep from the reader any facts that might help to reveal the truth.

b) Villafañe left the hotel that night after Oribe, as if he were following him. But to imagine Villafañe spying on Oribe would be absurd. Villafañe went out to enter "La Adela."

He made love to the girl. When they tell him later that one of the girls has died, he wants to know her name. Then he does not leave the wake until he has seen the three sisters of the dead girl (he is afraid she is the one who was with him the previous night, but he hopes it is not she). From the beginning he has feared the worst, and so he devises a ruse for Oribe and the Delegate to get him a photograph of her (he wants it for a souvenir). He says that he hates to see dead persons, because then he cannot imagine them as they looked when they were alive (but in this case the statement would be meaningless if Villafañe had not seen the girl before). He stays awake all night, he is very sad, he is in love with Lucy Vermehren (but I do not believe that a photograph and a more or less poetic nature would be enough to make him fall in love). He refers to Oribe's story as "the horrors" and he alludes to his feeling of "repentance" (Villafañe could only have spoken of repentance if he had been somehow responsible for Oribe's fate; he could only have spoken of horrors if the account given by Oribe had mirrored his own disrespectful version of an adventure that was purified in an atrocious way by death).

Finally, I must call the reader's attention to Villafañe's comparison of an episode from Vermehren's life to the surprise ending of a story in which one of the characters, previously considered as secondary, suddenly becomes the protagonist. I wonder if Villafañe inserted that sentence in his account so that one day someone would use it as a key to interpret the whole story.

I don't say that mine is the only interpretation. I simply believe it is the only true interpretation.

And now I must add a few words about Villafañe and Lucy Vermehren. Perhaps Lucy Vermehren received Villafañe like the angel of death who would save her, at last, from the tedious immortality imposed by her father. As for Villafañe, fate turned against him. It converted him into an instrument of death, but it did not defeat him. Nothing was able to defeat his tranquil virility, his incorruptible serenity. Once he said, "I like to think that Oribe's death was consistent with his life." He gave no explanation, but I believe I know what he meant. He added something about his "own death." At that time we were all talking about our own, and other people's deaths; there was scarcely any distinction between the two.

With regard to the calumny that implicates him in Vermehren's suicide, I venture to say that its only source was Villafañe's own manuscript. But that is not to suggest that Villafañe invented the indefensible calumny so the reader would reject it and believe it established his innocence.

My last memory will be of Carlos Oribe. I can still see him on the night of his departure, waving a straw hat and repeating this involuntary twelve-syllable line:

>"No, never, oh, no, never, forget about me!"

The poet's request was not unheeded.

A. B. C.